After losing his betrothed to a Lowlander, Laird Gabriel MacKinnon is charged with saving her cousin along with a brood of children from an impenetrable castle. Though, the lady he's been tasked to protect has been accused of a heinous crime, Gabriel has no fear of her. In fact, he's a little irritated at the prospect of delivering her to her kin. But this hardened, cold warrior just may find his heart melting, for the hellion brings out a passionate side he'd thought long buried.

A lady who will stop at nothing to see him fail...

Lady Brenna has had more than her share of hardships and when freedom looks to be on the brink of her horizon, she's not about to let some moody Highlander take it all away. She'll stop at nothing to keep her children safe—and to guard her heart—even though the warrior's heated kiss threatens to change every vow she's ever made and every belief about love she's ever known.

Praise for The Stolen Bride Series ...

"For fans of Highlander romance, this series is a must read!" ~*Night Owl Romance*

The Highlander's Reward-winner of InD'Tale Magazine's Best Historical Novel 2012

The Highlander's Reward- "The powerful yet sensitive Magnus and the saucy and beautiful Arbella are a winning pair in this Scottish themed romance that even boasts cameos from William Wallace himself." ~Publisher's Weekly Reviewer for the Amazon Breakthrough Novel Contest

Conquered
BY THE
Highlander

Eliza Knight

Dedication

*For Andrea, because you are an amazing,
beautiful, vibrant, smart and sassy lady!*

Prologue

Isle of Skye
Scorrybreac Castle
October, 1290

SHE should have eaten her supper.

A lass who disobeyed her elders would be punished. And now it seemed Brenna MacNeacail had brought the devil into their house. Mama and Da would surely blame her for it.

Huddling with her sister, Kirstin, in the nursery, she watched their governess, Meg, shove a chest in front of the door with every ounce of strength she had. Sweat beaded on her upper lip and her gray-streaked hair fell limply from her bun.

From below, they could hear screams and crashes as a battle raged inside their walls. Less than an hour had passed since the castle had been swarmed by enemy warriors and the warning bells of a siege had tolled. Just over an hour had passed since Meg had sworn Brenna would bring hellfire upon them for her wicked temperament. But what lass would eat lamb's tongue? Brenna was certain the unsightly fare had been Meg's way of revenge since Brenna had put a toad under her pillow.

And now hellfire had come.

Kirstin shivered, her lip trembling. Her sister's fear pulled Brenna back to the present. At any moment, Kirstin would break out into great sobs. Sobs that would pull the attention of the warrior devils up to the nursery. They'd hack them to death. That's what enemies did. They killed everyone. Brenna didn't want that. Of the two of them, Brenna was definitely the strongest. And she should be, she was born first. From the moment they'd left the womb, Brenna had been protective of her sister.

At twelve years old, she was practically a lady already, though she wouldn't have minded being a warrior. Da had seen to it that she was fierce and that she could wield a weapon, given it was the right size for her tiny frame.

Meg finished moving the chest, her heavy bosom heaving from her labored breaths. Swiping a meaty palm over her face, she turned in a circle then began shoving a table across the room, the sound of the legs scraping on the wooden planks drowning out the noises of the fighting below.

"Shh," Brenna cooed, trying to calm her sister. She tucked Kirstin's head against her shoulder and stroked her back. "Ye dinna want them to hear us."

Kirstin nodded, biting her lip. She clung to Brenna, just as they'd most likely clung in the womb. Mama was lucky to survive their births, as Brenna had been told time and again that it was a very difficult experience, and the reason Mama had not had any other children.

As such, Brenna and Kirstin were the heirs to the entire MacNeacail holdings and fortune. A vast one, if father didn't say so himself. Though their lands were not as far-reaching as some other clans, their treasury was filled with coin and various other assets.

"Girls, quit your fussing and help," Meg puffed, red-faced, as she lifted a chair on top of the table.

Brenna stood and gently tugged Kirstin up. "What should we do?"

"Help me bar the door."

Brenna straightened and shook her head, her gaze roving over the haphazard pile. "Nay."

Meg looked shocked and then glowered, putting heavy hands on her hips. "What? Do ye want to die then?"

"We need to escape, not bar ourselves in and wait for the devils to come knocking." Brenna spoke with authority and sense, two things Meg hated.

Their governess eyed her the way she always did, like she was trying to read Brenna's mind to find a way to knock her down. "How would ye have us escape? Through the door I've just barred?"

Brenna chewed her lip. Father had made her promise never to tell about the secret passage in their chamber that led down to the water gate. This was an emergency, though, and she knew he'd not be upset if she told Meg now.

"Through the laird's passageway."

Meg scoffed. "The laird's passageway? Rubbish. Get the other chair afore I cuff your ear." Meg turned her back, hauling another piece of furniture toward her pile.

Kirstin gripped on to Brenna's hand and stared at her with wide blue eyes. Brenna couldn't let her sister down. Couldn't let anyone down. She'd already gotten in to trouble once—all right, twice—today. That was enough.

"Come on, Kirstin," she said, ignoring Meg. She led her sister to the far corner of the room, behind their dressing screen.

"Brenna MacNeacail, ye little scamp!" Meg called.

They could hear their governess' pounding feet crossing the room. If she caught up to them before Brenna opened the secret door, Meg would surely tan their hides and they'd never be able to escape.

Brenna shoved against the small table with their washbasin on it, knocking the bowl to the ground where it clattered but did not break.

"Brenna..." Kirstin wailed. "I'm scared."

"All will be well," Brenna said, repeating the words her mother always said to soothe Kirstin. "I'll keep ye safe."

With quick fingers she pressed along the stones, looking for the one that was weaker than the rest. The pads of her fingertips grew raw from her frantic searching. Finally she found it, shoving hard, but she wasn't strong enough.

"Kirstin, help me."

Four hands pressed to the stone and the girls shoved with all their might against it. Sweat started to form on her brow from the exertion of it, and when it finally gave way, Meg wrenched Kirstin's arm snapping her backward.

"Kirstin!" Brenna turned around and glared angrily at their governess. "We need to escape. If ye want to stay that is your choice, but I demand ye let go of my sister."

Meg's eyes narrowed, her puffy cheeks gone nearly purple with rage. "Just who do ye think ye are? The laird hired me on to keep ye in line and even when death is upon us, ye would defy me."

Meg reached for Brenna, but she backed away, pressing against the secret door she'd just unlatched, revealing the darkened tunnel beyond.

"I'm the MacNeacail's daughter. My da hired ye as our governess and ye have a duty to protect us as well as teach us. Dinna be a fool, Meg. The best chance we have is to escape."

Meg's mouth fell open in surprise as she gaped at the passageway beyond. "Apologies, my lady," she murmured. "I didna realize this passage existed. Let us go."

Brenna grabbed hold of Kirstin's hand and ran into the dark. Meg brought a lit candle, closing the door behind them. And it appeared to be just in time. Beyond the door, she could hear the banging of axes as their chamber door was chopped down and the crash of Meg's pile as the men entered.

"We need to hurry. They will find us," Brenna said. "'Tis only a matter of time."

Meg held the candle high. "Do ye know where to go?"

"Aye. Da showed me."

They walked briskly down the stairs, Brenna and Kirstin holding tight to each other's hands as they went, their free fists wrapped in their skirts to pull the hem away from their boots. With every breath she took, she expected to hear the sounds of the men above discovering the secret tunnel. And though she did occasionally hear a bang that made her jump, no one marched through the door. No one called their names, shouted for them to stop. No one grabbed hold of them.

Hands outstretched, and only seeing a foot or two in front of her, Brenna touched the dead-end of the tunnel. All she had to do was find the right stone that would press the wall outward. It was higher than she thought, just out of reach. Blast her tiny frame. Her mother, too, was small and while her da had always found their slight forms to be sweet, Brenna found it a hindrance.

"I've got it, lass." Meg, who had at least six inches on the girls' heights, pushed the stone until it clicked.

They eased the door open, the scent of the salty firth a relief. They'd made it to the water gate. Now all they needed was to take a *currach*, one of the tiny row boats, and paddle away from Scorrybreac. That was their only chance for survival.

"Where will we go?" Meg asked, fear filling her eyes.

"We'll need to sail east to the MacKinnons. They are allies of our da."

"What if it's the MacKinnons who've attacked?"

Brenna felt like she'd been punched in the gut. She'd not thought of that. Searching her memory, she tried to see if she could recognize any of those who'd attacked, but from the window in their nursery and the dark of night, she'd not been able to make out the color of their plaids. "Then we are dead anyway."

With a curt nod, Meg ushered the two of them down the watery stairs toward the gate and, beyond that, to where several *currachs* lay on the rocky shore.

They were nearly to the quay. Meg bade them wait as she stepped out from the protection of the stairs. Only a second passed before Meg cried out in pain, stumbling forward. The torch clattered across the natural stone surface of the water gate as Meg fell forward. Brenna stared wide-eyed at the blood seeping through the back of her governess' gown. She'd been stabbed through. Shoving her sister into a crevice in the rocks, she said, "Stay here. Be silent."

Recklessly, Brenna ran toward Meg's body, seeing a lad not yet a man, but older than a boy standing just beyond where they could see from the stairs. "Ye killed her!" she cried.

He shrugged. "She was going to take ye away."

Rage, pure and raw filled her. "Aye! What of it?"

The lad pointed his sword in her direction, squaring off, and puffing out his chest. "I cannot allow that to happen. This castle will be mine one day, along with all of its inhabitants."

"Go away! Ye're not welcome here!"

The lad laughed and directed his sword at Brenna's throat. "On the contrary, 'tis ye that is no longer welcome here. But I'll make an exception seeing as how ye're to be my wife."

"Wife?" She was not old enough to be anyone's wife. She'd not yet had her menses. A betrothal contract must have been what the boy meant. She'd not be well and truly wed for several years to come, which would give her time to escape if needed.

But Kristen... Brenna chewed her lip and forced herself not to look behind her to be sure her sister was still hiding.

The lad nodded, his face contorting into something of an evil grin. "Aye. Now that Chief MacNeacail and his wife are dead, ye are the only one left."

Her mother and father were dead.

She was the only one left.

The only one.

He'd not seen Kirstin. Didn't know about her. Brenna sent up a prayer that at least Kirstin could escape, even if she had to sacrifice herself for a time and go with this fiend.

Still, she tried to negotiate, all while swallowing down the bile of fear and guilt. Meg's death was on her. Her parents' death was on her. She'd never forgive herself for causing such mayhem. She'd never disobey an order again. If only God would let her escape this sinister lad. "What does that have to do with anything? Ye've seized this place. Let me go."

"Nay, lass. Ye're coming with me."

Brenna shook her head, but she dared not move backward in case the lad advanced on her and saw her sister in the crevice.

The lad poked her neck with the tip of his sword and pain radiated from the spot. She felt a warm trickle of blood running down her neck, but still she remained strong.

Brenna held out her hands in supplication, sending a prayer up to heaven to receive her if that was the Lord's plan. "Why do ye not just kill me?"

The lad shrugged — a nonchalant, uncaring act that made her rage further. The lad could care less that he'd killed her governess, that his men had killed her parents and countless others. It wasn't important to him. She was important. Life was not important. Her blood chilled.

"Father's orders."

Brenna swallowed around the icy lump growing in her throat. "Who is your father?" she croaked.

"The MacLeod."

From what Brenna had understood, the MacLeod's had been trying to get their hands on her clan's land for decades. She didn't know why. No one had shared that bit of information with her. Seemed they had finally gotten their way.

Thrusting her chin out, she said, "Our allies will avenge my family's murder."

The lad laughed. "Doubtful. All of Scotland is rife with unrest. The little queen has died. Have ye not heard?"

All the blood drained from Brenna's face. If Queen Margaret, only slightly younger than herself, was dead, then indeed there would be unrest as no one would know who to name next to the throne. Why would they care about a small clan on the Isle of Skye when all of Scotland was up for the taking?

She may very well be without a friend in the world.

Her only chance was if Kirstin could escape, but her sister was so weak... She'd never survive in the wild on her own. If Brenna left her here, she might as well sentence her sister to death, but if she told this vile boy... He might kill her, too. She had to strike a bargain.

Folding her hands in front of her, Brenna attempted to look meek, but the sounds of boots pounding on stone through the tunnel she'd just come from startled her. The secret door was thrust open and her cousin, Finn, stepped through—not much older than the lad in front of her.

"Brenna!"

The vile lad grabbed her elbow, yanked her against him, and wrapped his arm around her ribs squeezing tight, his sword pressed hard to her throat.

"Leave or I kill her," he ordered.

Finn growled, pulling his sword from his scabbard. She was certain that if he tried, he could dispatch of the MacLeod lad, but not before her enemy slit her throat.

"Kirstin, go with Finn. Protect her."

Kirstin slipped from the stones and shook her head. "Nay, Brenna. Not without ye."

"There are two of ye?" MacLeod growled.

Risking his wrath, she stiffened. "Nay, there is only one of me," Brenna said. "Go! Finn, please!"

"I cannot leave ye," Finn said, his face contorted in indecision, for he must have known there was truly only one option.

Brenna locked her eyes on his, imploring. "Ye must. 'Tis her only chance."

"And what of ye?" Moisture gathered in her cousin's eyes.

The MacLeod boy pressed the sword harder to her neck, bringing a sting of tears. "Take the little bitch with ye else I cut off this one's head. Dinna think I won't!"

"Brenna," Kirstin sobbed, her entire body shaking. She reached toward her, but Brenna shook her head.

"Be strong, sister. Ye must. There is no other way. One of us must escape this."

Kirstin rushed forward, arms outstretched, which had MacLeod reacting violently, his sword flinging away from Brenna's neck and toward her sister. Finn grasped Kirstin around the waist yanking her back, just before the tip of the sword could pierce her skin.

"Go!" Brenna shouted. "Go, now!"

Finn grabbed hold of Kirstin's hand and dragged her, sobbing, toward the quay. Finn would protect her with his life, she knew that, and at least now her sister had a chance at freedom. Brenna shivered, for she was certainly doomed to a lifetime of suffering.

The boy laughed against her ear. "Ye're mine now. And dinna doubt, those two will not taste freedom for long."

Brenna pressed her lips together, holding back her sobs, resigned to her fate. Finn and Kirstin had to make it. They just had to.

The boy dragged her up the water gate stairs, through the small courtyard at the north side of the castle and through the door that led to the kitchens. They crossed the empty kitchen and into the great hall.

Sobs sounded throughout the castle as servants checked on the dead and cleaned up the mess. Blood stained the wood planks of the floor. The bodies of MacNeacail warriors lay lifeless, eyes gaping, mouths slack.

Brenna closed her eyes from the sight, relieved she'd not seen her parents, and not wanting to see them should she spot them after all.

Though she'd seen plenty of servants look woefully her way, none had tried to save her. And she didn't expect them to.

"Who's this?" an older man grunted.

"Brenna."

"Daughter of MacNeacail?"

"Aye, Father."

Brenna did open her eyes then to see the man who'd brought carnage to her home. She vowed that from this day forth, she would never forget his face, and one day, she'd smile over his dead body.

The chief called over his shoulder, "Get the priest. They marry today. Now."

Wed? A priest? This was not a betrothal, but a marriage in truth. Brenna's mouth fell open to protest, but the lad pinched her hard when he sensed her action, and then whispered, "Be lucky that 'tis I he will marry ye to as the old man is without a wife himself."

She clamped her lips closed, fully aware that she was accepting the lesser of two evils.

Chapter One

Isle of Skye
Dunakin Castle
June, 1305

LAIRD Gabriel "Wolf" MacKinnon was ready to kill someone.

Anger sliced a path through his veins, coiling his muscles. A snarl curled his lips. He gripped his sword tight and circled the bastard standing in the center of the bailey. Ginger hair pulled back with a leather thong, the warrior even grinned a little, creases cutting his tanned cheeks. His dark eyes sparkled.

Chief Lamont.

Gabriel's enemy.

Overhead, the summer sun broke free of any clouds and shone on them with glee — as if the heavens themselves were laughing at Gabriel's expense. *Bloody hell.*

"How dare ye step foot on my land after what ye did. Either ye're a damned fool or ye've got bloody ballocks of iron. If I were ye, I'd be preparing to meet my maker, ye whoreson!"

Nearly a decade had passed since the filthy maggot had stolen his woman and Gabriel was still spitting mad.

Lamont pulled his own sword from his scabbard, fury flaring in his eyes. Gabriel was glad the foolish grin had been wiped from his face.

A dozen MacKinnons drew their weapons, leaping forward, but Gabriel warned them away. He would handle the bloody jackanapes on his own.

"'Twas Montgomery's doing and ye know it," Lamont offered in defense of his actions.

Gabriel shook his head with disgust. "Dinna lie, I can see it plain on your face."

"My wife fairs well, in case ye were wondering."

If that wasn't Lamont's attempt to goad Gabriel's anger, he didn't know what could be.

The "Wolf" broke free and Gabriel let out a battle cry as he arched his sword bringing it down on Lamont, who, disappointingly, parried at the last second. The warrior was strong and their swords clashed, sparks flying. He held still, gripping on to Gabriel's wrist as he stared him straight in the eye. Fury gone, replaced with something close to pleading.

"I need to speak with ye, MacKinnon. We can fight later."

"What for?" Even the mention of *her* name sent his heart into aching spams. He'd fallen in love with Ceana Montgomery, sister to Laird Jamie Montgomery, eight years before and had been prepared to wed her when a deal had been brokered between the two bastard lairds and she'd been ripped from his arms. "Have ye come to gloat?"

Gabriel didn't wait for the man to answer, instead he leapt back and launched in to another attack. Anger blinding him to everything save revenge against the man who'd stolen away his bride.

"Dammit, Wolf, cease this. I'll not kill ye and Ceana would dismember me if I even injured ye."

"Ye'd better kill me, else I'll slice ye at the neck here and now." Holding his sword steady, Gabriel glanced back toward the keep briefly to be certain his mother had not come outside. There was no need for her to lay witness to his rage at their visitor and, even though he was laird, she'd feel obligated to make an attempt at breaking up their fray.

They continued to circle one another, attacking, blocking, until sweat poured down their spines and over their brows. A crowd had discreetly grown around them, no one making a sound for fear they'd be turned away.

Lamont ducked and twisted away. "Do ye think I'd travel so far simply to gloat? I've need of your help."

That gave Gabriel pause. He stopped his attack for a moment, but kept his sword pointed squarely at Lamont's throat.

"What is it? Is Ceana all right?" When he'd met her, she'd just been widowed, and happily so, given her marriage had not been a pleasant one. He'd loved her, wanted her, and then she'd been given away. He wanted to grab Lamont by his neck and shake him. To lift him off his feet and watch the breath dissipate from his body. "Ye'd better be making her happy."

Lamont smiled, a whimsical look that didn't suit the fierce warrior. Blast it all, the arse was in love with her. Gabriel ground his teeth.

"Ceana is well and happy. As am I."

Gabriel tightened his hold on the hilt of his sword. He didn't want Lamont to be happy, but if the man wasn't, that would mean that Ceana wasn't either, and he knew how heartbroken she'd been when her brother had given her the news that he'd not honor Gabriel's request for her hand. Hell, she'd sobbed on his shoulder for an hour and he'd been close to tears himself. But that was years ago and he'd not shed another tear for her loss, even if his heart had broken and never healed since.

Sweat trickled over Lamont's brow and he swiped it. "'Tis another matter I come to ye with."

"What?" Gabriel cracked his neck, loosening himself up for the next round of attack.

"Ceana's cousin, Lady Brenna MacLeod."

"The MacLeod's wife?" MacLeod land bordered the west of the MacKinnon holding and they'd been allies until four years before when the old laird died and his son took over. Having a violent and vengeful nature, the new laird had made it his plan to seize all of the Isle of Skye for himself. Perhaps he'd had a taste for it since he was a lad of sixteen and married Brenna MacNeacail after murdering and seizing her clan's castle and holding, which bordered MacKinnon land to the north.

Gabriel had never seen Brenna himself, but he'd been told she was a frail little thing, barely more than the size of a child.

"Aye. The MacNeacail's wife, Amalie, was sister to Jamie and Ceana's mother, making them cousins."

"What's this got to do with me?"

"We've heard about the trouble MacLeod has been giving ye."

"And?" Trouble it had been at first. A few cattle raids, a couple skirmishes along the road. They'd turned into more than just a nuisance when MacLeod had started ambushing their trading wagons, interrupting their markets and then pillaging villages.

The MacKinnon holding to the east controlled access to Loch Alsh and the mainland, as well as the Sound, which led into the Minch and the surrounding seas. MacLeod land also bordered the Minch, but they'd not conquered all the MacDonald's holdings whose access to the Sound of Sleet also fed to the mainland, though ships had to sail through the treacherous Minch. Having access to the narrow sound and loch to the mainland would have been a boon for the MacLeods and the only way to command it was for them to take control of MacKinnon lands. Which they'd not yet succeeded in doing. But not for lack of trying. Any day now, Gabriel expected a full on attack by the MacLeods.

"We want ye to fight." Lamont dug the tip of his sword into the ground.

"Fight?"

"Aye. Take on those MacLeod bastards."

"To what purpose?" Gabriel glanced at his men from the sides of his eyes and gave a little swipe of his hand. They started to back away, though they didn't disperse completely.

Lamont cocked his head and studied MacKinnon. "I think we both know to what purpose."

"I'll not kill another laird. That will only be inviting every MacLeod to my doorstep itching for a fight." The entire Isle of Lewis, thousands of warriors. Even the MacLeod holdings on the Isle of Skye vastly outnumbered his own.

"Ye need not kill him, Wolf. Have ye not heard?"

"Heard what?"

Lamont raised his brows, seeming surprised that Gabriel was oblivious to whatever news he was about to impart.

"Rumor has it, his wife's done the deed herself. But now she and her wee ones are being held prisoner by the

MacLeod's younger brother. She managed to get a letter to Ceana begging for help."

Gabriel chewed on that bit of information. The wee lass had killed her husband? Must have done it in his sleep. A slip of a woman like that would be hard pressed to kill a mouse caught in a trap.

"And?" Gabriel prompted, still not entirely sure what the hell it was that Lamont wanted.

"The lass needs help."

Gabriel waited for him to say more, but he didn't, leaving the space between them thick with unanswered questions. Gabriel let out a small groan. "Are ye expecting me to rescue her?"

Lamont's face lit up, as if he'd been hoping Gabriel would come to that conclusion and he wouldn't have to actually make the suggestion himself. "And the wee ones. Their uncle has threatened to kill them and I wouldn't put it past him. He needs them dead so he can be laird."

Lamont, after unmanning him, wanted to see him further emasculated by playing rescuer and nursemaid? "Nay. Not a chance."

Gabriel shook his head prepared to call over his guards to have Lamont tossed out of the gates on his ear.

"Wolf, I beg ye. Ceana begs ye."

He ground his teeth again, the crunching noise it made music to his already pained ears. "Ye're jesting."

"Not at all. I swear it." Lamont crossed himself.

Dammit! The man was serious. And Ceana wanted his help, too. Aye, he'd lost her, but after all these years, he would still do anything for her.

Gabriel let out a loud, irritated groan. "How many wee ones?"

Lamont spoke softly and slowly as if he were trying not to awaken a bear. "Four. Three lads and a little lass."

MacKinnon rolled his eyes. "Ye just expect me to ride up on my horse and gallop away with a lady and her four bairns?"

Lamont shrugged. "Well, if ye could take the castle that would be even better, considering the eldest boy is set to inherit as laird."

A murderess and her, no doubt, unruly children. "How old is he?"

"Fourteen summers."

Gabriel rolled his head from side to side, cracking his neck. He needed to weigh his options. If the laird was dead and his fourteen-year-old son was going to inherit, then he'd likely be advised by a group of elder clansmen. They could end up being like his father, content with continuing the arsehole's plan for Skye, or they could be men that were loyal to the lad's grandfather, MacKinnon's old ally. Then again, Lamont mentioned that the boy was being held prisoner with his family and that their uncle wanted to kill them all.

If their uncle was as power hungry as he was being made out to be, which seemed fairly obvious, then MacKinnon may have an even bigger problem.

"Do the men have no loyalty to their new laird?" Gabriel asked.

"The lad?"

"Aye."

"Seems the uncle's named himself his nephew's advisor and will rule until he comes of age."

Just as he feared. Gabriel got straight to the point. "What's in it for me?"

"Lady Brenna."

Oh, this just got worse and worse. "Ye cannot be serious."

"Deadly."

"An old hag? She's borne four children already. What good is she to me?"

Lamont raised his brow. "She's not as old as ye may suspect."

"With a child of fourteen? She's past her prime, Lamont. I see ye've just come to insult me. Get off my land."

"No insult, Wolf. I've asked for your help, and if the woman is not what ye seek, then what is? Ships? Coin?"

"Have ye a ship for me?" Gabriel could always use more ships.

"The MacLeods have plenty. When ye rescue the lass and her bairns, steal away on a galleon or two."

Gabriel snorted. "Ye're something else."

"Will ye think about it? Time is of the essence. I must know by morning if ye're willing to help."

"And if I'm not?"

"Then I'll need to find someone else who is."

"Who?"

Lamont shrugged. "'Haps your neighbors, the MacDonalds."

Gabriel frowned. The MacDonalds already surrounded him on two sides. The last thing he needed was for them to surround him on a third and have their heads swell at the increase in power. That would be dangerous for him.

He stared hard at Lamont, knowing that had to have been the man's angle all along. The spark of knowing in his eyes gave it away.

"Ye'll have my answer by morning." He'd let the man stew on it overnight, even though Gabriel was already certain what his answer would be: on the morrow, he'd be preparing for a siege. Truth be told, he wasn't only doing it for the fact that he didn't want the MacDonalds to have more power should they succeed in their siege of the MacLeods. He was doing it for Ceana. Because even though eight years had passed, he still felt the loss of a life they could have lived together. It had not been her fault she'd been given to another. He would do anything she asked of him. "Come inside. I'll have a room made up for ye, and ye can sup at my table."

"My thanks, MacKinnon."

"That doesna mean all is forgiven between the two of us." He'd never forgive Lamont. Even the span of nearly a decade had not dulled the ache of that loss. He had no wife, he had no heirs and, after losing Ceana, he'd not even bothered to try to find another.

In fact, at aged thirty-six, he wasn't certain he'd ever marry. Ceana's wasn't the first marriage he'd attempted to enter into. Before her, he'd been betrothed to Lorna Sutherland, sister to Laird Magnus Sutherland, and, ironically, now married to Jamie Montgomery — Ceana's brother — these past eight years. How was it that he'd lost two brides in the span of a few months? And Montgomery appeared to be at the heart of them both.

They'd been allies. Hell, Gabriel had joined his men with Jamie Montgomery's in the fight against the English that same year. The English had killed Gabriel's sister, brutally, and he'd been ripe for revenge. He still felt the pain of Annabelle's death. He'd been a raging, feral animal on the battlefield, giving no mercy, and it was there that he'd garnered the name Wolf.

They'd won and an alliance had been formed between the MacKinnons and the Montgomerys. Until Lamont happened along.

Gabriel gritted his teeth and sheathed his sword as he climbed the stairs to the front entrance of Dunakin Castle. Situated high on a rocky knoll that jutted out, overlooking the Strait of Kyle Akin and Loch Alsh, the scent of seawater washed over him in a gentle breeze. 'Twas late afternoon already and within a few hours dusk would settle upon them.

What he wouldn't give for a quick swim in the Akin before Cook was ready to serve supper. He opened the door, his *guest* following. His housekeeper, Una, greeted them at the door.

"My laird," she said with a curtsy.

"Please make up the guest chamber for Laird Lamont."

"Aye, my laird."

"See that he is made comfortable and an extra place set at the laird's table for supper."

As soon as Lamont had gone off with Una, Gabriel turned back around and went outside. He nodded in the direction of his men who were still training in the bailey and made his way toward the postern gate and the stairs that led down to the water.

As soon as he stepped on the rocky beach, he shed his clothing and walked out into the water, diving in as soon as the cool water hit just above his knees. He sank beneath the surface, letting the water run over his back, through his hair. Still his blood burned with memories he'd tried to force aside and a past that was best left there. Coming to the surface, he dragged in a breath, the warm air contrasting with the chilled water, and then he began his swim. Arcing his arms over his head, he reached forward, extending each to maximum length and then pulling them back through the water. His legs kicked forcefully as he plowed through the depths.

Gabriel was a powerful swimmer. Had always been. The movements came easy to him. When he was a lad, he'd thought it was possible he'd been born from water folk and gifted to his clan. He could swim for hours at a time and, in fact, when a man was tossed overboard on one of his galleons, Gabriel was the one who dove below to save him. He never seemed to tire of swimming. Kicking his feet, his legs and arms powered him a mile out toward Loch Alsh, his mind blank of everything save pushing his muscles hard.

He floated on his back, staring up at the sky and contemplating Lamont's unfortunate visit for a good quarter of an hour before he turned around and headed back to shore.

Perhaps this undertaking of saving Lady Brenna and her bairns would be just the thing he needed. He'd not seen a battle since the year before when Montgomery had called on him to help with a clash against the English at Stirling Castle. He'd narrowly escaped with his life and the bloody Sassenachs still held the fortress. Gabriel had come back to Dunakin, intent on training his men harder, because he was certain the War for Scottish Independence would soon travel northward once more. How could he protect his people and his own lands against the English if he had to worry about his neighbors, too?

His men needed to see a little battle, to have practice that was closer to the real thing than simple mock battles in the bailey and fields.

And he wanted to do something for Ceana so that she knew he harbored her no ill will. Perhaps, this one last act of kindness on his part would also allow him to let go. She was happy, as Lamont had said. She no longer loved him, or if she did, it didn't matter.

Truth be told, his heart had ached so fiercely, he'd wanted to forget about her. But it didn't matter. Every woman he'd attempted to flirt with had fallen short. Every one of them that he'd brought to his bed, he'd been able to pleasure, but wasn't able to take pleasure himself. Och, but he was a fool. None compared to Ceana.

He'd worked his way through dozens of women in the hopes of drowning out her face and the sound of her voice from his mind. And until now, he'd mostly succeeded.

Perhaps the worst thing was that he was nearly certain he was no longer in love with her. Aye, his heart would always hold a special place for her, but somewhere along the way he'd moved on. And maybe that was part of his sense of rage—cold-hearted bastard was what he was, for he'd forgotten her. He'd been content in his unhappy solitude.

Until today. Until that blasted Lamont had to come through his gates and flaunted his happiness and all the rage and pain Gabriel had felt before unearthed itself from where he'd kept it safely buried.

Well, he needed to see it reburied. A lass tonight, a stiff whisky and battle on the morrow ought to do it. And he had to get Lamont the hell off his land. He never wanted to see the cur again.

By the time Gabriel walked naked from the water, his breathing had just the right labor, proof of a fruitful workout. It did his spirit good. He whipped his head to the side, flicking his wet hair from his forehead and wiped the water from his face. Without skipping a beat, he dressed and walked back up the stairs toward his keep.

Supper would be in an hour or so, and before that, he needed to talk with his second-in-command, Coll. He'd also need to warn his mother that he'd be leaving soon. But, he rather thought she might find joy in that prospect as she'd been one of those telling him to quit moping about. Shaking his head at what a quandary he found himself in, Gabriel entered his castle, surprised to find his mind a little lighter after his swim.

Chapter Two

Isle of Skye
Dunvegan Castle

LADY Brenna leapt to her feet when her chamber door burst open and her eldest son, Theo, was thrust back inside. The door quickly slammed and the sound of the lock turning echoed in her silent shock. She scrambled toward him, tripping over her tapestry rug, but he caught her in his arms.

"Ye're shaking," she said, cupping his face and looking into his eyes. "What happened?"

Her other children, Gillian, eleven, and her five-year-old twin boys, Nevin and Kenneth, hurried close, but Brenna waved them back. Her pure white

36

wolfhound, Snow, ignored her flutter of fingers and nudged her muzzle against Theo's palm.

Theo closed his eyes a moment, his throat bobbing as he swallowed. At fourteen, he wanted so badly to be a man grown, but he was still just a lad. And one that had been through one overly traumatic event after another.

"Tell me, love," she whispered, edging closer.

His body was stiff and he looked ready to snap.

Snow sat down, taking up guard beside them both and Brenna ran a hand over her crisp, yet soft, furry head. Her son opened his eyes and met her gaze, the irises the same blue as her own, his raven hair just as unruly.

"More of the same," he muttered. The lad sounded dejected, tired.

It broke Brenna's heart to see him so.

A full month had passed since their fates had changed. And Brenna wasn't certain it was for the better. With one demon dead and gone, yet another had arisen to take his place. Tormented for the last fifteen years by her husband, the late Chief MacLeod, his death should have been a blessing—and she didn't feel an ounce of remorse at his passing—but his younger brother, Thomas, had taken it upon himself to hold them hostage as he attempted to get at the root of Ronald's death and any other secrets Dunvegan held.

The torrent of usual questions tumbled from Brenna's lips. "Did ye tell him ye were not witness to it? That I killed him?"

Theo's chin wobbled, but he quickly clenched his jaw, the sound of his grinding teeth making Brenna wince. Oh, her poor lad. When had he ever been able to be just a boy?

"Aye, mother. He's still looking for father's treasury, too."

Blasted beast. He would make them prisoners and steal their coin, too? "And ye told him ye dinna know where it is? That your father never shared the information with ye?"

Theo nodded, pain contorting his face. "He doesna believe me."

"There is nothing else for your uncle to believe. I killed Ronald, that is all anyone need know." When Theo broke his gaze away to stare at the ground, she plucked his chin, forcing his gaze back up. "With your father gone, ye are the laird."

"They will not follow me. Not with Uncle Thomas keeping me locked in here. He's poisoned the clan against us."

Brenna shook her head. "He is angry that his brother was killed at the prime of his life. Our people will soon see the right of it." Even though she said the words, Brenna didn't believe it. The people of the clan had been poisoned against her many years ago. Saw her as weak. She'd been brought into their clan as the daughter of an enemy. They'd been told not to trust her. And when Theo came to her aid more than once against his father, they began to despise him, too. Their prejudices against her naturally clamped on to her offspring. If her children loved her, if they protected her, then they were the enemy, too. Even if the clans' people didn't believe her children to be against them, they still followed the moods of their leader. Their laird would have been angered if they'd done otherwise. Their mighty and brutal chief.

Ronald's brother, Thomas, was just the same and she was full aware that Thomas wanted the lairdship for himself. If his naming himself advisor to the new young laird, ruling in his stead until Theo came of age wasn't enough of a clue, then the fact that he kept Brenna and her children locked up like prisoners was. What council kept their laird behind a locked door?

How could she have faith in the people of MacLeod if they did not rise up against Thomas and demand that he let Theo go? She couldn't. The people were not on their side. It was a sad and disheartening fact. And she had no faith in them at all—except for two.

Luckily, Brenna had a couple of servants on her side, servants who'd helped her so many times over the years that she'd lost count. Her personal maid, an elderly clanswoman named Sarah and her husband, Angus. They'd been with her since the beginning and knew she wasn't a threat, that though she was borne of an enemy clan, she herself would not harm them. Behind closed doors, they scoffed at the rest of the clan for believing such rubbish.

Brenna had given a letter to Sarah, who passed it on to Angus, who then smuggled it out to her cousin Ceana, Mistress of Clan Lamont, pleading for assistance. She prayed nightly that Ceana would be able to help. That they would take Brenna and her children away, whisk them off to the Lowlands for their own safety. If they had to keep hidden until her son had not only come of age, but amassed the skill and army to fight for what was his, then that was what they'd do. By all rights, MacLeod and MacNeacail lands were his and she would see them restored to him.

The last fifteen years had been pure hell, but Brenna hadn't forgotten who she was before she'd come to Dunvegan. Brenna MacNeacail was a fighter. She was strong. With her cousin's assistance, she'd take her children to a place where they could be safe.

"Mother, I will not let Thomas hurt ye." Already a foot taller than she was, Brenna had to crane her neck to look into Theo's eyes.

"I know, son. But when it comes down to it, ye are the one who needs to survive this. Ye are the only hope your sister and brothers have. The only hope of our people, both MacLeod and MacNeacail."

Thomas had been given her family's seat when Ronald had captured her and murdered her family all those years ago, and he'd ruled with a bloody fist just as his brother did. Apparently, though their father had been mostly a just man, the two brothers had grown greedy and vicious. Power hungry.

Well, now there was only one to contend with. Better than two of them. Good riddance.

She could still see Ronald's prone, bloody body. His head bashed in by a fire poker. The same fire poker that had been removed from where it usually rested beside her empty hearth. The weapon that had ended her fifteen-year marriage and could have set her free if Thomas had not been visiting at the time.

Ronald would never hurt her or her children again.

"Aye, Mother." Theo nodded resolutely and she led him over to the table by the hearth and urged him to sit.

"Thomas called on ye before ye had time to break your fast. We saved ye breakfast." Brenna nodded to Gillian who'd hidden the meal when the guards had come to collect the remains of it.

Brenna was pretty certain that her captor thought to starve the truth from her boy, but that wouldn't work. Theo had been raised by a man far more brutal than his uncle. Humiliation and deprivation were daily thrust on Theo daily by his father, and he'd grown a thick skin, and a strong heart, because of it. Gillian, too. The lass had suffered much, and even recently had been threatened with marriage, though she was only eleven. Seeing as how he'd married her at age twelve, the fiend didn't see a problem with it.

Despite that, 'twas her youngest bairns she worried over more. Nevin and Kenneth favored her late husband's looks with their ginger locks that came down to their chins in straight, even lines. The only difference between them and Ronald was their light brown eyes that showed kindness. He'd taken a liking to the twins, coddling them when he ignored his older two children. They missed their father and blamed her for his death, as they rightly should. For, 'twas her fault.

The two boys held hands and stared at their brother with blank expressions. As of late, they were hard to read, but she was certain she'd know soon enough just how they felt. The young lads were more prone to tantrums in the last month. Gone were the cheery bairns she'd known them to be the last five years, replaced with shells of their formers selves. They mourned their father's death and it broke her heart to see them suffer.

As Gillian served her brother his ration of bread and butter, Brenna knelt before her twins and hugged them tight to her. Snow inched her way forward until she sat beside Brenna. The hound was a blessing. She'd had her the past two years — since she'd birthed her last stillborn bairn. Snow had been a gift from Ronald — an apology for how he'd handled her while with child. She'd been determined to hate the hound but, as it turned out, Snow was the best friend she had at the moment.

Brenna pressed her lips to the temple of each boy, breathing in their sweet scent. Being a twin herself, she understood their tight bond. And every time she gazed on them, she was reminded of the sister she'd lost. She'd never received word about her cousin Finn or her darling sister, Kirstin. Though she kept them in her prayers, she was almost certain Kirstin and Finn had been taken on the road, so when she prayed for their safety wherever they may be, she also prayed for their souls. If they'd survived their escape, wouldn't she have heard something over the years, even if 'twas only rumor?

Nevin pushed against her shoulder while Kenneth sunk against her. Now that was different. Normally, Kenneth was the one to push away.

"Oh, my laddies," she whispered. "Ye know I love ye?"

"Nay," Nevin said with a pout while Kenneth remained silent. "Ye're a sinner. Sinners canna love."

Brenna swallowed hard past the pain of her son's words. He did not know any better. In his eyes, she was a sinner. And Uncle Thomas had been certain to push that thought into the young ones' minds. Did they not realize they, too, were locked up like prisoners? Oh, how could they? They were still bairns, innocent of all things unrighteous in the world.

"I know ye're hurting," she started. "I wish I could take away your pain."

"I want Da back."

"Me, too," Kenneth piped in, finally pushing against her.

Brenna sank back on her heels, letting them go as they turned their backs on her and walked across the room to the corner they'd taken up as their own. In comfort, Snow placed her large head into Brenna's lap, and Brenna leaned forward to kiss her between the eyes, affording her a slobbery lick of an overlarge tongue.

In the corner, her boys had picked up their wooden horses and warriors and were playing a mock battle. Their little voices carried over the room and with them, the sounds they made to portray swords clashing and hooves pounding the floor. Their innocence made her smile, even if they were rejecting her at the moment. They had not been witness to the killing of Ronald. Kept in their nursery on the top floor, they'd not been witness to his caustic verbal abuse of her, how he locked her away in her chamber whenever he liked, nor the way he handled the bedding. To his ill-treatment of anyone. Sometimes, she'd almost preferred that he would simply beat her rather than torturing her mind endlessly. Ronald didn't have a nice word in his head or a kind bone in his body.

But their two youngest children had only ever seen him at his best, and though she hated to admit it, for the most part he'd been a good father to the two of them. But he only saw them when it was convenient for him, which never amounted to more than a few times a month. On those days, he would bring them treats, toys and then he'd play games with them that he knew she and their nursemaid, would never allow.

Gillian's light hand touched her shoulder. "One day they will know the truth, Mama."

Brenna shook her head. "Nay, darling, let them remain innocent of it. We've all suffered enough. If they want to remember their father as a great man, let them."

Gillian sighed with disappointment and removed her hand. Speaking as a lass far older than she was, she said, "Better for them to hear it from ye, as they will surely learn the truth and then blame ye all the more."

Brenna smoothed her hands over her plain, green gown, nudged Snow off of her lap and then pushed to her feet. "Mayhap I will. In time."

Just as Theo had her coloring, so did Gillian. And in another year or two, the lass would be her height as well, which wasn't much more than tiny. Brenna's head barely reached the saddle of her horse when standing on tiptoes. Birthing children had, at least, given her feminine curves.

"Mother," Theo said from across the room. His voice had gained in strength since he'd first returned.

Brenna returned to the table where he ate, her feet feeling as heavy as her heart. He'd already devoured the bread and was greedily drinking the watered ale they'd saved for him.

"We have to find a way to escape." His eyes were hard as he stared at her.

Brenna suddenly got the feeling there was something her son had kept from her. "What haven't ye told me, Theo?"

He took a large gulp, wiping the remnants on his sleeve. Lips closed, he seemed apt to refuse an answer.

"Theo—" Brenna closed the distance between them, placing her hand on his palm. "We are in this together. We must be honest with each other if we are to survive this."

"Do ye not see? We will not survive if we do not escape."

"What are ye saying?" What had that bastard told her son?

"Thomas aims to pick us off one by one. Starting with Nevin and Kenneth."

Brenna's breath stole from her throat and she had to grasp on to the table for balance. Snow came up behind her, holding her wavering body in place.

"He aims to make an example of them both, and to ye."

Brenna rubbed her temples, shook her head. "Nay, he could not have meant that. He'd not hurt them."

"Worse, Mother. He will kill them."

"Why?"

"Because, he thinks we are withholding information from him."

"He is right." She let out a deep sigh. She'd not wanted to tell Thomas about the treasury because the coin within it, amounting to a vast fortune, belonged to her son. She'd hoped to withhold it from him and keep it for when they escaped, but that was clearly not an option now. "I will tell him where the treasury is."

"That will not be enough," Theo said. "I could see it in his eyes, Mother. It won't matter if ye tell him where the crown jewels are. He wants us all dead because he wants to be Chief MacLeod. We stand in his way — your three sons stand in his way, as does your daughter."

All the blood had drained from Brenna's head, her limbs, pooling somewhere in her boots. She was cold, tingly and close to falling over. Even at Ronald's worst, he'd never threatened the lives of his children — her, aye, but never them. Ronald's words could crush anyone with a soul, and he'd threatened many times to send her out into the wild as he had her sister, where she'd die before night fell. When one of his outbursts on the stairs led to him brushing past her at a speed that her overly pregnant belly could not handle, she'd lost her balance and her child. He'd never accepted the blame, accident though it was, but rather stated it was her fault for causing him to snap.

A month trapped in this godforsaken chamber, nearly that long since she'd sent word to Ceana, and she'd heard nothing back. Had her cousin abandoned her? It would seem so. Theo was right. Their only recourse was to escape. She'd be damned if she'd give Thomas her children's coin or their lives.

"Mother," Gillian, who sat across from her brother at the table, said. "Theo's right. I've heard the servants talking. They fear him, too. They say he's worse than Da."

Gillian's face was pinched with worry. Brenna pressed her other hand to her daughter's, clutching on to both of her older children, her sources of stability. "We will escape. We need to come up with a plan. Thomas was smart to put us in this tower room. There are no secret passages here, not like at Scorrybreac." The tunnel she'd led her sister and governess through. The tunnel that had led to Meg's death, her sister and cousin's disappearance and her own capture.

'Haps it was best there was no secret passage here as the one at her childhood home had not served her well at all.

"I have an idea that might buy us some time," Theo said. "Uncle is quite disturbed by anyone who sneezes or coughs. He fears a plague will take him one day."

Brenna smiled at her son. "Brilliant. I think we can easily come up with a plan to at least keep us safe from his interrogations for the short term. Hopefully enough time to form a plan of escape."

Chapter Three

AT the edge of the wood, over the rocky crag, Gabriel called a halt to his men and stared through a rough passage of trees toward Dunvegan Castle. In late afternoon, the sun shone down on the castle through a few white, fluffy clouds. Set far back from the road, the castle had a high wall and several guards on the gate tower. There were only two ways to approach the castle — over the wall or from the loch at its back where a sea gate cut into the outer curtain wall.

Any warrior would have a hard time finding a castle more difficult to penetrate. Dunvegan was a mighty fortress, and if it weren't for Lamont's suggestion and veiled threat of offering the duty of saving its inhabitants to Gabriel's neighbors, he'd not be there now.

Sweat trickled down his back from their long ride in the summer heat, causing his linen shirt to cling to his spine. His horse, Ghost, was slick, too, from riding.

"'Tis a mighty fortress," Coll said. "I've not seen it afore now."

Gabriel rolled his head to the side, cracking his neck. "I've been many a time. When the MacLeods were our allies." Odd that he'd not laid eyes on Brenna while he was there. She would have already been married to Ronald MacLeod at the time. "'Tis here that I traveled and met with Jamie Montgomery, the old MacLeod and the Mackenzie afore we fought for the Bruce. Afore Da's passing, and afore the swine Lamont took something from me."

Coll raised a brow.

"That which we do not speak of," Gabriel muttered. Everyone in the clan knew about his resentment of Lamont. Hell, Coll had been the one to clean him up after drinking himself into a stupor the night he'd found out. Slanting a sideways glance at his best mate, he added, "That which I am completely over, as well."

"I'd never say otherwise, my laird," Coll drawled. The two men had known each other since they were in swaddling clothes, even fostered together at the Mackenzie's castle. If anyone could call his bluff it was Coll, and no matter how many *my lairds* the sot used, Gabriel knew just what each of those uttered syllables meant. Aye, his comrade respected him and his position, and though he'd never show any insolence in front of any of their clan, he snuck them in when they were one-on-one. Coll had been his second-in-command since Gabriel's father passed away and Gabriel had been named the new laird — nearly seven years now.

When Gabriel had been to Dunvegan before, he'd been his father's second-in-command, and had been doing most of the clan negotiations for several years at that point as his father had been afflicted with an ague that left him bedridden. Gabriel had always wondered if the death of his sister hadn't pushed his father over the edge, as it had not been much longer after that the old laird passed in his sleep. A death that Gabriel had been greeted with upon his return from battle. His poor mother had lost her husband and daughter within months of each other and Gabriel had not been himself since. In essence, Lady Cora had lost all three of them.

He was determined to come back from this siege more himself and, in fact, he'd already felt that way since three days past when Lamont came knocking on his door. 'Haps he was well and truly over his pain. 'Haps he'd only needed to hear that Ceana was happy in order to let go.

There was a shift on the ramparts that caught his attention. The guards were changing — what little there were, less than half a dozen.

All Gabriel had to do was get in, take control of the castle and get Brenna MacNeacail MacLeod and her four bairns out. He hoped he wasn't too late. There had been an edge to Lamont's plea for help that left Gabriel feeling uneasy. Why did he get the feeling there was more to it than simply MacLeod wanting to kill off the bairns? Or was he reading too much into it? Wasn't it terrible enough that an evil lout like Thomas MacLeod would want to kill children?

Gabriel glowered at the castle, mentally willing Thomas MacLeod to step out onto the battlements so he could put an arrow through his heart. He'd never liked the grimy bastard. Nor his brother.

"How do we go about it?" Coll asked.

Gabriel squinted, staring hard at the castle, glad for the distraction of Coll's question. He'd been surprised at the lack of scouts roaming the woods. They'd only encountered exactly two pairs. One duo that hid in the trees and another that simply patrolled a road below when they passed by, hidden over a ridge. Four warriors to patrol miles and miles of roads, moors and woods surrounding the castle. 'Twas a pathetic attempt. Why did MacLeod even bother? The old MacLeod had been a lot more careful. Whole platoons of men traversed his lands.

When he'd died and his eldest son, Ronald, had taken his place as laird everything changed. Arrogant fool. It would seem Ronald MacLeod's younger brother was even more arrogant than his predecessor. He'd not think anyone would try to lay siege to his castle, especially not from the inside.

Turning his attention to his second-in-command, Gabriel muttered, "The sea gate is the only entrance.

'Twill be hard to simply trudge up to the gate and beg entrance. We'll have to scale the wall here at the north. They'll not be expecting it. We'll wait until the sun has set, give the men several hours' rest." They'd traveled three days at a hard pace from Dunakin Castle, keeping mostly to the coast of the Sound for the cool breeze the water afforded them, until they'd had to cut across MacKinnon land just before reaching the town of Kiltaraglen so news would not travel that a band of fifty warriors was making their way somewhere. From there it had been rough passage over the rocky terrain of the isle, across the moors and wading through burns. A summer rain had doused them for the first two days and even now he wasn't certain his plaid was completely dry.

"Aye, my laird, I think 'tis best."

Lamont had informed Gabriel that at least half of the MacLeod men were stationed at Scorrybreac, the MacNeacail stronghold, another day and a half's ride away. The MacLeods had lost at least four score of their warriors when the old laird had sent them to help the Bruce. If Gabriel had to guess, that meant Dunvegan had only fifty, maybe seventy-five, warriors at most. Gabriel had brought only fifty men with him, but having trained them himself, he knew they were each worth at least three warriors in a battle. In fact, while the MacLeods had lost a great number of men supporting the Bruce, Gabriel had only lost half a dozen, and of that six, two had been from infection.

"I will take twelve men with me. Leave two men here with horses for the thirteen of us. The rest of ye make your way down to the marsh near the sea gate but remain hidden. Once we're inside, I will have a man open the sea gate, and the rest of ye ride in with haste as the castle will be alerted to our presence."

Ordinarily, Gabriel might have approached the gate and requested an audience with the laird, but from what he'd heard of Thomas MacLeod, negotiating with the man would be not only impossible, but likely turn into a bloodbath. There was every possibility that a slaughter would be difficult to avoid and he'd react when and if that time came. But for now, he wanted his men to practice their skills at being elusive, and what better way than to sneak into an impenetrable castle?

They spent the next hour making two crude ladders using rope they'd brought with them, and long branches for the frames, shorter ones for the rungs. Fallen trees were released from their roots to make battering rams. When he was comfortable that the ladders would hold their weight, and that the rams were of good size and weight, he gave the go ahead.

To the men staying with the horses, he said, "Be on alert, we may return and need to withdraw with haste if we are caught going over the wall." Then he added to Coll, "Set up archers to take out any guards on the curtain wall that attempt to push our ladders over, or that come looking to begin with."

The sun had seemed to take forever to set, but at long last the horizon had darkened leaving the MacKinnon warriors cloaked in black. Torch flames lit the wall every twenty feet or so, and through some of the arrow slit windows, he could see the lights from candles or hearth fires. The moon and stars afforded some light, but not enough to give them away in the shadows.

Gabriel took the briefest of moments to gaze at each of the candle-lit windows. Could he catch a glimpse of Brenna? Was she looking out now? Or was she shackled in the dungeon?

Taking twelve of his most seasoned warriors, save for Coll, who he left in charge, Gabriel and his men took off at a slow pace through the woods, two men carrying each ladder. The battering rams remained behind with the other men. They were careful of any MacLeods that might be scouting the area, again surprising him when they found none. At the bottom of the crag, just before the ground turned into wet marsh, Gabriel and his men paused. He stared up at the castle, taking in each crenellation groove and measuring the height of the wall.

The impenetrable fortress sat on a mound of rocky hill, all the gorse bushes and grasses cut away so that no one could lay in wait. It was about ten paces from where they were to the bottom of the motte and another dozen feet up to the base of the curtain wall. The ramparts were clear on this side, making his job almost too easy.

Did Thomas MacLeod really think he was so safe that he needn't have men walking the wall?

Gabriel raised his fist and gave a low owl hoot indicating to his men that he and the dozen he'd chosen were moving out. They picked their way slowly over the rocky, wooded terrain and up the ridge at the base of the curtain wall. Dropping to their bellies, they slowly crawled up the cleared rise. They made certain to keep low and quiet, not even swatting at the bugs that tasted the sweat on their skin. Once each warrior had made it to the wall, Gabriel raised his fist again and nodded, not risking the owl hoot. They stretched to standing. Backs pressed to the wall, they remained still, listening to the sounds on the other side.

He was glad to hear the clatter of people rummaging around and the hum of voices on the other side. From the lack of sentries guarding the wall he'd have thought the place was abandoned, but clearly the men were more interested in pleasant pursuits rather than fortifying their castle. Where was MacLeod? The bloody whoreson didn't seem to give a fig about his castle.

He held his fingers to his lips when, finally, two guards passed by above. They chattered on about a couple of women they'd bedded the night before and how one of them had been more than sotted on whisky and could barely remember it. Though they walked the wall, the one thing the idiots didn't do was actually safeguard it. Their conversation didn't skip a beat as they walked past the invading men fifteen feet below.

Gabriel rolled his eyes. Aye, he wanted the siege to be quick, but he was at least hoping that it would be challenging. So far, this had been laid back enough to be disappointing. He waited for the shams' voices to disappear altogether and then signaled his men. Both ladders were quietly placed against the stones. At the bases, a man held each one steady, while the first two men climbed—Gabriel being one of them. Once he and ten of his men were on the wall, the two at the bottom would remain as lookouts, keeping watch from below and prepared to put up the ladders if needed.

Dagger between his teeth, sword in one hand, Gabriel climbed using his free hand and his feet. In case he met a foe at the top, it was best he be well armed. He made quick work of the ladder, going over the rampart wall in fifteen seconds flat, as did, Donnan, the warrior at his side. Each of them immediately crouched out of the way of the next round of warriors to climb, and faced the opposite direction, prepared to fend off any oncoming guards, but none seemed the wiser.

Torches flickered, bouncing shadows on the wooden planks of the rampart floor, and though he heard plenty of sounds from below in the bailey, there was no trudge of boots. The ramparts had no railing, any skirmish that would take part could leave a man in danger of falling over the side. A drop of fifteen feet, if he had to guess. A man would live, possibly crippled, if he didn't land on anything that killed him.

The next two warriors, and then the next two after that, landed behind Gabriel until all eleven of them were over the wall. Too damned easy.

Frowning, he nodded to his men. Six of them would go to the right of the wall and take out any men they found, while he and the rest took out men to the left. They'd meet in the middle on the opposite side, behind the high tower of the castle. He led the way around the ramparts, keeping close to the wall so they didn't alert any of the guards below — if there were any.

A set of stairs led from the ramparts down near the sea gate and another set on the opposite wall. If he had to guess, there was another set behind the keep.

From the sounds of it, those in the bailey were doing a lot more whisky drinking than anything else. Raucous laughter floated up from below where Gabriel had spied at least half a dozen guards sitting around a bonfire. There appeared to be only two guards up on the ramparts, unless the two he'd heard earlier had abandoned their post, or another couple had joined their comrades. If his men to the right had encountered any guards, they were quiet in dispatching them.

The distinct sound of boot heels on wood gave Gabriel pause. He held up his hand and nodded to his men. The two guards were swiftly approaching, their bawdy banter gaining in resonance with their clomping boots.

Gabriel grinned. At last he could put his sword to use. He and his men waited beyond the glow of the torch, ready to take out the two fiends. They were quickly within view, clearly not paying attention. One of them even took a swig of whatever liquor he had in a small flask. Gabriel almost, *almost*, felt bad for them. But not bad enough to let them pass by, nary the wiser.

Without warning, Gabriel stood, lunged and used his dagger to slice the one's throat, simultaneously using his sword to dispatch of the other straight through the heart.

Donnan grabbed the second warrior by his shirt before he fell over the side and they quietly piled the two dead warriors along the wall in the shadows, hoping no one had caught sight of them. When no warning came from below, all Gabriel could do was shake his head. The old MacLeod would roll in his grave if he knew what was going on at his own castle.

With quick steps, they continued on the ramparts, circling around the back of the large keep where they met up with the other men.

"Ramparts are clear on our side," Gabriel whispered.

"All clear on ours," Lorne, brother of Coll, replied.

Gabriel gazed up the length of the tower. At least three stories high from where he stood, one floor below and likely a cellar. There was a door a few feet away. He tried the handle and found it unlocked. They could easily steal inside, but they needed to get the sea gate open for the other warriors waiting in the woods.

"Lorne, take the men and get the gate open quickly. Coll should be ready to flood the entrance with the rest of the men. Donnan, ye come with me. We're going to see if we can find the prisoners. Two of us should be able to sneak about inside unseen."

"Aye, my laird," the two men answered.

Lorne signaled to the other warriors to follow him and they made their way back around the ramparts toward the stairs that led to the sea gate opening. There was no turning back now. In a matter of minutes, Gabriel would have five helpless lives to protect. A murderess and her four bairns. The thought made him snicker for a moment. Would she try to kill him?

She could try, but she'd not succeed. Gabriel was easily ten times the man her late husband was. If she knew what was good for her, she'd simply submit to him and allow him to take her and her children from Dunvegan.

Somehow, he knew deep down that she'd not be so easily accommodating. After all—she'd *killed* her husband.

With a sigh, Gabriel opened the door to the castle and headed into the dark.

Chapter Four

"WHY do we have to lie under the blanket, Mama?" Nevin asked.

Brenna stared down at her two boys who lay in their special corner under a thick plaid. Snow lay at the boys' feet, protecting them as she oft did at night.

A small handful of whitened ash from the hearth, smeared on their cheeks and forehead gave her children's pallor a decidedly sickly look, which was only emphasized by the dim light of the candle.

"'Tis a game, loves," she answered with as much of a playful smile as she could muster.

Behind her, Gillian and Theo had also smeared ash on their faces, and now Gillian was climbing into the only bed in their chamber. Theo stood in the corner beside the door so when it opened, the guard would not see him standing there. They'd lit the hearth hours before with a single log, slowly heating the room, and when one burned through they added another. In the heat, all three of her boys were happy to disrobe to their long, linen shirts and Gillian to her shift. They were covered in sweat, and if one of the servants were bold enough to enter their *sick* room, the heat of their bodies would make them guess fever, at which point the guards would report to Thomas and he would undoubtedly fear the worst.

"Mother, your face," Gillian reminded her.

Brenna nodded then turned back to her boys. She held her fingers to her lips. "Now, remember, we must stay quiet about what we've done, or else we will not win." Then she pulled out a playing card that made her feel utterly guilty all the way to her core, but that she knew was necessary if she were going to get the twins to cooperate. "Your Da is watching from the heavens." She pointed toward the roof. "And he wants ye to play."

"Are ye certain?" Kenneth asked, his little face scrunching up with worry.

"More than certain, my boy." She winked and hoped that the smile she forced still made her boys feel as though it was simply a game.

A heavy game it was, for it was a gamble with their lives. If they were found out, likely Brenna would be separated from her children, an act she'd been worried over since the day they'd been imprisoned. She'd fight to the death before she allowed that to happen.

Using the remnants of the ash on her hands she scrubbed her face and then turned to Theo and Gillian for their approval. Her daughter beckoned her forward, smoothing out a line on her cheek.

"Perfect. Ye look positively dreadful."

Brenna smiled at the mirth in her daughter's eyes, glad to see some joy coming back to her. Theo was the only one of them who looked truly worried. Immediately, Brenna felt contrite and wiped the delight from her face. With a sigh, she tucked the blanket up to her daughter's chin and went to the window. Peeling back the fur covering she peered down at the bailey below. Men sat around a bonfire guzzling whisky. No one guarded the gates or the walls.

Since Thomas had taken over, he'd not seemed to care a fig about the safety of the castle. He'd even told her their reputation was enough to keep their enemies at bay. It only made her more afraid. If any of their foes caught wind of the lackadaisical way he managed the castle then they'd likely be besieged within a day, a week at most. Ronald had been more proactive in the castle's fortifications than Thomas, but neither of them had been as staunch in their security as their father, the old laird.

He'd been her saving grace in the time that she was here, despite the fact that it had been his idea to take over her clan's castle, and he'd been to blame for her family's death, and her subsequent marriage. She'd not quite forgiven him for his transgressions against her, but she'd accepted his protection whenever her husband went mad enough that the entire castle could hear his ranting and raving.

She shook herself from the brutal memories and let the flap at the window fall back into place.

"Are ye ready?" she asked gravely.

Their plan had come a little farther than when they'd first perceived it. Knowing the men would be well into their cups, their strategy had grown decidedly bolder. Truth be told, Brenna was too afraid not to take action tonight. Over the hours since her son had been questioned that morning, worry had rotted her gut. She was sick with it. A mother's sixth sense told her she needed to get her children out of the castle with haste. Tonight. *Now.*

"Aye, Mother," Theo said. The other three also murmured their agreement.

Taking a deep breath and closing her eyes for a moment, Brenna scrubbed her hands through her hair making herself look in disarray, then she headed for the chamber door.

With two fists she banged frantically and shouted, "Help! Please, someone, my bairns are ill! We need a healer!"

Snow bounced from her spot in the corner, rushing to her mistress, attempting to help her. She scratched at the door and clawed at the floor, while Brenna banged and screamed over and over. Someone was bound to hear her at some point. But when her hands grew raw and painful from banging, her voice hoarse, still no one came. She sagged against the door to draw in breath and give her body a rest. Snow, too, sank to the floor, panting.

"Where are they?" she asked no one in particular.

Thomas had not had their door guarded. Having the door locked from the outside and nearly every item in their chamber that could be used as a weapon removed, he'd not thought he needed a sentry. The chamber was at the very top of the keep's tower, well away from most, and with nightfall giving the inhabitants of the castle permission to drink and entertain themselves in many bawdy ways, was it any wonder that no one could hear her calls?

"Dinna give up, Mother." Theo's voice was full of strength.

Pressing her temple to the door, she turned to stare at her lad. Breath heaving, heart pounding, her shoulders started to ache something fierce from the thumping she'd given the door. Theo returned her regard, his jaw clenched tight, resolute. He wouldn't give up. He wasn't going to let her either. The eldest of her children and the first to be born and survive. He'd been just as fierce in her womb as he was outside of it. She'd been younger than he was now when she brought him into this world. She'd be damned if she was going to let anyone take him away from her.

Brenna managed a smile and nodded. She faced the door once more and was about to pound when she heard someone jiggle the handle from the other side. Gaze riveted on the handle, she couldn't make her mouth work. Why did they not simply unlock it?

Shaking herself out of her temporary stupor, Brenna slammed her palm on the wood. "Open the door! We need help! We need a healer!" she called.

The handle jiggled again and she heard the scrape of metal on the lock. Snow growled low in her throat, ears perked, eyes flicking from the handle to Brenna's face.

A curse sounded along with the scratching of metal and then finally there was an audible click. Brenna bounced away from the door, giving a quick glance at Theo before the door banged open hiding him from view.

A stranger stood in the doorway, taking up the entire expanse. Shoulders as wide as the door frame, and just as tall, he glowered down at her with haunting blue eyes. Behind him she could hear the shuffling of someone else, but she couldn't see him other than to recognize his plaid was not MacLeod, and neither was the stranger facing her.

Snow stood on all fours, hackles raised as she growled threateningly, teeth bared. A caring nursemaid she was, she could also be a fearsome guard. The warrior looked at the dog, whistled and flicked his hand. Snow ceased her growling, contemplated the man and then retreated to her place in the corner with the boys.

Brenna's mouth fell open in shock and horror. How could he command her dog in such a way? And Snow! Traitor!

"Who..." She swallowed around the fearful lump that had formed in her throat, then forced herself to stand tall when she really wanted to retreat. "Who are ye?" she demanded.

The warrior was over a foot taller than she, his golden head bumping against the top of the door frame. When he stepped into the chamber, he actually had to bend slightly to the side and duck. There was nothing small about him. Muscles pulled at the confines of his shirt. Her gaze was riveted to the broad expanse of his chest, the silver brooch that held his plaid at his shoulder sparkled, a single emerald in the center glinting in the light of her candle. She held her breath as she scanned him from the top of his kilt all the way to the end just above his knees. Strong calves were encased in leather boots. He was covered in weapons. A sword at his back, one at his waist. A dagger strapped to his belt, bracers on his forearms, and a needle-nose sharp instrument in one hand. A warrior. Ready for battle. By the time her gaze roved back to his face, she was trembling.

Hard and fierce blue eyes stared down at her, sending a shiver racing over her skin. His flaxen hair was cropped short; the same shade of hair covered his chin in a short beard, lining a strong square jaw. His face was broad, but not overly so, and could have been cut from marble, the angles were so precise. His lips were set in a determined line, but even that fierce look didn't take away from their shape. The V indent at the top that gave them a mesmerizing outline. To be certain, Brenna had never seen a man more handsome, or more terrifying, in her life. Not even Ronald or Thomas ever frightened her by their sheer presence alone. And there was nowhere to go. Rooted in place, her gaze locked on his, she waited for him to tell her just who the hell he was.

Brows arched in assessment, the warrior scanned the room, taking in the sight of her children.

"Where is the fourth?" The timbre of his voice was gruff and deep.

"The fourth?" she asked, buying for time.

"The eldest lad."

Oh, dear, sweet heavens. Brenna's heart constricted painfully behind her ribs. Had Thomas sent this man to kill her son? Was he an assassin? That would explain the colors of his plaid. Thomas wouldn't want her children's deaths on his hands. He'd hired mercenaries. Out of the corner of her eye she caught movement from behind the door. Theo was going to make himself known, but she couldn't allow that.

"He is not here," she lied.

The warrior ceased scanning the room to meet her gaze, his eyes narrowing as he scrutinized her.

"Not here?" he asked.

Her belly tightened and her mouth went dry. *Remain strong, Brenna.* Already once in her life she'd failed someone who looked to her for protection, and poor dear Kirstin had paid the price. Brenna never had closure where her sister was concerned as she never knew what happened to her. Well, she'd be damned if she was going to let this man succeed with his mission of taking her son.

"Aye. He's gone."

The fiend had the audacity to look put out. He grimaced and rubbed at the stubble on his chin. "Where is he?"

Brenna jutted her chin forward. "I do not know."

"Have ye any idea when ye expect him back?" The warrior's voice had taken a sarcastic tone as if he were simply paying a social call to her lad.

She refused to take the bait. He wanted to anger her, but angry, her wits would wilt like a flower in the beaming sun. "None at all."

The warrior took a step closer to her, slowly, the sound of his boot heel on the wooden-planked floor echoing in her head. His companion entered the room. She flicked her gaze toward him, suddenly fearful he'd shut the door and reveal the hiding place of her son. Thankfully, his companion turned his back, she presumed, to keep watch in the corridor.

"Mama, is this still part of the game?" sweet Nevin asked.

Brenna remained still, unflinching even at her child's innocent question. "Aye, love, dinna say another word," she crooned.

The warrior stared even harder at her as though he were trying to read her mind and the way her head suddenly felt pushed around, if she believed in such sorcery, she might have thought he'd succeeded.

"Come here, lad," he called to Nevin.

"Stay away from my son!" Brenna leapt in front of the stranger, shoving her hands out, trying to keep him from approaching her child. Her palms met with a wall of muscle that sent a jarring shudder up her arms.

The warrior simply glowered down at her, lifted her at the waist and set her aside. She tried to bound back in front of him, but she only ended up bouncing off the muscles of his arm and onto the floor.

The moments it took to recover her breath, he'd walked around her and knelt to the ground, smiling at her twins.

'Twas a decidedly sweet move she wouldn't have thought a fierce one such as he to be capable of. And yet, it was also, inexplicably fearsome. He looked like a wolf leaning over his prey.

Heat suffused her face, and she bared her teeth, wanting to run at him, to leap onto his back and wrap her arms around his neck, to squeeze the breath from him. Likely he'd flick her off like a fly, as he'd just done.

"Dinna move, lads!" she warned.

Nevin and Kenneth tossed back their plaids and jumped to their feet, ignoring her plea to stay in the corner.

"Remember what I told ye," she rushed.

The laddies beamed up at her with their tiny, pearly white teeth and light brown eyes. "Aye, Mama," they said in unison.

It almost broke her heart.

The wolf turned a glower on her. "I'll not harm them. Calm yourself wench."

He leaned closer to the lads and whispered something she couldn't hear. Brenna flicked a worried glance at Gillian, who still lay in bed, and stared back at her wide-eyed, close to tears. If only Brenna had a weapon. She spied the mean looking dagger strapped to the back of the warrior's belt. If she could grab hold of it, she'd have a weapon. Yet, in his vulnerable position, and with his companion at the door... Could she do it?

'Twas risky, but it was her only chance at protecting her children from this would-be assassin.

Whatever he whispered to her twins had them giggling and nodding. The beast was lowering their defenses, opening their hearts and gaining their trust. Such innocents had no idea what kind of danger they were in. The monster! He was no better than any of the MacLeods using children in such a way.

The wolf tousled her laddies' hair and then sent them back to their corner. When he stood and turned around, his eyes rested on hers. Her heart skipped a beat. A very slight smile curved his lips, making him even more handsome and, for a moment, disarming her, but the smile quickly faded.

"Sweet bairns," he murmured.

When his gaze slid to Gillian, fury filtered through Brenna, returning with a vengeance. She leapt between the warrior and her daughter and held her hands out, baring her teeth.

She hadn't been not much older than Gillian when her world had been turned upside down. She'd rather fight to the death than hand over her beautiful daughter to this feral animal.

"Dinna come near her. Dinna even look at her, ye foul beast!"

"My, ye are a feisty one. I'd not heard that about ye."

"Ye know nothing about me. And I know nothing about ye, other than ye would prey on innocents!"

The warrior rolled his eyes. "I dinna prey on the innocent. I'll not harm the lass, any more than I did your youngest bairns," he said, his voice too soothing for her taste, then his gaze slid over the chamber again before settling on the door. "Come out from behind the door now, lad."

"Nay!" Brenna shouted, rushing around the giant to stand between him and Theo, arms outstretched. "Get out of here! Go! Ye're not welcome here."

"Unfortunately, ye have little choice in the matter. I *am* here and I'm not going anywhere just yet."

Though she couldn't see, she could hear the creak of the door hinges and footsteps as her son stepped free of his hiding spot.

"Theo, nay!" she cried. She spread her arms wider, feeling feral in her need to protect her child.

"Stand down, Lady Brenna, I'll not hurt your eldest son either. None of your children will suffer at my hand. Ye have my word. Step aside now."

He was walking closer, his impressive size filling the room to bursting. There wasn't room enough for them both. How could she trust him? How could she allow him to come near her children and just what was she going to be able to do about it? She was at least half his weight, if not a third of it. Sheer size alone was against her.

Brenna was close to fainting. Her head swam and she swayed on her feet. She didn't believe a word he said. Not one uttered syllable. Too many lies had passed too many treacherous lips. She'd spent most of her life in captivity, a few promises from a stranger — a threatening intruder at that — wasn't going to change anything.

Fight or die.

That was all there was left. Gearing up all the strength she had left in her, she rushed at the wolf.

Chapter Five

WAS the lady mad?

The dirty, little imp was charging him. She came at him with arms raised, fists flailing and with such fierceness, he found it hard to move as he was too busy admiring her temerity. Her hound also leapt to her feet and made a good effort to protect her lady, biting savagely at his rear, but a sharp command from him sent the dog back into her corner.

Gabriel grabbed Lady Brenna up in a bear hold, his arms pinning hers to her sides, and when she kicked at him, he trapped her legs between his thighs, holding tight. She bucked, tried to slam her head against his, but he reared back keeping well away from her. Despite the fact that she wanted him dead, the contact of her body against his had his blood pumping madly. Tiny though she may be, the lass was full of curves in all the right places. Her breasts pushed against his chest, her labored breathing causing their contact to tighten and loosen and then tighten again. Between his thighs, hers were lithe with muscle and softness. Saints, but he wanted to run his hands over her back and down to her arse to feel if it was just as supple as the rest of her.

Lust fueled his blood, surging straight to his groin. It had been a long time since he'd felt true desire for a woman. What was it about this one that made a difference? Her face was covered in soot, her gown grimy and she spit fire like a demon from Hell.

She was younger than he'd expected. A mother of four should have had lines at her eyes and gray streaking her hair, but the lass had skin as smooth as silk and hair the color of night.

"Ye bloody, rotten sot! Let me down! How dare ye?" She cursed like the lowliest of men as she wriggled fiercely in his grasp. He wouldn't have been surprised if she spit in his face, but she apparently did have some manners after all.

"Cease this," he ordered, giving her a slight shake.

She locked her eyes on him, the blue having gone darker with pure rage. "Never! I'll never surrender!"

When her older son started to charge Gabriel, Donnan whirled from the door to grab the boy from behind.

Did she not understand what she was doing? Her mad tantrum could ruin everything.

"Ye'll have every guard in the castle up here and then where will ye be?" Gabriel growled into her ear. "We've come to help ye, not to harm ye."

"Why should I believe ye?" she said, still struggling wildly against him.

"Why would ye have cause not to?"

Lady Brenna let out an unladylike snort. "Did ye not have to pick the lock to enter our prison?"

"I had to do a lot more than pick the lock," he tossed back.

All of a sudden, she stilled. Her sapphire-colored eyes widened and looked off past him at the wall. He could tell she was listening. Searching for sounds, and with her shouting done, she could hear them. Or at least, he assumed she could, for he could hear the sounds of a battle being waged in the bailey below.

"What is happening?" she asked, eyes skating back to his, indignation replaced by fear.

Gabriel loosened his grip on her, already feeling guilty at how he'd had to manhandle her since breaking through her locked door. But there'd been no other choice. In her madness, she wasn't willing to listen to sense and, truly, he couldn't blame her. She was a mother trying to protect her children. "At this moment, my men inside the castle will have lifted the sea gate, allowing more to penetrate the castle walls. Likely, my second-in-command is leading a battle in the bailey below and he's almost guaranteed to win."

Lady Brenna shook her head, a mass of raven locks falling all around her face, and a wave of subtle spicy essence coming with it. "Nay..."

"Aye," he said softly. Gabriel hated the way she sagged, as if all the ire in her taut, little body had just vanished.

Her lip trembled before she bit it hard. When she spoke, her voice had lowered an octave. "And ye want to steal me and my bairns? Ye want to kill us all?"

"Nay."

Her eyes searched his, frantic. "Aye."

Gabriel groaned at the aggravating back and forth. "Did ye not hear me say I'd come to help ye?"

"How can ye help me? Ye are besieging my home. Those who come to conquer, leave little in their wake save destruction." Pain filled her eyes.

Gabriel did not know much about this woman, nor the trials of her life, but he did know a few minor details, and from the look in her eyes, he could tell there was a whole lot more. Happiness had not touched her often. From the way she fought for her bairns, they were the only light she could see. That struck a chord inside him. Made him want to help her all the more than simply for Ceana's sake, or to keep his neighbors from gaining power.

Gabriel was not normally the type of man to fall for tears. But the softening of his resolve was due to a lot more than her rampant moods. The woman was something to be reckoned with, a force that, for a moment, made him want to change who he was. To desire something more than what he'd settled for.

"As I said, we've come to help." The lady trembled in his arms and he suddenly felt every bit the wolf his enemies called him. "If I set ye down will ye cease fighting me?"

Slowly she nodded, but he wasn't entirely certain he could believe her. "And ye'll not call for your hound to attack me?"

The barest hint of a smile flashed over her lips and then was gone. "Nay."

Gabriel loosened his grip on her, chagrinned that she actually enjoyed the feast her dog had made of his arse. He didn't feel any blood running over his skin, so he was certain the hound's teeth hadn't broken through, but he'd likely have a bruised rear for a day or so. Damned animal.

He bent his legs until her tiny feet touched the floor and then let go of her thighs. When she didn't kick him, he let her go from his embrace, already missing the heat and suppleness of her form against him.

As he let her go, Donnan also released the boy and he rushed to his mother's side, putting his arm over her shoulders, glaring up at Gabriel.

"How dare ye manhandle my mother!" He looked every bit the young warrior. "I'll kill ye if ye ever touch her again."

Gabriel raised a brow at the young lad's ferocity. "I admire your spirit, lad, and I'll take your threats into consideration."

"They aren't threats. 'Tis a promise." He glowered up at Gabriel hard enough that a vein popped out of the lad's neck.

Gabriel grinned. "Ye'll make a fine warrior."

"I'm already a warrior," he seethed.

Gabriel shrugged. "Ye've still much to learn." When the boy started to protest, Gabriel raised his hand for silence. "We've no time for your prattle. Gather your things."

"I will not let ye take him," Lady Brenna seethed.

He could feel the anger radiating off of her body. If he didn't quell her, she'd tumble into another maelstrom. "Ye'll be coming along, too."

She shook her head. "This is our home. We've already been imprisoned twice, I'll not let ye do it again."

"Twice?"

Her mouth fell open and then she slammed her lips closed. "I meant once. I'll not let ye take us as your prisoners."

Gabriel said nothing, simply studying the expression on her face. She'd been a prisoner in her marriage and a prisoner again when her brother-by-marriage stepped in.

"Ye'll not be my prisoners." His voice softened when he spoke.

Unable to help himself, with the pad of his thumb he brushed away a black streak lining her cheekbone. "Is that ash on your face?" he asked only to see what her answer would be. He'd noticed the soot the moment he walked in. At first he'd simply thought them dirty, but when her youngest bairn mentioned a game, he'd figured it had gone deeper than that.

Her lower lip trembled, but she managed to hold herself together. The strength in this woman was admirable. He'd met some men who didn't have as much grit as she.

"Never fear, lass, I'll not harm ye. Ye have my oath."

She broke her gaze from his and stared at the floor, shaking her head. She didn't believe him and he didn't blame her. How long had it been since she'd been able to trust anyone?

"We need to go now," he said.

"Why? If your men will win the battle in the bailey, why should I leave with ye? Why not keep us here?"

Gabriel blew out a breath, praying for patience. "I've been tasked with retrieving ye."

She tapped her foot, gaining back some of the spirit he'd seen in her moments before. "By whom?"

And his patience was gone. "Woman, we dinna have time for your questions. We must be on our way."

Her expression contorted in outrage. "I'm the lady of this castle and I'll not have ye speaking to me with such disrespect."

"Are ye going to attack me again? Because I assure ye, I will not be so nice the second time."

"Nice?" she scoffed.

"Aye." Gabriel bared his teeth and pressed his face close to hers. Despite the soot on her skin, there was a sweet cinnamon scent about her. Again, his blood stirred with desire.

What in bloody hell was wrong with him? Since entering this chamber, he'd experienced more disturbing feelings than he had in nearly a decade. There was something about this lass that threatened to unravel him. If he didn't get her deposited quickly into Lamont's hands, he was likely to go stark raving mad.

Ignoring her, he turned to her eldest son and said, "Lad, if ye be a warrior, then protect your younger siblings. We need to get the lot of ye to safety afore your uncle sends a troop of imbeciles up the tower stairs to find the five of ye and we've only two of us to defend ye. We dinna want to get stuck here. Best to be on our way."

"But ye said yourself that your men were defeating those in the bailey."

"And ye think your uncle is down there fighting?"

The boy shook his head, face paling beyond the ash covering his skin.

The lady stepped into his view once more, giving her son a brief nod. The boy went first to his sister, handing her a gown and blocking Gabriel and Donnan's view as she dressed. The lad was good and caring. He'd be a fine man someday, despite his sire.

Brenna gazed up at him with dejection, which made him feel guiltier than he had before. "Please, tell me, who sent ye? I'd be much obliged if ye would divulge the information to me before I trust that ye'll see us to safety."

Gabriel raised a skeptical brow. "Will ye cease fighting me?"

"My laird…" Donnan warned, standing by the door. "We'll soon have company."

The lady clutched at Gabriel's arm, heat searing a path from his wrist to his shoulder. Even now, he could hear the sound of booted feet pounding on the stairs.

"Please, tell me."

"I must have your total cooperation." He wasn't going to give in unless she did. Trust went both ways.

She chewed her lip, but nodded in agreement. "Aye."

"By your cousin."

Her eyes widened with hope. "Ceana?"

For some reason, that spark of hopefulness in her eyes sent a rush of relief through Gabriel. Why he cared for this woman's feelings was beyond him at the moment. "Aye."

"Ye still haven't told me your name."

"I am Laird MacKinnon."

Her face paled and she backed away from him. What did her sudden change mean?

He didn't have long to ponder it as the march of boot heels in the corridor grew louder.

"They come," Donnan said.

"Get back," Gabriel ordered Brenna and her children.

Without hesitation, she backed her children into the corner, shielding the young boys and the girl, the hound also acting as a guard, but Theo refused his mother's protection.

"Give me a sword," he demanded of Gabriel.

"I've promised to protect ye, not see ye harmed."

"I can protect myself."

"Protect your mother and your siblings." Gabriel took the sword at his hip and tossed it to Theo, pleased when the lad caught the hilt in his hand.

"Who the hell are ye?" Demanded a man at the entrance to the chamber who was at least a dozen summers younger than Gabriel. "Get away from my family, ye bloody bastards!"

Gabriel drew the claymore from the scabbard at his back and grinned at the whelp. "Thomas MacLeod, I gather?"

"None other. Prepare to die!"

Gabriel actually had to laugh at that. Such dramatics. The whelp didn't even know how to hold his sword correctly. No wonder the castle wasn't well fortified. "'Haps ye ought to be saying that to yourself, laddie."

The younger man's face turned purple with rage and Donnan had himself a good chuckle.

Behind Thomas were several guards, each of them looking just as angered as their leader. This was going to be sad. Entertaining, aye, but deeply lacking in any type of battle Gabriel had hopes of engaging in.

"Attack!" Thomas called, pointing his sword at Gabriel.

The MacLeod guards trotted around Thomas, swords outstretched and prepared to fight off Gabriel. Their faces showed their weakness and fear. These were not the same MacLeod men he'd fought beside years before at Stirling. What had happened to them? Who were these imposters?

Fending them off was effortless, just as it had been getting into the castle. He parried and struck each one down, not bothering to kill them, but knocking them out all the same. When he was done, he looked to Donnan who'd done the same. A pile of three unconscious men at each of their feet.

"Come now, that was too simple. Haven't ye got any warriors that fight back? Where did ye find this rabble? Will ye not challenge me yourself?" Gabriel asked Thomas.

The man's face had gone from purple to ashen. "Ye killed them," he shrieked. "Do ye know who I am? Who we are? All the MacLeods of Scotland will come for ye."

"I doubt that," Gabriel drawled. "Seems ye've no idea who I am, nor that I was an ally of your father, fighting at his side against the English. The MacLeods respected your father and all that he stood for, but ye've shamed your family. Ye and your brother."

"Shamed?" The cur's mouth fell open in such an exaggerated motion, Gabriel wondered if he'd stomp his foot like a petulant child, too. "Ye sneak into my home like a demon, kill off my men and attempt to abduct my family and ye call me shameful?"

"I'd not have to sneak in at all if ye were honorable."

"*And* now ye question my honor?" Thomas' face was back to being purple.

Gabriel shrugged. "'Tis not hard given the circumstances."

While the little runt sputtered, Donnan was nearly doubled over in laughter.

"Now, truth be told, I was sent here to seize the castle and its inhabitants." Gabriel affected boredom. "I told the man that asked it of me that I'd not kill ye. Hmm… Nay, in fact, I said I'd not kill the laird." Gabriel smiled cruelly at Thomas. "But ye are not the laird are ye?"

"I bloody well am!" Thomas shouted, taking a menacing step forward.

Behind him, Gabriel heard the indrawn breath of Brenna and Theo. Their hound growled.

Gabriel raised his brow. "I think there are a few here who would beg to differ, Thomas MacLeod."

"They can beg all they want. They can beg for their lives. 'Tis mine. I've earned it and I'll be damned if I'm going to let ye take it from me."

"Ye see, the thing is, I dinna need to take it from ye, because it's already mine." With that said, Gabriel marched forward and struck the hilt of his sword against Thomas' temple, knocking the man unconscious. He slumped to the floor. "What is wrong with this place? Everything has been entirely too easy," he muttered.

Then he felt a pinch at his back which grew into a searing pain. Whirling, he caught sight of Brenna's alarmed face, the sword he'd given her son now bloody in her hands. The room erupted into chaos. Theo grabbed the sword and held it toward Donnan who'd leapt across the room in one bound to grab Lady Brenna. The twins burst into tears and Gillian fainted.

Brenna trembled fiercely as she knelt beside her unconscious child, Gillian's head cradled in her lap. Her gaze was on his, expecting and unwavering. What was it she expected him to do? Act out? Harm her as she'd surmised he would do from the moment he entered?

Reaching around, he felt the warm slickness of blood on his fingertips. She'd stabbed him. The fiery wench had bloody stabbed him!

Ballocks!

Anger overpowered any pain he might have felt.

Gabriel let out a roar that shook the rafters, and while Donnan disarmed Theo, Gabriel grabbed hold of

Brenna's arm and whipped her close to him. Eyes locked on hers, he glowered fiercely.

"I told ye that if ye attacked me again, I'd not be so nice to ye the second time around," he growled like the wolf he could be. "Welcome to not so nice."

He had to admit, out of all the men he'd fought this night, the only one who'd been able to draw blood was a woman half his size.

Chapter Six

VIOLENT shivers stole over Brenna. Despite the warmth of her room, and the heat of the warrior's body pressed so boldly and mightily against hers, she was chilled all the way to the bone. His arm wrapped around the small of her back, tucking her belly to his, her breasts to his chest, her hips to his…

What had she done?

She was an incompetent fool. Only an imbecile like she would take a sword to a man and not only *not* kill him, but barely wound him. Power radiated from his every limb. She was in danger of being crushed simultaneously by his hold and her own fear.

"Please, dinna hurt my mother," Theo pleaded.

In the corner, Gillian, who had revived from fainting, hugged the twins and they sobbed like mad while Snow couldn't decide between protecting the children and safeguarding her mistress.

"Mother, didn't mean it!" Kenneth shouted. "'Twas an accident."

The warrior raised his brow, having the impudence to look jovial at the moment. "Was it an accident, my lady? Did the blade slip from your boy's hand into yours and then magically thrust its way into my back?"

She licked her lips nervously. Her children need not bear witness to his violence. Jutting her chin forward, she said, "Not in front of my children. Punish me somewhere else."

The mirth left his face, replaced by anger. "I *should* have ye whipped."

Blood dripped from his back onto the floor in tiny droplets. Nausea built inside her and, try as she might, she couldn't force it away.

He squeezed her tighter, their breaths mingling. He leaned closer, his lips just an inch from hers. His gaze lowered to stare at her mouth. Would he kiss her? She was both afraid and shockingly entranced.

"But I suspect ye've already been punished enough," he hissed.

Brenna held her breath, refusing to move, refusing to say a word.

"Have ye not?"

Was it a trick? He'd told her straight out he wouldn't be nice the second time she attacked him. How could he simply forget it? She'd seen the blood soak the back of his shirt. She'd cut him. Wounded him.

"I…" She swallowed. What answer was he looking for? "I've…" She couldn't make her throat work. Her neck felt tight and her stomach was in such knots she expected to lose what little breakfast she'd eaten.

"Ye insult me with your assumptions. I'd never frighten an innocent child. Nor a harm a broken woman."

Broken woman? That got her ire up, mayhap because for the last fifteen years *damaged* was exactly how she felt and perhaps more because she didn't want to feel that way any longer. "I'm not broken," she seethed and wriggled against him.

The man had the gall to grin, his grip not loosening the slightest around her waist. "Nay?"

"I stabbed ye," she pointed out the obvious. "Seems there is only one person in the room with a wound."

He chuckled. "Aye, ye did that. But 'twas more from fear than malice, aye? And let us be honest, our wounds are not always visible. Sometimes we bleed on the inside."

"I am no more wounded on the inside than ye are small. Put me down!" Every time she wriggled against him, trying to be set free, her body met with corded sinew and her skin sizzled, her body at complete odds with her need to get away. Her skin just wanted to be closer.

MacKinnon gave off a wolfish grin. "Ye've taken note of my size."

Och, the insolence! "How could I not? Ye're bigger than... bigger than anyone."

He lowered his voice, the husky timbre skating over her skin in a forbidden caress. "I've taken note of your figure as well."

"Lecher," she ground out.

"*That*, I am not. Is it a crime to notice a woman is well-formed?"

Well-formed? She didn't know whether to be insulted or not. And how did one respond to a comment like that? Slapping seemed appropriate, but she'd just stabbed him. That would not go over well. Saying thank you would also likely not go over well since he looked ready to kiss her, and judging from the way that thought made her belly flip and her heart skip a beat, she might like that too much.

She settled for the most proper of responses. "'Tis not appropriate. Especially in mixed company."

"Och, apologies, my lady. I forget myself and my audience." His grip loosened, shocking her to the core.

Would he truly let her go? So easily?

Where she'd been on tiptoes, pressed against him, her heels touched the floor and the heat of his body gave way to a cool inch of space. Brenna frowned against the slight ping of disappointment.

"Alas, we truly must be leaving now afore any of these pests wake and decide to try their hand once more at defeating me. I need to see a healer about this wound. And 'tis at least three days' ride, if not more, to Dunakin Castle."

Suspicion welled inside her. "Dunakin? That is not where Ceana resides."

"Nay, 'tis not." He did not expound on his response.

She shook her head. "But ye said—"

"I know ye have no cause to trust me—"

She cut him off just as he'd done to her. "Nay, I do not."

MacKinnon frowned. "And I dinna care if ye do. Ye and your bairns are coming with me if I have to tie ye up myself."

The thought of being tied and tossed over his horse sent a shiver of fear tearing through her. Nay, that was not what she wanted at all.

"Mother." Theo's voice sounded strangled. Her lad was struggling with indecision. They'd just witnessed so very much violence, Brenna couldn't bear for them to witness any more.

Brenna straightened her shoulders and tried to act calm and collected for her children's sake. "Gather your things."

She might not be able to trust MacKinnon, but they'd been allies of the MacNeacails when she was a child, perhaps she could implore him on that count. At the very least, he was getting her and her children away from Thomas. Though she hated her brother-by-marriage, part of her was also thankful that MacKinnon hadn't killed him. There had already been enough death in this castle over the past several weeks.

The twins picked up their carved toys and Gillian and Theo started to make piles of their clothes and personal items.

"Will ye allow us a few satchels?" Brenna asked when she took note of the piles being built and not even with her own things.

"Nay, my lady. We must go now." He turned to the children. "Take only what ye can carry."

Seeing their stricken faces, Brenna quickly added, "Ye'll be back, loves. Put your things in the chest and they'll be there when we return." Locking her gaze on MacKinnon, she said, "We will be back."

He gave a curt nod, then took her by her elbow, leading her from the chamber. The men on the floor had started to stir. MacKinnon's guard gathered the children behind her, walking at the back of their short line and closing the door with the downed men inside. MacKinnon tossed him the spindly dagger he'd used to pick the lock and his guard jammed it into the keyhole. With a few twists and turns the click of the lock sounded.

"That will keep them contained for awhile," Gabriel muttered.

He led them down the stairs, past the empty great hall and into the courtyard. Lit up by torches and the bonfire, she could see the courtyard was a mess. Overturned carts and barrels, discarded cups and food.

The ground ran wet and she was certain it wasn't only water. Her feet sank into the mess and she feared on the morrow when the light shined on her boots and the hem of her gown, she'd see blood.

Dozens of his men gathered around the courtyard, all looking as fierce as MacKinnon. Not a MacLeod in sight, save for the bodies strewn upon the ground.

"My laird," a man called out and approached.

In the dark, she couldn't make out much more than he was nearly as tall as his laird and just as muscular. Were all the MacKinnons giants?

"Coll, the status?" MacKinnon questioned.

"The castle is yours. Survivors were imprisoned. Servants agreed to either flee or remain behind, loyal to ye and ye alone. The walls are fortified."

Oh, dear lord, she hoped her loyal servants, Sarah and Angus, were all right. Her belly did a little flop as she gazed around the courtyard, intent on finding them. They were not in sight. Saints, but she hoped they'd surrendered.

"Good. I'll leave Donnan in charge here with two score of our men. Ye and the rest will go back to Dunakin with me. Check the stores. And I've locked Thomas MacLeod and his cronies in a chamber in the tower. See that they stay there for a time afore joining their comrades below."

"Aye, my laird. Well done. Dunvegan is yours."

His.

Brenna looked up toward the ramparts of the curtain wall. Men walked in moving shadows the length, no doubt wearing the same plaid colors as MacKinnon.

They'd been so easily taken. This castle was no longer hers, nor her children's. It was MacKinnon's.

Just as she'd feared she might not be able to trust his clan fifteen years before, she couldn't now. If her sister had ever made it to them, wouldn't he have sent word? Well, perhaps he wouldn't have if Kirstin and Finn were able to explain that the MacLeods were at fault. And even then, if he'd known and not come to her aid, didn't that speak volumes? Then again, if he had found her sister, wouldn't he have mentioned something about her upstairs?

Brenna didn't know what to think. What to believe.

She stared hard at the back of MacKinnon's head as he talked with the man he addressed as Coll. How could she trust a man who was for all intents and purposes, her enemy?

Servants milled around the bailey, appearing to make an attempt at cleaning up the mess of the battle. MacKinnon's men were piling bodies into a wagon they'd uprighted. She covered the twins' eyes from the sight of it, wishing she had someone to cover her own. After all these years, she supposed she should be used to carnage, should not feel so queasy, but numb instead. Well, she didn't. Every loss of life, every drop of blood, every inflicted wound affected her.

Tiny hands slipped into hers. Kenneth on one side and Nevin on the other. Her heart melted at the contact. Neither of them had approached her, sought comfort from her, since their father's death the month before. Strangely, this enemy had brought the boys closer to her. Whatever it was he'd whispered had brought about a sudden change she was grateful for.

She clutched their hands, delighting in the small squeezes they returned.

"I'm scared," Gillian whispered beside her.

Snow sat beside her daughter, leaning into her, providing comfort.

"All will be well," Theo said, echoing words from her past that still haunted her dreams. "I'll keep ye safe."

The same words she'd whispered to her sister as they sat huddled in their nursery at Scorrybreac. The same words she'd promised and then all had not been well. In the end, she'd not been able to keep her sister safe. A guilt and blame she'd carry heavily with her for the rest of her days.

Those words carried a heavy weight with them. A dread. An omen of terrible things to come.

For just the barest of moments in her chamber, she'd thought that perhaps this man wasn't as dangerous as she feared. After all, he'd spared punishing her when she'd taken a sword to his back, but witnessing the carnage in the bailey... She now knew just how dangerous this man could be.

An idea formed, a horrifying revelation really. Perhaps it wasn't her cousin, Ceana, who'd informed MacKinnon after all that Brenna needed saving. Because why would Ceana then have this laird seize her castle? Nay, it must be that he'd intercepted her letter to her cousin and had made a plan to attack and besiege the castle and kidnap her and her children. For what? A ransom? Had he, too, heard of the vast MacLeod treasury?

They had to escape. Somehow. She'd go along with him for now, but the moment there was a chance, she was going to take her bairns and run.

Brenna cleared her throat. "Do ye not wish to rest after your long journey? If the walls are secured, then why rush out of them?"

MacKinnon swung to face her, and thank goodness for the dark, because she was certain his expression would have terrified her had she been able to see it fully in the light.

He marched toward her, stilling just a few inches away. "Dinna question me. I've already explained, though I need not do so."

Despite the pounding of her heart, Brenna managed to keep her voice steady. "Right. My cousin awaits me. But surely a few hours difference will not matter."

He made a sound that she could only interpret as very irritated. "Ye test me, my lady. Let me warn ye, I'll not play games with ye. We leave as soon as my back is sewed."

No matter what he said, she wouldn't back down right away. Never would she do so again. The past was the past, and she was a new woman now. "But the children... They are tired. If we wait until morning — "

The laird growled. "Ye'll do as I say. I've seized your castle, taken ownership of it. That means I own everything inside including ye and your bairns. Ye'll do as I say or suffer the consequences. I've already let your transgressions from the tower go, but I shan't do it a third time. Dinna try me again, else ye find out that Thomas and Ronald were pups compared to my wrath."

Brenna swallowed back her anger, her fear. Every word uttered was a whip against her flesh. A sound lashing that she ought to cower from, but instead, she stood taller, straighter, thrust her chin forward and faced off with her enemy.

"I was never, and never will be, owned by anyone." Her voice was cold and even as she spoke.

The light of a nearby torch flickered on his face. A cruel smile covered his lips. "Is that so?"

She matched his smile. "Aye."

Locked in a stare down, he finally turned away and headed in the direction of the keep, calling for the castle healer.

Brenna stood in shock, not knowing what to do. He'd not tied her up. He'd not left anyone to guard her. She doubted his men would open the sea gate to let her leave, but still...

Did this mean she'd won their argument? Was he just going to let her... go?

She turned in a circle, hands pressed protectively to the twins' chests, taking in those around her. The MacKinnon warriors went about their business and the servants appeared to be minding their own business.

"My lady."

Brenna startled, focusing her gaze on Angus. Thank the saints he was still here and appeared unharmed.

"Angus," she breathed out. "Where is Sarah?"

He smiled and nodded. "She is well, in the kitchen cooking."

"Oh," she breathed out a sigh of relief. "I feared for ye both so much."

"Dinna fash yourself, my lady. We'll survive. We always do. His lairdship says ye're to come inside."

Without speaking, she nodded shakily and headed back toward the keep with her children and hound in tow.

They made their way into the great hall where MacKinnon sat, with his back to her, at the table. His shirt was off and the length of plaid that had been at his shoulder trailed onto the floor.

She was struck speechless by the sight of him. Muscles curled and bunched over tanned skin. Her breath caught in her throat and a shiver of awareness stole over her. *Again.*

Pushing those sensations away, she focused on the wound on the left side of his back. Only about an inch or two wide, it seeped a minimal amount of blood. She could still feel the sensation of the blade sinking into his flesh and how she'd jerked, panicking at the last minute. She'd not pushed hard on the blade, probably only sank it into his body an inch at most.

A flesh wound really. God's bones, but she thought that was all he thought of it.

"MacKinnon," she said softly, edging closer, afraid he might turn around, bare his teeth like a rabid wolf and threaten to bite her. "Ye asked to see me?"

With turned, he said, "Lady Brenna, ye're going to sew me up."

Chapter Seven

THE heat of her gaze permeated his back, even from this distance. If he turned around, he was certain he'd see in her eyes the same sensations coursing through his body. Attraction. Desire. Need. Fury.

Why they seemed to have this strong connection— this push and pull—he didn't know. What he was aware of, was that he needed to cool it now before he was in too deep. If there was one thing he was certain of, it was that he wasn't going to give his heart away to a woman ever again.

Aye, he needed a wife, he needed an heir. Lamont had suggested he marry Brenna and, considering he'd besieged her castle, it was entirely in the realm of possibility. No one would naysay him, save perhaps the bride, and given he was on good terms with Robert the

Bruce, he'd see no objection there. But Brenna MacNeacail MacLeod came with a whole lot more than what he needed, what he thought he could honestly handle. After the heartache he'd endured, the endless battles, what he wanted was a simple life.

Brenna was anything but simple.

Nevertheless, when he'd caught sight of the hatred burning in the castle healer's eyes, he'd come to the logical conclusion that the crone had lost a dear one in the skirmish that took place when he besieged the castle. Hence, he'd sent her away and called for Brenna to do the deed. After all, she'd been the one to cause the wound, shouldn't she be the one to mend it?

"There are pallets over there." He pointed toward the corner of the great hall where he'd asked a servant to lay out several makeshift beds for Brenna and her family. "Have the bairns get some rest afore we travel."

Her soft voice washed over him as she lovingly told her children to go lay down. They walked past him, their massive, white hound in tow. Brenna's love for her children reminded him of his own mother. Having lost her daughter, Annabelle, to the English a decade ago, his mother would be pleased for the female companionship Brenna would provide once they arrived at Dunakin.

He'd have to be sure to tell his mother it was only temporary though. Brenna would have to go and reside with her cousin and in four years' time, her son would be old enough to take control of his holding. During that stretch, Gabriel planned to form an elder council that would respect Theo and advise him in a way that would be good for their clan.

Gabriel would also have to prepare himself for what he eventually needed to tell the lady. Theo would remain with the MacKinnon clan to foster while Brenna took her younger bairns with her to the Lamont holding.

At Brenna's approach, Gabriel stiffened. He took a sip of the whisky in his cup, breathing in the burn that wound its way down his throat.

"Have ye sewed a wound afore?" he asked.

"Aye." Her soft voice was like a caress on his back.

"I've all ye need right here." He patted the table with the whisky, a bandage, sewing needle and thread.

"No salve?" she asked.

Gabriel shrugged. "No need."

Though she didn't say anything, and he couldn't see her reaction, he could feel her frown on his back.

"I'll get a salve," she said.

He gritted his teeth as she left the great hall, but rather than argue, Gabriel took another pull on his whisky, swishing it around his mouth. The whisky was damn good. The MacLeods might be a thieving lot, but their distiller certainly knew his way around a barrel.

Gabriel found his gaze roving toward the corner where Brenna's children rested. The wee bairns had cuddled up beside their sister who was the spitting image of her mother. Theo sat beside them and looked on fiercely. He met Gabriel's regard and jutted his chin up, defiance in every crease of his frowning brow. If any of the younger MacKinnon lads had looked at Gabriel like that, he would have taken them to task. But, he sensed that Theo wouldn't do well with such a reprimand. Theo needed support in his new role. If anything, he also needed to know that he was safe. Which he was. Gabriel wouldn't let any harm come to Brenna's children.

The lad had quickly become the protector of his rather large family. The moment his father passed, he'd taken on the responsibility of his siblings and his mother.

A mother who was rumored to have killed her husband.

Yet another reason Gabriel should stay as far away from a union with the woman as possible. He didn't want to end up dead.

Then again—if she was a murderess as accused, wouldn't she have simply run him through? There was hesitation on the end of the blade and regret in her eyes. Not the reaction he would have expected from a woman used to killing.

Gabriel nodded his head at the lad and beckoned him forward.

Theo glanced at his sister and brothers, whispered something to the lass who sat up straighter, meeting Gabriel's gaze. The lad stood and sauntered forward with a swagger that oozed a confidence Gabriel knew he didn't quite possess.

"My laird?" Theo said when he was a few feet away, stopping and placing his hands behind his back in a position of ease.

"Have ye ever had whisky, lad?" Gabriel asked, downing another dram.

Theo glanced at the flagon on the table and shook his head. "Nay, my laird."

"'Tis a man's drink," Gabriel said.

Theo shrugged. "I've seen women drink it, too."

"Have ye now?"

"Aye."

Gabriel raised his brow. "Your mother?"

Theo's mouth fell open then he clamped it closed, as if he wasn't quite sure how to answer the question. The lad wanted to protect his mother's image, Gabriel guessed, and that made him smile.

"I've seen women drink it, too. I only meant, that perhaps ye're a man now. Care for a nip?" Gabriel had his first taste of whisky at Theo's age and he'd thoroughly detested it. In fact, he'd been nearly twenty by the time he developed a tolerance for it and only then, because it was the manly thing to do. Now, as a man in his thirties, he'd learned to appreciate finely barreled spirits.

The boy let out an audible breath that he'd been holding. "I dinna think 'tis a good idea."

Gabriel shrugged. "Up to ye, but if ye ever think to have a drink, I'd like to be the first to have one with ye."

"Why?"

Gabriel nodded his head toward the children in the corner.

"Ye've had to grow up fast, lad. And ye've done a good job of protecting your siblings and your mother. Not many have the ballocks to do what ye've done."

Theo's eyes widened and he rushed, "I've done nothing! Nothing!"

Gabriel was taken aback by the boy's intensity.

"What's going on here?" Brenna all but ran at full speed into the great hall, wrapping her arm through her son's, her other arm loaded with small vials.

Keeping his face neutral, Gabriel locked eyes with Theo and waited for the boy to answer his mother. But he seemed more inclined to keep quiet and Brenna's gaze was burning a hole into Gabriel's head.

"MacKinnon, what have ye done to upset my son?"

"I commended him on doing a fine job of protecting his family."

Brenna looked taken aback, her gaze jerking to her son's face. "Is that so?"

The lad's lips were thinned, face pale and he nodded. "Aye, Mother."

The lady's face was pinched and Gabriel could tell she didn't believe either one of them. He waited for her to argue, for her to rage at him for distressing her child, but she remained quiet. Finally, she nodded and patted Theo's arm.

"Go and get some rest," she murmured.

The lad stared extra long at Gabriel before backing away and returning to the pallets in the corner.

"What did ye truly say to him?" Brenna asked as she laid out linens and jars on the table.

"Just as I said. Why should he get upset about it?" He sensed the two of them were hiding something and he couldn't quite figure out what it was.

"He's been through a traumatic ordeal," she answered simply, then moved around to his back, dismissing him.

Her fingers pressed to the area around his wound as she examined him. The whisky had dulled the ache and not even her palpating the area could bring back a sting. In fact, all he felt was the warmth of her fingers, the tingle of her caress. She was gentle. Soft. How many wounds had she tended before his?

"I need to clean it," she observed.

He nodded, closing his eyes as she worked.

"Ye seem quite deft at wound care," Gabriel pointed out.

"Aye." She did not expound on her answer, leaving him filled with more questions than answers.

After cleaning the wound, she threaded the needle and started to sew him up. The prick of the needle was barely felt as all of his concentration was on her breath fanning over his bare back while she leaned close to examine her work.

"How long were ye married?" he asked.

That question did break her concentration and he felt a painful jerk of the needle.

"Long enough." Her tone left no room for question. She didn't want to talk about her marriage to Ronald MacLeod. Odd for a woman who should be in mourning. Then again, she had been accused of killing the fiend.

Gabriel wasn't going to let it go so quickly. "Long enough to have a brood of bairns," he said.

Her breath blew out forcefully on his skin. She was getting irritated. And she didn't respond.

"Long enough to hate him?" he prodded.

Her fingers stilled at his back. "Ye want to ask me something. Just ask it, warrior. I've not patience for your games."

The whisky made his mouth work before his brain could stop him. "Why did ye kill him?"

There was a jerk on the needle again and he winced.

Brenna moved around him to gather the linens and salve. "What did ye hear?"

"I heard that ye killed him."

"And now I've stabbed ye."

"Quite a reputation ye've garnered."

"And yet, ye've allowed me to sew ye up. Are ye not afraid I might try to harm ye again?"

"I'm not sure how much harm ye can do with a sewing needle." He chuckled.

The lass tormented him by leaning closer, her face to the side of him as she braced herself against the back of his shoulder. The needle appeared before his face, between two of her fingers and she spun it. "I could poke your eyes out. Wouldn't that make a warrior's life much more difficult?"

Her tone was calm, soothing almost, and underlying it, a hint of teasing.

"Indeed, it would." He turned around so that he could look at her face, but doing so may have been a mistake. Her eyes were full of mirth and her lips... they were tantalizingly close. His gaze roved over her face, settling on her mouth, and he couldn't help but wonder what it would be like to kiss her, at least once.

To taste her fire, to subdue her, to slide her supple body against his again, but this time to claim her. To claim her as his.

Blood rushed through his body, settling between his thighs, making him hard and adding power to his need. Saints, but every time he looked at her he had difficulty not imagining what it would be like to bed the lass.

A flush of pink tinged her cheeks and she shoved away from him, breaking the spell.

"Apologies," she mumbled. "I seem to have forgotten myself."

Gabriel wanted to turn around, to tell her it was all right to lose yourself every once in awhile, but truth be told, he needed the distance.

Aye, he could be one of the conquerors who staked their claim on the castle, the land and everybody within it. He could say it was his right to bend her over and drive himself deep into her warmth. He could claim it was his right to do whatever the hell he wanted.

But Gabriel wasn't a monster.

Neither was he a saint.

"Be done with it, lass. We've no time to tarry." His voice was harsh.

Her fingers trembled as she rubbed the salve over the stitches making Gabriel feel even worse for his gruffness. But he wouldn't apologize. He needed her to be done so he could get away from her.

"Lift your arms," she said softly.

He did as she bid and gritted his teeth against the feel of her arms wrapping around him as she bound the linen at his waist.

"I'm finished," she said.

He still couldn't look at her. Gabriel nodded and poured himself another dram of whisky.

"Should ye be drinking that much if we are to leave, MacKinnon?"

"Ye begged leave for your children to rest, did ye not?" Even he winced at the surly tone in his voice.

"Aye. Am I to assume then, that we will leave in the morning?" All the warmth and mirth had left her voice. She was all crisp and proper and he expected her to put her hands on her hips as she demanded more from him than she already had.

"Ye need not assume anything. That is the way of it. Go sleep with your bairns."

He shoved off the bench, whisky and frustration coursing through his veins. After besieging the castle, he, too, needed to get some rest before they left. He'd been up all night and had barely slept during the three days it took to travel to Dunvegan.

"Come, I'll take ye to a chamber where ye can rest." Her hand slipped around his bicep. She was still trying to be biddable. 'Haps because he had given her children a reprieve to rest.

"I'll sleep with my men," he grumbled.

"If I may dispute such an idea, my laird, I think it best ye sleep in a bed, in case ye've need of my attentions."

Gabriel winged a brow and whirled to face her. "Your attentions?" Bloody hell, was the lass offering... "I assure ye, that I'll not be needing anything from ye this night." Even if he was tempted to sell his soul for a taste of what she had beneath that gown.

But damn it all, if she insisted, he'd had enough whisky that his will could be turned.

Brenna's mouth fell open, her hand dropped from his arm and she stared up at him with a mix of horror, along with a spark of anger. "I was referring to your wound, sir, and not *anything* else, least of all what your rogue mind has cooked up, I can promise ye that."

Gabriel took in the full force of the tiny whirlwind before him. Hands on her rounded hips, raven hair flying in a mess of curls around her head, blue eyes sparking ice. Her breasts pushed against her gown, rising and falling with her rapid breaths. He took her in from the top of her head all the way to her toes and didn't hide the fact that he was doing so. Or that he appreciated the subtle swell of her nipples as they hardened beneath his perusal. She was beautiful. Enchanting. *Mo chreach...* What was in the MacLeod whisky?

"Best get to bed with ye afore I change my mind," he said, voice husky with need.

"Scoundrel," she seethed.

Gabriel closed the distance between them with one step. He could feel the heat of her body, smell her spicy cinnamon scent. His eyes fixed on her lips, if she didn't walk away right now, he wasn't going to be able to help himself.

"I never claimed to be anything but."

She didn't move.

Hell and damnation.

He leaned forward and brushed his lips over hers.

Chapter Eight

LIPS, warm and supple touched hers.

Startled, for half a breath Brenna leaned into the subtle touch of his mouth, breathed in his masculine essence. Thunder sounded in her ears and shivers raced over her skin. In that short moment, she felt as if she floated away from Dunvegan, away from everything, swept up in a single heartbeat of pleasure.

The kiss was brief. One moment he was touching his velvet lips to hers and the next he was walking away, leaving her dazed, confused and light-headed.

Ronald had never kissed her in a way that was so pleasant. And she'd been tied to him so young that she'd never kissed another besides a few practice pecks with a servant lad.

Until now.

Laird MacKinnon. She didn't even know his given name, only that his gentle kiss belied the intensity she felt pulsing within him. Belied the gruffness of his tone and the curt way he'd dismissed her. The man was filled to the brim with restrained passion.

Brenna watched him walk away. Eyes roved over the way his muscles worked as he went. The breadth of his bare shoulders, the length of his spine, the stretch of his muscular legs, the swish of his plaid with his swagger.

"MacKinnon," she called.

He stopped in his tracks but did not turn to face her. Her heart lurched up to her throat.

"Ye canna do that," she said, though her protest was half-hearted.

She said it more because her children had witnessed his uninvited kiss. Truth be told, if he wanted to kiss her again, she'd allow it, if only to explore it more. To examine the exact rate at which her heartbeat kicked up a notch and how long it would take before she let out the breath she held. To see if his kiss would be pleasurable all the time or if it had only been that way because she was so surprised by it.

When it didn't appear that he would turn around, she took a step forward, not realizing how shaky her legs were. His kiss? Nerves? She didn't know, but she didn't trust herself to walk the dozen paces toward him.

"'Tis not proper," she said softly. "I am a lady."

In the few hours since her freedom from being held prisoner, the month without her caustic husband, Brenna was starting to find her voice. The lass she'd long since buried yearned to be set free and to grow. She'd held *her* tucked away deep inside for so long.

"I apologize for taking liberties without asking," MacKinnon said, surprising her.

Asking? She would have most certainly said no, even if she were curious. Eyes on his back, she studied the set of his shoulders and jumped a little when he turned around to face her. Though it would have taken her at least ten to twelve steps to reach him, he was back in front of her within three and looming over her enough that she had to crane her neck to look at his face.

"I'll not apologize for doing it though." His voice was low enough that she was certain no one could hear the scandalous words he spoke. "In fact, I want verra much to do it again, which is why I'm leaving the hall, because kissing is not something either one of us should be doing."

Stunned, eyes wide and lips parted, she watched him retreat again. Heat filled her chest, smoothing up over her neck and cheeks.

The further he walked, the more retorts blasted in her mind. She wanted to race after him, force him to treat her like a lady, because she'd seen more of his kindness in the past few hours than she'd seen from any man since the death of her father-by-marriage.

Aye, the MacKinnon was a fierce warrior. A man who commanded respect from his clan and even from his enemies. He was bold, having easily snuck into the impenetrable Dunvegan Castle. In all her fifteen years here, she'd never even seen a deed such as that attempted.

But he was also a man tormented by something inside. A man, who she didn't doubt, never shared his feelings with anyone.

There was also the inexplicable truth—she found him intriguing. He startled her. Moved her. Made her want to be the woman she was meant to be.

How was that possible? Was it simply the rush of being free? The knowledge that she would soon, hopefully, be reunited with her family? That there was a light at the end of the tunnel that had been her misery for so long? The fact that a world of opportunities had been opened for her children?

Brenna dragged in a shallow breath, brushed aside the frantic ramblings of her mind, and turned away from her enemy's back. For he was her enemy. 'Haps not overmuch now, but in a few years' time, when she would support her son's defeat of MacKinnon to gain back Theo's legacy and the chiefdom of MacLeod, the fierce Highland warrior would certainly be her adversary.

Across the room, Nevin and Kenneth slept. Their heads lay on Gillian's lap. Her daughter and eldest son stared at her with pale faces and wide eyes. They worked hard to keep their emotions at bay, but a mother always knew the true feelings of their hearts.

She made her way back over to them, contemplating grabbing the whisky flagon MacKinnon had left behind. A wee nip would do her good in falling asleep and calming her nerves, but she left it, not wanting that same wee nip to dull her senses and wit.

"He kissed ye," Theo said when she was but a few feet away. Anger sliced his words.

Brenna shook her head, brushing aside how much the action had truly moved her. "'Twas nothing."

"A man does not kiss a woman and it means nothing," her son said, frowning.

"In this case" — Brenna kept her voice calm — "it meant nothing."

"Why would he do it then?" Her son wasn't going to let the topic drop.

Gillian and Theo looked on her with a concentration she'd grown to love about them. They were intelligent, curious children.

"'Twas but a truce being made." Mayhap the lie would even convince herself.

"And a kiss can seal a truce?" Theo asked with the raised brow of a youth desperately wanting to challenge the words of his elders.

"Aye. A truce."

"What truce?" Gillian asked.

"That is a matter between the MacKinnon and me. Ye need not worry over it. Ye're safe, and he's given us this night to rest before we travel, so close your eyes and sleep."

Her children dutifully obeyed, though Theo grumbled something under his breath she couldn't quite catch.

Brenna lay down beside her children, but sleep did not come. Instead, her mind replayed everything that had happened over the last month. The death of her husband. The worries of her children. Thomas charging through Dunvegan, turning the guards on her and threatening all of their lives.

Then there was the siege of her castle and clan, which was also a blessed reprieve from her prison. The MacKinnon. His kiss. The man was formidable, handsome, and elicited emotions from her that she felt powerless to control, but determined to do so all the same.

At some point as she lay there, two MacKinnon guards took up a post by the great hall entryway. Were they there to protect her and her children or to bar her from escaping?

She might have been liberated from her bedchamber, though she wasn't truly free.

But the end was in sight. She just had to keep repeating that to herself. Aye, MacKinnon could have stolen her letter to her cousin. Or he could truly have spoken for her. She would find out soon enough, and she'd pray it was the latter, for if not, she had more to worry over than ever before.

Rolling over so she could no longer see the guards, Brenna forced her rapid thoughts away and let the soft sighs and snores from her children lull her into sleep.

THE bailey of Dunvegan was full of MacKinnon warriors. Half slept on pallets, the other half took up their posts on the wall and by the gate. He'd sent two inside to watch over Brenna and her children, unsure if any of the servants still loyal to Ronald or Thomas would exact their revenge upon her.

Gabriel took a pallet extended to him by one of his men. He rolled it out and stretched his body over it, lying on his back, ignoring the pinch of pain at his stitched wound, eyes up at the darkened, star-studded sky. His head swam from both the whisky and the events of the night.

He swiped a hand over his face, then rubbed it through his hair. What the bloody hell had he been thinking kissing the lass?

He'd been resolved to keep a distance from the woman. Resolute in his choice that he'd not heed Lamont's advice and marry her. And then, recklessly, he'd gone and kissed her.

The soft touch of her lips on his had been a slice of heaven. The scent of her, the feel of her, the not so subtle rush of desire and pleasure that a simple touch of his lips to hers brought.

Damn it all, he wanted the woman.

Wanted her under him, over him, all around him.

Worse still, she wanted him back. He could see it in her eyes. Pushing aside her trepidation, left a whole layer of fiery woman that begged him to kiss her once more.

Brenna MacNeacail MacLeod could not have been more different than Ceana Montgomery. 'Haps that was part of why he felt so drawn to her. Ceana had been quiet, kind, a hint of humor in her teasing smile.

Brenna could be those things, too, but there was an underlying intensity, passion and fearlessness about her that fascinated him. The woman had been through much and still she'd come out of it strong.

He was starting to wonder quite a bit about the events that led up to her husband's death. By all accounts, she should have been charged with his death and executed, yet her brother-by-marriage had kept her alive.

Why?

Not for the loyalty of her late husband's men.

For the children?

They were fiercely loyal to their mother, though the two younger lads could be swayed easily. He'd found that out by asking where their older brother was when he'd first encountered them in the chamber. When he'd whispered to them to obey their mother because she wanted only for their safety, they'd rushed to do his bidding.

What other reason could Thomas have to keep her alive?

Guessing wasn't going to help. The man himself was still locked up in the chamber where he'd kept Brenna for weeks. Perhaps the best way to get the answers he sought was to ask Thomas himself.

Gabriel shoved off of his pallet and sought a barrel of water. He dunked his hands into the cool liquid and splashed it on his face, wiping the excess over his head and down the back of his neck. He repeated the action a few more times until he felt well and truly clear-headed.

Donnan was asleep on a pallet, but Coll leaned against a wooden beam that held up the ramparts, his eyes on his laird.

Gabriel nodded for his attention and Coll approached.

"I need to talk with Thomas MacLeod," Gabriel said.

"He is still in the chamber, but we had his men removed to the dungeon."

"Good."

"Shall I accompany ye, my laird?"

"Keep watch here. I'll return shortly."

Coll nodded and went back to his post by the support beam.

Gabriel made his way back into the keep, but avoided the great hall. His men nodded to him as he passed, going up the winding circular stairs toward the upper chambers.

He unlocked the door to the chamber holding Thomas and found the man asleep on the bed. He bolted upright at Gabriel's entrance.

"Ye bloody bastard!" Thomas shouted, leaping from his perch and rushing forward.

Gabriel stopped him with a hand at his throat. "Calm yourself, cur. I have questions for ye."

"I'll not answer a single bloody one of them," Thomas said through bared teeth, spittle flying from his lips and narrowly missing Gabriel's face.

"Keep your silence if ye wish, but it will only make me use methods most unpleasant."

The man clamped his mouth closed, forcing Gabriel to squeeze his neck until his face turned red. Thomas struggled with his will to keep silent and his need for air. When his face turned purple, he weakly grappled at Gabriel's fingers and opened his mouth, gurgling noises coming out.

"Do ye wish to answer my questions now?" Gabriel asked.

The whoreson nodded.

Gabriel dragged him toward the overturned chairs by the hearth, righted one and shoved him down.

Standing in front of him, Gabriel pulled his dagger from his belt and held it at the tip of Thomas' nose.

"What happened to Ronald MacLeod?"

"The bitch killed him," Thomas shouted. "She beat him with a fire poker and left him to bleed on this verra chamber floor." The man pointed to the floor as he spoke.

A tapestried rug had covered part of the wooden planks and Gabriel was willing to bet if he peeled it back, he'd find a darkened stain.

"Why did she kill him?"

Thomas shrugged. "How the hell should I know? She's an evil, vile bitch."

"Ye've known her since childhood—was she evil then?"

Thomas flicked his regard toward the wall, not meeting Gabriel's gaze. "She's always been a mouthy wench."

"Did your brother abuse her?"

"He was no less kind to her than any other husband is to a wife."

The hair on the back of Gabriel's neck rose in warning. "Are ye married?"

"Nay."

"Was your father unkind to your mother?"

"My mother died when I was young."

Gabriel assumed it was safe to understand Thomas had no idea what he was talking about when it came to how a husband should handle his wife.

"Did Ronald abuse the children?" Gabriel prodded.

"Spoiled the brats rotten."

He'd not expected to hear that. "Tell me this, MacLeod, why did ye not charge her and execute her for your brother's murder?"

This time Thomas' gaze returned to Gabriel's, his eyes hard.

"I was investigating my brother's death when ye charged your way in and murdered my men."

Gabriel pursed his lips, studying the whelp. "Are ye incompetent?"

The question startled Thomas, and he jerked his head back, his face screwing up into a perplexed frown. "What kind of question is that?"

"Ye've had the lady and her children locked up for nigh on a month and yet ye're still investigating. I merely question your competence, as it seems such would not take so long. And why lock your niece and nephews away? What wrongs have they committed?"

"I didna want them to run away. Her children are unruly. 'Twas for their safety."

The MacLeod bairns were the furthest thing from unruly. Gabriel seriously doubted that they'd been locked up for their own safety. Thomas was after something else.

Thomas' eyes shifted around the room, as if he were searching for something, or biding his time to come up with a better lie. "If ye must know why I kept her locked away instead of killing her when it's what she deserves, 'tis because I plan to wed her. Still."

Gabriel's chest tightened and a fierce anger pinged its way through his veins. This jackanapes, marry Brenna? *Never*. Brenna deserved so much better. She deserved a man who could appreciate the passion within her. The fire she tried so hard to keep banked.

Raising a skeptical brow, he forced Thomas to look at him. "Why? If she killed her husband, why would ye risk it?"

"My brother didna teach the bitch well enough how to behave. I plan to do so."

Gabriel flexed his empty fist, the hand with the dagger itching to slice off the fiend's nose. "And give his widow and children a home?"

Thomas shrugged.

Gabriel didn't believe him for a minute.

"Ye're lying. I'll have the truth afore I leave or I'll have your head."

Chapter Nine

"WAKE."

Brenna woke with a start, sitting straight up, eyes bleary, arms outstretched to protect her children. Snow leapt in front of all five of them, standing guard.

It took her a moment to figure out where she was and who was speaking, but when she did, her breath left her in a rush of relief, though her blood rushed through her veins in a rising panic all the same.

The twins remained asleep but Gillian and Theo both sat up, stretching out the kinks in their bodies. They looked ready to bolt, also momentarily confused as to their whereabouts.

"MacKinnon," Brenna said, her voice gravelly with sleep.

Her hound, Snow, crept forward to sit beside the conqueror, nuzzling as he stroked her head. The brute truly had taken almost everything from her. Even her blasted hound.

Despite having slept on a pallet in the great hall in a castle that was besieged by an enemy, she'd managed a deeper slumber than she had in the past month.

That only spoke to the way MacKinnon made her feel safe, a sensation at complete odds with her situation and how she *should* feel.

"My lady." He reached out a hand to her and she stared at the outstretched appendage. "Take it," he said when she didn't grasp it.

Take it. Take his hand. Touch him. Accept his help. Consent to leaving with him. Sanction his siege.

If she took his outstretched palm, then all of the thoughts flying through her mind would come true. If she didn't take it, then… what? She'd hurt his feelings? Prove she could stand on her own? Show she didn't need him?

Brenna stared up at the man who'd changed everything for her in just a few hours' time. He stepped closer, his hand closer to her, his face urging her to take it.

She swallowed around the dryness of her throat, indecision never having been a weakness of hers. Giving in, aye. Acquiescing, aye. But those were choices she made in order to survive.

With a subtle shake of her head, she pushed to stand on her own, her children following suit.

"I can stand of my accord. I'm not as weak as ye may think me," she said, a hardened edge to her tone.

She'd allowed him to kiss her yesterday. And then he'd stalked away talking of how neither of them should have done it. Why feed the irrational desire that seemed to spark whenever they were near by touching his hand?

"I've thought many things about ye, my lady, but never have I thought ye to be weak." Even this early in the morning, the man had the power to enchant her with his words.

Brenna regarded him, studied the flat, serious line of his lips, the earnestness of his blue eyes. Would she ever get used to how handsome he was? He must have a thousand lassies chasing behind for a chance to hold his hand and she'd just turned him away. Turned him away, berated him for his offer of gentlemanly assistance and then been given a compliment for it. The man was a puzzle.

"Thank ye," she whispered, for that was what one said when given a compliment and she'd not have him add ill-mannered to whatever list of attributes he had assigned her.

"Cook has made a small meal to break your fast and then we'll be on our way." He indicated she should come and sit at the table.

But rather than pay attention to the rumbling in her belly, she felt immediately inadequate. "Apologies,

MacKinnon, I should have asked Cook to do that. I should have asked her to prepare provisions for our journey."

"There's no need to apologize. Ye needed rest and I'd rather ye had it than running around begging orders from the servants."

"Thank ye," she said, ducking her head.

She couldn't remember the last time she actually felt taken care of. For so long she'd been the only one she could count on. As a child, she'd been the one to care mostly for her sister. Even as a child, wed, much had been expected of her.

It had only been recently that she'd felt a certain relief from her children. Gillian and Theo had truly been godsends the last few years in how they'd grown and eagerly undertook their duties. Without them, she'd be much more worn out than she was.

Perhaps, it couldn't hurt to allow this Highlander to help her a little bit. He seemed willing and able. And she was tired…

"Come to the table," he said, coaxing her from her thoughts.

Brenna nodded, waving to her children to follow. Nevin tugged on her skirts, begging her to pick him up and though he was already half her size, she scooped him up and cuddled him close.

"I'm sorry, Mama," he whispered into her ear. "For what I said."

Emotion welled in her chest and she stroked a hand lovingly over her lad's soft hair and the line of his back. "All is forgiven."

What spell had MacKinnon cast over her twins? They'd hated her before he arrived and the last thing she expected was an apology. She'd been resolute to the fact that her bairns would likely hate her the rest of her days for taking their father away from them.

The table had been set with porridge, honey and blackberries. The children scrambled for places at the table and Brenna's mouth watered. It'd been a month of bread, some cheese and ale. If she had her way, she'd never eat another loaf of bread again. Snow nosed her head around the benches, but then scampered off when Angus whistled near the door, a meaty bone in his fist.

Seeing that after her children were seated there was only one place setting left, she turned to MacKinnon the Conqueror and asked, "Where is your bowl?"

"I will eat with my men," he said.

She frowned eyeing the golden porridge, the scent of Cook's alluring nutmeg making her belly grumble all the more.

"Do not eat, children," she warned, turning her gaze back to MacKinnon. "What have ye done to our food?"

He looked taken aback, narrowing his brows and staring at the bowls.

"Is it not to your liking? Cook said ye oft had this afore ye were imprisoned."

He'd checked to see what she liked to eat? Trying not to be baffled, she forced herself to concentrate on the conversation.

"It looks wonderful, but I have to wonder, I have to have my suspicions. Ye've been too kind for a man who has besieged us, laid claim to our land and my son's birthright. What best way to get rid of us without blood on your hands than to tamper with our meal."

Now MacKinnon frowned in earnest. "Ye think I poisoned your breakfast? Ye think me cruel enough to poison a woman and her children?"

Brenna shrugged. "'Tis the way of things with war."

MacKinnon moved quickly, one moment standing a few feet away and the next advancing on the table. He lifted her bowl, scooped a massive bite of oats and shoved it in his mouth, staring at her with open hostility. Grabbing the bowl of blackberries he tossed a handful into his mouth and then drizzled honey onto his fingertips and licked them clean. He washed it all down with an entire cup and ale, then held his arms wide.

"Am I dead? Think I'd poison myself?"

Brenna felt instant regret at her accusation, but it couldn't be helped. "I thank ye for proving me wrong. I'd hate for our deaths to be on your conscience."

He grunted. "That I doubt. Ye dinna give a damn about my conscience." He waved to a waiting servant. "See that the lady gets more porridge and ale. Refill the bowl of blackberries." Then he bowed low to her, a cruel smile on his face. "Enjoy your perfectly well-prepared meal, my lady, for on the morrow ye'll be eating what I prepare for ye."

A tremor shivered up her spine, but she held herself rigid, hoping he hadn't noticed.

Brenna took her seat and when a new bowl of steaming porridge was placed in front of her, she kept her attention only on the meal. Her confrontation with MacKinnon had spoiled her appetite. The sweetness of the honey, blackberries and oats barely touched her tongue as she methodically chewed and swallowed.

Around her, the children babbled and complimented Cook on her meal. Fresh cups of goat's milk were placed before them, and they drank as though starved, which they'd mostly been.

When their meal was finished, Sarah presented them with a bowl of warm water and linens.

"His lairdship requests that ye wash your hands and faces and present yourselves in the bailey," Sarah said with eyes downcast.

Brenna bit the tip of her tongue to keep from retorting that she didn't follow MacKinnon's orders. Truth be told, she wanted to wash the grime from her face. After the events of the night before, she and her children still had faces smeared with ash.

So she placed her hand gently over Sarah's. "Thank ye for all ye've done for me. Ye are most loyal."

"Think nothing of it, my lady."

The water had been scented with rosemary and was fresh feeling as Brenna scrubbed her face. The children followed suit and when they were all finished, she turned in search of someone she could speak with — namely a MacKinnon guard — about changing their clothes before they left. They need not know that she also planned to grab coin to keep on her person for when she escaped with her children.

"Can I be of service?" A tall guard with dark hair and green eyes approached. He was almost as large as MacKinnon and wore his colors.

"Aye. I'd like for us to change our garments before we join *your* laird for the journey." She put emphasis on *your*, as she never planned to bow to MacKinnon. As far as she was concerned, her son was the only laird she owed allegiance to.

"I'd have to ask him as he is most eager to leave."

"We will not tarry overlong. Ye can even accompany us if that makes ye more comfortable with allowing us to do so."

He thought about it a moment and then nodded. "Aye, my lady. I will accompany ye."

"Verra well." Brenna took her two young ones' hands and led them toward the stairs with Gillian, Theo and the guard in tow.

Just as they reached the bottom stair, MacKinnon himself entered through the great front doors, causing Brenna to stop in her tracks.

"What are ye about?" he asked. "Donnan, where are ye taking them?"

"The lady requested a change of garments for herself and her family."

MacKinnon looked them over, she assumed ascertaining that they had washed themselves as he requested.

"I'll take them. See that all the horses are prepared."

"Aye, my laird."

MacKinnon stood still, his eyes boring into hers as the man left through the same doors he'd just entered.

"Do ye truly plan to change or were ye hoping to escape?"

"I've no hope to escape," she answered, probably too quickly. "There is only one entrance and ye've made certain your men guard it well." She hoped to appeal to his ego.

He raised a questioning brow. "Aye. I guard everything and everyone that I owe protection to. Including ye and your bairns."

Brenna nodded, not having an answer. She wasn't quite certain whether his protection was a good or bad thing, for he seemed to wield it like a threat and she'd never met anyone like him before. No man with a sense of honor so strong. She'd not be able to get at the coin with him following her around without revealing its location. He looked well off, perhaps one night she could steal his own coin pouch before she escaped.

"Come, I will take ye to your chamber. I've removed Thomas MacLeod from the room."

"He is alive?"

"Aye."

"Why?"

"Should I have killed him? Or would ye prefer that duty?"

Brenna gasped and moved to cover her young boys' ears. "Dinna say such. I'd never —"

"Wouldn't ye?"

She shook her head vehemently. "Nay. There has been enough bloodshed. I simply thought ye might have..."

"I am not a cruel man for the sake of being cruel, my lady."

"I am coming to understand this," she acquiesced. And she was. She spoke the truth.

He held out his arm, indicating she should go first up the stairs. "To the young ones' chamber first."

They headed up the stairs to the nursery and Gillian helped her to change them quickly while Theo talked in soft tones to MacKinnon. What were they saying? When the laird made her child laugh, she wanted to jump from where she pleated Nevin's kilt to ask what the bloody hell was so funny, but she refrained.

They finished with the boys and headed to Gillian's chamber, which was beside Theo's. MacKinnon allowed Theo to change on his own while she assisted Gillian into a new gown. Once completed, they headed to Brenna's chamber and she paused in the doorway, shocked to see that the room had not only been put back to rights, it had been dusted, the floors washed and the fresh scent of herbs spread throughout.

She whipped around to face MacKinnon, poised to ask him if he'd ordered such done, and why, but the look in his eye gave her pause. He leaned against the doorjamb, a sense of pride in his gaze, as he studied her with earnest.

"Could I have some privacy?" she managed. "And my daughter to help me?"

He gave a curt nod and shut the door.

Brenna dressed in silence, her daughter helping to brush her hair and plait it freshly. Her thoughts returned to the coin chest. Ronald had hidden it well — though she'd spied on his hiding place — and she had to pray while she was gone that MacKinnon's men wouldn't tear the castle apart in their quest for it.

"Laird MacKinnon seems kind," Gillian said.

"Aye. But we must always be aware of kindness in our enemies, for it is likely a trap to take down our defenses."

"Ye think him an enemy? But he rescued us."

"He saved us from your uncle, but did he then vacate the castle and leave us to ourselves? Nay. He is taking us away."

"To Cousin Ceana. For protection," Gillian argued.

"So he says."

"Ye dinna believe him?"

"I dinna know what to believe." Brenna kept her fears to herself, not wanting to scare her child. She patted Gillian's hand and then tugged her in for a hug. "For now, we must trust that he has our best interests at heart. We are safe, I know that much."

"Aye, we are safe."

They walked to the door and opened it, faced by her three lads and MacKinnon.

"Our journey begins now," MacKinnon said, quirking a grin. "I trust ye will not delay us any further?"

Brenna blew out an irritated breath. "Ye might as well be prepared now, wolf, ye'll not be arriving at Dunakin as quick as ye reached Dunvegan."

"Wolf?"

He'd not cared a wit about her telling him his trip would be delayed when he was in a hurry, but instead asked about the name she'd given him in her head?

"Ye canna be serious," she muttered, attempting to move around the hulking man. "Let us go."

He shoved off the doorjamb, standing tall, his arms still crossed over his chest, blocking her path. "Did ye hear someone name me such?"

This time, Brenna focused on him, studying the intensity in his blue eyes. "Should I have?"

"Many have called me Wolf before."

"Is that your name? For ye've not told me what it is."

He nodded slowly. "To most."

"'Tis fitting."

"How so?"

Unable to look away from his eyes, feeling as though she could drown in their deep blue pools, she whispered, "Because whenever I look at ye, I feel like I am being hunted, that ye would devour me."

He winked slowly, a wicked grin forming on the lips he kissed so well with. His gaze roved from her eyes down to her toes, stopping at every curve of her body until she tingled.

"Then I am aptly named, my lady."

Brenna could have fainted, for all her breath left her, and a rush of heat filled her body. Indeed, he *was* suitably titled and she couldn't help but wonder just what being his prey would entail.

Chapter Ten

THE children saved him.

For if there'd not been any children about, Gabriel would have closed the distance between himself and Brenna in record time. He would have wrapped her up and kissed her most improperly this time. Not a gentle brush of his lips, but a full on claiming. Just the thought of it sent blood rushing straight to his groin and he shifted, grateful for the sporran that hid the sudden lift of his plaid.

The way she gazed at him just then was enough to make him waver in his stance, before gaining control and gruffly spouting, "We leave now."

He turned on his heel and marched toward the steps when every inch of him strained to return to her.

What happened to his vow to stay away from the lady? What happened to the intelligent part of him that knew meddling with her would only complicate his life?

Desire had a facetious way of making all else seem trifling.

Quick steps of little boots followed and then he found his fisted hands being pried open as two young ones pressed their palms to his. He glanced down at one and then the other, his heartstrings tugging. They were sweet lads. Unlike the older two who favored their mother's coloring, the twins looked much like the old MacLeod, his ally, before he'd gone gray. Their little ginger heads craned back to look up at him with warm, brown eyes.

Gabriel had not spent any time truly with children. Aye, there were plenty of them amid his clan, but most were apprehensive of him, thought him a giant, whispered his moniker, *Wolf*.

He felt slightly guilty about that. He'd spent the last eight years stomping around his clan like an injured, angry, hungry animal. But these two lads, they weren't afraid of him. In fact, they'd seemed to have taken a liking to him from the moment he'd picked the lock on their prison door.

"Lads," their mother called, worry in her voice as she and the older two children rushed forward.

Gabriel hated that a part of her feared him — for he also knew she felt something more for him, even if it was desire only.

He glanced over his shoulder at her pinched and worried expression. "They are well." He tried to speak calmly, but he was afraid his voice still came out gruff.

She winced and nodded, and he saw her daughter's hand slip into hers. The lass feared him, too.

Gabriel gritted his teeth and concentrated on the task of descending the narrow circular stairs with two little ones clinging to his hands. It was a feat he'd never attempted before and certainly very challenging. In fact, he thought he might have to give thanks to his mother for having done the same with him when he was a lad.

At the bottom, he waited for Brenna, indicating that she should head out the door first. He told himself it wasn't because he suspected she wouldn't follow, but rather because he wanted to protect her back.

She eyed him warily and then proceeded through the door, the light of morning breaking into the dimness of the castle.

In the bailey, horses stood amidst the warriors and servants who rushed about preparing for their departure. Brenna snapped her fingers to her hound who played with another and had ceased to follow her mistress.

"The animal stays," Gabriel directed.

"We do not leave without Snow." Brenna had turned around to face him, challenge in every line and curve of her body.

Gabriel shook his head. "Nay. She'll never make it."

"We'll not be riding at as quick a pace as ye think, my laird. She goes, or I swear to God, ye'll not get me out of this bailey except in pieces."

Gabriel grimaced. "I'd be happy to arrange such," he growled.

Brenna gasped. "Ye wouldn't."

"Try me."

"Ye're cruel."

"I am just."

She shook her head, pressed her lips together. "There is nothing just in taking away my hound."

"I am not taking her away. I am telling ye to leave her behind." Gabriel didn't understand what the problem was. 'Twas just a hound. Why must she fight him at every turn? Why could she not simply agree to do his bidding?

"I beg of ye," tears sparked her eyes, "I must take her. I need her."

Och! Hell and damnation! How could one woman's tears tug at him so? He'd rather have her fighting than this.

Groaning, he said, "Fine. But if she lags behind, we'll not stop for her."

"She'll not lag, I swear it," Brenna said, straightening her shoulders.

"I've procured three horses for ye. The twins will need to ride with someone."

"And I suppose ye think that's ye?" she asked, fire in her eyes.

"Nay. I thought of ye and your daughter."

Brenna glanced at Gillian who nervously smiled.

"I think it best for them to ride with Theo and myself," Brenna answered.

Gabriel shook his head. "Nay. Theo is nearly a man, I need him to protect his family, not care for wee ones. That's women's work."

The transformation that came over her was astonishing. He watched her fiery eyes blaze flaming daggers, her mouth contorted into something of a growl, and a red flush covered her cheeks. Even spitting mad she was a thing of beauty.

Beside him, the hound stepped back, a sign that Gabriel ought to do the same, but he'd never cringed from a struggle, let alone feared a woman.

"Might I have a word in private?" she asked, the honeyed words belying her anger.

Gabriel grinned, unable to help himself. Maybe he'd kiss the wrath from her. "Of course."

They stepped away from the children, around the back of the tanner's tent. Gabriel had to tuck his hands behind his back because he wanted to touch her face and see if it was as hot as flames.

"I insist that one of the boys ride with Theo."

"I canna allow it."

"Ye dinna understand."

"Enlighten me."

She glanced toward her children, fidgeting slightly. "Ye see, Gillian, she does not do well with a horse. If she is to ride, she must ride alone, else one of the boys may end up under a hoof."

"What do ye mean she does not do well with a horse?" Gabriel was well and truly baffled. What child of Highland descent couldn't ride a horse? Let alone a child as old as the lass.

Brenna was nodding, as if that gesture would convince him she spoke the truth. "She had an accident as a wee one and is quite frightened of them."

"Fears must be conquered."

Brenna rolled her eyes. "Save your inspiring speeches for when we reach our destination. I will not have one of the twins ride with her as the likelihood of all of us reaching Dunakin alive will be slim, for I assure ye, I will come after ye if one of my children is harmed."

Gabriel grinned, finding himself all the more entranced by her. Hell, he wanted to slid his fingers through her hair, tug her to him, and show her just how much she enticed him. "I will get your family safely to Dunakin, my lady, but I'd be remiss if I did not admit the thought of ye coming after me warms my heart." He pressed his fist to his chest and delighted in her angry reaction.

The lady stomped her foot, put her hands on her hips and leaned forward, her neck craning up so she could meet his gaze. "Ye heed my words. If ye be a wolf, then I am a lioness and I will protect my bairns with every breath and every beat of my heart."

Without warning, he reached out and stroked her cheek, cupping the side of her face, his thumb rubbing the point of her cheekbone. She jerked at his touch, but even that simple stroke on her skin seemed to take some of the bluster out of her. Her eyes grew hazy and just like that he was swooping low to kiss her again. He brushed his mouth over hers, swiped his tongue teasingly against the corner of her lip and over to the other side. She sucked in a ragged gasp.

Devil take it, but he was ready to lay her down where they stood. He needed to stop. Needed to put at least a foot of space between them, but he couldn't. Her hands rested gently on his chest, neither did they pull him closer or push him away. Silent invitation to continue?

'Haps.

He paused, waiting to see if she'd push him away. When she didn't, Gabriel slanted into the kiss, pressing his lips harder, testing her resolve. She sighed, her lips parting and he took that as an answer to his silent question. He slid his tongue between her lips to gently stroke against hers. Need exploded inside him, heat barreling its way through his body, blood pooling in his groin. He was hard. Harder than stone and dear lord…

This was madness.

Gabriel regrettably pulled his mouth from hers.

"I believe ye," he whispered, eyes locking on hers. "Now believe me, I will not let any harm come to them or ye. I know ye think me the enemy, but I am not."

She gently pushed his hands from her face. "That remains to be seen." Her voice had come down an octave or two. Perhaps it was true that a gentle touch could tame even a lioness. Or mayhap she was just as moved by the passion of their kiss as he was.

"I will prove it to ye," Gabriel said.

Gaze bemused, she asked, "How?"

"When we arrive at Dunakin, ye will see that I did not lie about your cousin." However he had kept the truth of his plans for her eldest son from her. But the lady would have to agree. After all, he offered Theo an opportunity that, as of right now, he did not have.

Gabriel would take care that Dunvegan thrived while training their future laird. What better opportunity could he have? Lamont lands were too far away for the lad to be any good to his people. If he remained with MacKinnon, he could even go and visit his people several times a year. She would have to see reason in that.

"For your sake, I pray ye have not lied about Ceana."

Her threats were endearing, and he was certain that once she was on her way to Lamont, he would miss them.

"I assure ye, though I'd enjoy a battle with a temptress such as yourself, I speak the truth." He grinned and winked. "Now, the matter of the lads. Would ye prefer them to ride with the warriors so ye're able to care for your daughter if needed?"

The offer was kind and he could see she struggled with her answer.

"My warriors will protect your boys with their lives, I assure ye."

"'Haps that would be best." She frowned. "Did ye kiss me to distract me?"

Gabriel laughed softly. *I kissed ye because I had to. Because ye're too enticing not to kiss.* "Aye."

Brenna glowered at him. "Dinna do it again."

She turned from him before he could respond and approached her youngest two, crouching down to tell them of the riding arrangements. The lads hooted with joy, striking their fists into the air. Gabriel decided that where Gillian and Theo were cautious and reserved, the twins must be wild and fearless.

He found himself smiling down at the children, and then he happened to look at Brenna, and his chest tightened. She'd not waited for him to answer. Did that mean she didn't want him to agree to not kiss her again? Because, if she let him, he'd take her back around to the privacy of the tanner's tent and kiss her once more.

She stared up at him with a mixture of angst and wonder. He felt the tug of a connection between the two of them, and convinced himself it was merely the children and their mutual need to keep them safe. That it had nothing to do with the two incredible kisses they'd shared.

Even still, he wanted her to trust him.

This time when he reached out his hand for her to grasp, she hesitated only a moment before placing a palm against his. He gently pulled her to standing.

"I promise ye, ye are safe with me."

Despite his softly spoken words, her hand started to tremble and her face paled. She wavered on her feet, and he reached forward, his hand around the small of her back to hold her steady.

"Are ye all right, lass?" he asked.

What had he said to cause such a reaction?

She nodded, batting away his hands, her gaze turned away from him. "Aye. Let us be on our way. The sooner we leave, the sooner we arrive."

The connection he'd felt was broken, leaving him perplexed. Perhaps the lady was much like her older son. She wanted to be in charge. She didn't want his help. And he supposed he knew that well enough given the interactions that they'd had. But didn't she realize that she needed his help?

Without him, she'd still be locked away in that chamber going through God knew what at Thomas MacLeod's hands.

On pain of death, the bastard had admitted much, including his search for a vast treasure within the castle and his suspicions that Lady Brenna had not, in fact, been the one to kill Ronald MacLeod. The way he'd sneered and muttered, *Like father, like son,* had been all too haunting in Gabriel's opinion.

Had Ronald killed his father?

Had Theo killed Ronald?

Gabriel turned away from the lady and called out, "Mount up!"

He led them to their horses, and when he attempted to help her mount, she brushed him aside, lifted her leg and placed her foot into the stirrup, swinging herself effortlessly over the horse. Theo helped his sister onto her mare and the twins bounced away amidst calls of joy with the two warriors Gabriel had assigned to keep care of them.

"My laird, I wish ye well on your journey," Donnan said.

Gabriel grunted then nodded his head for Donnan to walk away from hearing distance from the rest of the crowd.

"I know ye'll keep this place safe and help the people to thrive. At all costs, keep Thomas MacLeod locked up, but cared for. We need not have the bastard die on us."

"Aye, my laird. I will."

"And there is a rumor of a treasure. I charge ye with keeping it safe."

"With my life."

"It belongs to the lad, Laird Theo, and no one else."

"Aye, my laird."

"I'll return in a month's time, after I've gotten the lady situated and returned to her cousin, and I've secured Scorrybreac Castle. Then I'll figure out just what to do with Thomas MacLeod."

"Aye, my laird. All will be well whilst ye are away."

"Given that ye'll be here awhile, when I return, I'll bring your wife and bairns with me."

Donnan smiled. "I'd be grateful, my laird."

Gabriel clapped him on the back. "I dinna know why."

Donnan laughed. "The tender touch of a woman never did a man harm." His laughter quickly faded and he eyed Gabriel warily. "Apologies, my laird."

Ordinarily, a comment such as that would have thrown Gabriel into a storm of anger and vengeance, and he waited for the hot rage to take hold, and when it didn't, he simply grinned and patted his friend on the back again. Somewhat amazed at his own reaction, Gabriel said, "Right ye are, my friend, right ye are."

Donnan appeared speechless, a smile frozen in place on his face as he nodded and clapped Gabriel back.

"See ye soon, Donnan."

"Safe journey, my laird."

Gabriel returned to the horses, making sure that the saddles of his charges were tight. He stopped at Brenna, checking hers. She stared down at him as he did so. He gripped her ankle without thinking, the delicateness of it felt even through her boot. She jerked away from him, but not before he saw the flare of the same heat in her eyes that charged through his blood.

He'd be lucky to get her off to Lamont before he ravished her. A ravishing he would thoroughly enjoy and regret, for Brenna may have been the healing balm he needed to push away the pain of his past, but she was not the woman for him.

Tearing himself away from her, he mounted his black warhorse, Ghost.

"Ride!" he bellowed, and the thunder of the horses pouring through the sea gate echoed on the stone walls of the stronghold, chiming the ending of one quest and the start of a new one.

Chapter Eleven

BRENNA lied.

Well, it was more of a withholding of information, truly.

Gillian not only didn't have a problem with horses, but she rode quite well. 'Twas Brenna who was inclined to anxiety around the beasts. Mostly because she'd not ridden in fifteen years. Climbing atop the beast had been easy, she'd not forgotten how to do such, and in the years since she'd been taken from Scorrybreac, she'd not grown much taller, so her foot had easily stretched as high as she remembered it needed to go to reach the stirrup.

She flicked the reins with the rest of them and urged the mount into a trot. Though it had been a number of years since she'd ridden, her body and mind recalled the steps quite easily. Hands trembling, she mumbled to herself, hoping that no one noticed her nerves.

Though their father had not favored them, Gillian and Theo had been taken riding often.

And Brenna had been invited a time or two, but she knew her place as ultimately a broodmare to her husband. Riding wasn't an enjoyable pastime to her.

Besides, her arm still tingled from what had happened on the way from Scorrybreac to Dunvegan all those years ago.

She'd struggled. She'd fought hard against the guard who held her. And she'd fallen, her arm trampled by a horse. The break had been clean and they'd set it right away. The pain had been unbearable, made worse by her circumstances and the jostling ride all the way to Dunvegan. Ronald had not wanted a lame bride, neither was he willing to halt their journey in order to give her a few days' rest. She supposed she ought to be grateful for the fact that he'd made certain her bone was at least set. Her arm had healed perfectly and it only ached a little during raging thunderstorms and snowstorms.

Brenna flexed her fingers, willing the tingles to go away. She knew they weren't really there, more of a sensation her mind was creating. The last time she'd been on a horse, it had not been of her own volition, and though she'd climbed this one willingly, it had only been to avoid being tossed over a guard's lap.

A jerk in her horse's gait brought her back to the present and she tightened her hold on the saddle to keep herself balanced. The mare's feet sunk into the rocky beach and then into the marsh, causing her steps to be slightly unsteady. Brenna breathed deep. In through her nose, out through her mouth, telling herself not to fall. Not to be afraid. That this, too, would pass and soon she'd have her own two feet on solid ground.

As soon as they cleared the marsh and turned onto the road that led through the forest, she started to feel a little better. The horse's stride had improved and she didn't feel as though she was holding on for dear life. Or that her breakfast would make a reappearance.

Snow trotted alongside her for a little while, but made her rounds amongst the horses carrying all her charges.

Brenna's gaze slid to the side, taking note of the small smile on Gillian's face. The lass loved to ride, felt that it was freeing. If only Brenna could harvest some of her child's joy and let it spread through her.

Gillian caught her mother's stare and smiled wider.

"Ye ride well," Brenna said.

"As do ye. I didna know ye could ride." Gillian frowned slightly, looking perplexed.

"I learned when I was a child," Brenna said softly, hoping her daughter would not ask her anything more.

"How come ye never rode with us?"

No such luck. Brenna simply smiled and said, "I had other duties to attend to." How could she have said: *I loathed your father. He would likely not have let me ride anyway if I'd agreed for fear I'd run off.*

For she'd threatened just that more times than she could count. And he only asked her to torment her anyway, to remind her of her fall.

"'Haps we can ride together when we reach Cousin Ceana's holding." Gillian stared at her expectantly. Brenna was suddenly filled with deep emotion as she gazed into the innocent hope of her daughter's eyes. She had so much to live for. So many dreams yet fulfilled.

"Aye, lass, I'd like that."

On her other side, Theo sat his horse tall and stoic. His gaze straight ahead. Pride in his seat. She couldn't help but be proud of him herself. He'd been through so much trying to protect his family. He was a good lad.

Brenna studied his rigid profile, wishing she could gather him in her arms and hold him like she'd done when he was young. To sweep her fingers over his brow and take away all the pain and angst. To make him carefree and calm again.

Then again, Theo had never really been a carefree child. He'd been born into a tense environment and had yet to experience life without strife.

Something unfavorable between Theo and Ronald had happened a month ago that had triggered her son's usually doggedness to shatter. She had yet to find out what had caused the argument with his father that started the calamities leading up to today, but she had no doubt he would tell her soon.

Ahead, her little lads were mostly quiet. She couldn't see them, as the guards' hulking bodies hid them from her view, but she could hear a small boyish laugh every now and then.

And then there was MacKinnon.

His horse was gorgeous, sleek and strong. And he was just as refined. Dressed as though he were going into battle, he was an impressive sight. He'd donned a shirt since she'd sewn him up, and if she hadn't been the one to inflict and then patch-up the wound herself, she wouldn't have known he was injured. She wondered if he was the type of man to reinjure himself without thinking. As much as she despised him, she couldn't allow his injury to become infected either. It did help to think that if she were to allow him to become ill then she and her children would suffer as a result.

With each turn of his head as he kept watch of their surroundings, she observed the set of his jaw. Severe.

Did he do anything without that extreme and deeply penetrating intensity?

He rode with the same passion he exhibited in all else and just watching him made her skin tingle. Made her recall the sweep of his lips on hers, the velvet heat of his tongue and how her body had come alive. And *that*, made her head swim.

Never had it crossed her mind that a kiss could feel like that. That a man's touch could momentarily take her away from reality.

"Mother," Gillian said, interrupting her reverie. "Do ye think we will be safe on our journey?"

Biting the inside of her cheek, Brenna nodded. "MacKinnon has promised us his protection. He will keep us safe."

"And Ceana? Do ye know her well?"

"I've not seen her since I was verra young. But when we played as children, she was kind."

Movement ahead had Brenna's concentration breaking once more as MacKinnon appeared to slow, but the rest of the men continued at their regular pace.

What was he doing?

As the distance between them lessened, her heartbeat increased until she heard it pounding in her ears. She drew in a breath and held it, hoping to calm her nerves at his approach, but that only made her chest burn.

She exhaled just before he motioned Theo ahead and took her son's place at her side.

"How is the horse, my lady?"

His leg brushed against hers and she shifted jerkily, trying not to fall.

"She is fine."

"And your daughter?" He peered around Brenna toward Gillian and frowned. "She rides verra well."

Brenna gave a curt nod and kept her gaze ahead, feeling his eyes boring into her profile. "Aye."

"She does not seem uneasy."

His tone was skeptical. He was not going to let the subject drop, and now she could feel Gillian's eyes on her, too.

"The mare is gentle," Gillian piped in. "Thank ye for choosing her. She's making the journey easy."

Brenna blew out a sigh of relief and silently sent up a prayer of thanks for having such wonderful children.

"Aye, thank ye, MacKinnon, for making such good choices in mounts," Brenna added.

"I'd not have *any* of ye uncomfortable."

"We will be fine. I thank ye for your concern," Brenna said softly, not missing his implication that it might be she who was uncomfortable.

The man was far too perceptive for her liking. She wasn't used to a man acting as though he truly was concerned for his fairer sex companions. It was confusing to her, and left her brain feeling muddled, and the twenty-inch thick imaginary wall she'd built up to protect herself felt as though someone had yanked a core stone from its foundation.

She chewed her lip, wishing he would leave her side, but he didn't. He faced the front and continued at the same pace beside her.

Theo kept turning around to look at his mother, no doubt trying to gauge if she were safe. She tried her best to smile at him, though her lips wobbled with her nerves.

For so long, Brenna's children had been her source of strength. The reason she'd lived and withstood so much. A feeling churning in her gut told her that this journey was going to partially change that. She was going to have to learn to rely more on herself and she was going to have to let her older children learn to trust their own judgments and decisions.

But, was she ready to let go? Was she ready for them to grow up and away from her?

She glanced at Gillian, who looked so lighthearted. At that age, Brenna had been ripped away from everything she knew and thrust into a role she'd not been ready for at all. A role that changed who she was at the very center of her heart.

A role that she'd not ever give back, for it would mean losing her children. And she'd fight to the death for them.

With that in mind, and having MacKinnon beside her now, she asked, "Ye've not yet said, will Ceana be waiting for us at Dunakin?"

Would this all be over in just three days' time? Four or five at the most?

"Nay."

Brenna gasped, yanking hard on the reins and earning an irritated whiny from her horse. "What?"

Her mount stopped dead in its tracks, getting a slight bump from the horse that trotted behind her. Snow took the opportunity to collapse and catch her breath.

MacKinnon called for the riders to halt and he grabbed her reins, pulling her close enough that their legs brushed again, heat transferring from his body to hers. She gasped, trying to will the warmth in her cheeks to abate.

"Only I call a stop to the caravan," he said with a frown.

"I'll not move another inch away from home without knowing just where ye are taking me and why."

Silence reigned around them as everyone fought to pretend they were not paying attention.

MacKinnon's glower could have frozen her into stone, but she straightened her shoulders and lifted her chin. Aye, she could be stubborn and her governess had told her that time and again.

"'Tis dangerous for us to be stopped like this in the middle of the road. Ye put all of us in danger with your outburst." He spoke in low tones, as if he hoped to keep their conversation private where there were not dozens of ears only feet away.

Brenna matched him glare for glare. She'd not let him make her cower. Nay, Ronald had been the last man to ever make her cower. With his death, she was released from the bonds she'd been placed in fifteen years before. A new Brenna was born and this one wasn't going to take anything lying down ever again. "Ye told me ye were taking us to my cousin, that ye'd keep us safe, but if she is not at your castle, then why should ye not escort us to her instead?"

The muscle in his jaw ticked and his blue eyes had grown darker in color. "I can protect ye best at Dunakin from the MacLeods who will know soon what has happened to Dunvegan and ye and your children.

They'll know what ye did and they'll want revenge for killing their kin."

So their departure and the lure of Ceana had to have been a trick. Brenna worked hard to keep her voice from shaking. "And my cousin? Was that a lie?"

"Nay, my lady."

"I do not understand." He sounded so genuine. Was he that good of a liar?

"I will explain later."

Brenna shook her head. "Explain now."

His frown deepened. "Ye have to trust me."

Trust? How could she put her trust into the hands of a virtual stranger?

Tears of frustration burned her eyes and she willed them away. Didn't want MacKinnon to think her weak for crying. She wasn't doing so to get her way, or from sadness, or fear. Nay, but from lack of control and being at the hands of a man and his clan whom she did not know. As a child, she'd thought the MacKinnons might be allies with the MacNeacails but one never knew when clans would turn against each other for land. Both their holdings butted against Loch Portree and the Sound of Rathsay.

There were so many reasons why she shouldn't trust MacKinnon.

His face softened and he reached out, covering her hands with his own where she tightly clutched at the reins.

"Lass, my lady," he murmured softly. "I do not pretend to know all, but I do know ye have been through a lot in the course of your life. I promise, I only seek to make it better from here on out. But ye must trust me. We are not safe stopped on the road like this. When we make camp this night, we will speak more extensively."

Brenna gazed into his eyes, feeling warmth seep over her. She slid her tongue over her teeth, thinking hard, and coming to terms with one thing: if he'd intended her harm, why would he not have done so at her own castle?

He'd done nothing so far, save prove he could be trusted. She could tell herself that she had no choice, and truly, she didn't have many. But she *could* choose to believe him.

She had to put aside her fears and the stigmas from her past and take a leap of faith, if not for herself, then for her children.

Slowly, she nodded, the jerking movement not as fluid as she'd hoped. "All right," she whispered.

The smile he sent her was stunning and tugged another stone from her curtain wall.

With a final squeeze of her hands, he withdrew, leaving her limbs to feel the loss of his strength.

MacKinnon gave the signal that they should move out and Brenna dutifully urged her horse forward. She dared not look at her children, for she feared what she'd see in their eyes. Concern, pity, fear.

She didn't want to see them look at her like that.

"Mother, would ye look at those wee things," Gillian said, her voice full of joy.

Brenna turned to see what her daughter was talking about, spying two squirrels chasing each other, rolling as they wrestled in an apparent love squalor. They climbed a tall fir tree and sat on the limb overlooking the caravan, watching as they passed.

"Weren't they funny?" Gillian asked.

"Aye, love," Brenna said, smiling.

'Twas then she realized, her older children didn't pity her. Neither one of them had expressed any fear of MacKinnon. Theo, still bothered by the events that had taken place over the past month, seemed pleased to partner with MacKinnon. Gillian and the twins, she'd not seen them this untroubled since they were young and innocent.

What was this man doing to them? Changing them all.

"Do ye think the one is courting the other?" Gillian turned in her saddle to spot them again.

"Nay, lass. The courting of squirrels is quite vicious. Likely those were two young squirrels at play," MacKinnon interrupted, with a wink in Brenna's direction.

Brenna ducked her head to hide the heat that filled her cheeks. How could he make her feel like they had an intimate connection? Saints, but she felt like he could see inside her. And she didn't so much mind that thought, which troubled her all the more.

"Like Theo and I?" Gillian giggled. "If he had a treat I wanted, I'd chase him up a tree, too."

"Och, aye. I dare say, if your mother had a treat, I'd chase her, too. There's no telling what one would do for a strawberry cake."

"Strawberry cake?" Gillian asked.

"Aye. Dunakin's cook makes the sweetest, most savory strawberry cakes."

"I've never had one," Gillian said, excitement lacing her words.

Theo tossed over his shoulder, "And likely ye never will as I'll be sure to seize the lot of them when we reach Dunakin."

"Not if ye value your life," MacKinnon said with a laugh. "My lady mother will see to it ye eat nothing but stale bannocks if ye steal her sweet treats."

Brenna's chest lurched at the jovial conversation between her children and, begrudgingly, with MacKinnon.

"What of ye, my lady? Do ye like sweets?"

Brenna nodded. "Aye. But I'll not have a strawberry cake."

"Why is that?"

"I cannot." She felt heat fill her cheeks. Ronald had often berated her for her affliction to strawberries and her insistence that her children not ever taste one. 'Twas odd, because other berries did not cause such a reaction.

"Mother gets ill from strawberries," Theo offered.

"Ill?" MacKinnon asked.

"Aye," Gillian nodded.

Brenna stayed silent, waiting for him to scold her for her weakness.

"Well, then, I'll see to it that Cook learns another recipe for cakes while ye're in residence, for ye need not go without. 'Haps blackberry."

Brenna caught herself before her mouth fell open in shock and she stared up at MacKinnon with what she was sure was a mixture of disbelief and amazement.

He would do such a thing for her? Why?

"Ye need not, MacKinnon. I'll not be with ye long enough."

He shrugged and smiled in that disarming way of his.

"'Twould be my pleasure, for ye've a beautiful smile, and what kind of host would I be if I did not deign to see it."

Host. Host?

Brenna nodded, trying to hide her confusion. The more he spoke, the more he smiled, the more he winked, she found her foundation crumbling as though each of his niceties was another stone being flung from a well-built trebuchet.

He could spin the words a hundred different ways to make them sound prettier, but there was one thing he was not and that was her *host*. MacKinnon had stormed her castle, seized it from her and then taken her away.

Well, he may have captured her home, herself and her children, but there was one thing she'd not allow him to conquer and that was her soul.

"Come, now. We must be on our way. We've already tarried overlong here." MacKinnon flicked his reins and urged the caravan forward.

Chapter Twelve

WITHOUT the cover of the forest, the sun beat down on the riders, but at least covering the rocky knolls and descending into the valleys, a breeze blew from the river warding off some of the summer heat.

Gabriel had ridden with Brenna and her older children for a time. He liked to see her smile and had tried to coax more, but at some point, and he'd seen just when it happened, she'd shut down.

When he'd talked of seeing her smile. But he couldn't help it. 'Twas a sight he'd only witnessed a couple of times since meeting her, and he was not a man to withhold a compliment from a beautiful woman when it was deserved.

Several hours had passed. They'd need to stop soon to give their mounts a break, seek release of more personal matters and to eat the nooning. He'd not have Lady Brenna thinking ill of him for pushing her children too hard, even though the bairns had all taken a liking to him. She, on the other hand, was proving harder to open up.

Not that he should care. In fact, he should be happy not speaking to her for the rest of their journey and then sending her off with Lamont when they got to the castle.

But that would be a lie.

As bitter as he'd become over the years, he couldn't deny the fact that Brenna struck something inside him. That she offered hope with her bright eyes.

"Halt!" MacKinnon called, when they reached an area beside the river that was protected by trees. There was also plenty of grass for the horses to graze. Shade and privacy for the riders.

The caravan stopped and his men went about their duties, dismounting and tethering horses.

Gabriel dismounted quickly and approached Brenna who had not yet done so. The white hound she insisted on bringing had lay down beside her mount, as if it didn't expect his mistress to dismount at all. Brenna's face had paled as she looked toward the ground and her horse shifted restlessly on its feet, causing the hound to leap up and find a resting spot a few feet away.

Gabriel swiped his hand over the horse's muzzle, rubbing between its eyes as he looked up at Brenna.

"May I assist ye?" he asked.

She shook her head. "I think I'll just wait here until we are ready to leave."

Gabriel raised a suspicious brow. "'Twill be an hour afore we do, and then we'll not stop again until we make camp for the night."

She looked away, but not before he saw the fretfulness in her eyes.

"Let me help ye," he said. When he'd seen the way her daughter delighted in riding, and Brenna took a more reserved approach, he'd wondered whether or not she was the one in fact who was nervous around horses.

Brenna shook her head. "Leave me to myself."

"I canna."

Her gaze whipped violently back to him, defiant. "Because ye are my *host*?"

Gabriel was taken aback by the vehemence in her tone and the way she'd swiveled to face him with such anger and resentment wiping away any other emotion from her face.

"Because, I'll not have ye spouting unfavorable tales to your cousin of my treatment of ye." He gripped her waist and yanked her down, holding her tight against him, as he'd done in her chamber when she'd fought him. "I'm not a cruel man by nature, Lady Brenna, but I can be if pushed."

"Bastard," she seethed.

"Dinna make me into a monster that I'm not." She seemed to bring out the best and the worst in him.

"Only a monster could have succeeded in taking a well-fortified castle the way ye did."

"Nay, lass, any man with half a wit could have. Ye're protected more with me and my men on the road than ye were in that castle. With little guards and most of the ones there sotted on ale and whisky, ye're lucky someone didn't try to besiege the castle from Thomas MacLeod before I did. I promise ye, they'd not have been as nice as I've been, nor would they have given a fig for a lady's comfort, or the safety and care of her children. I'll not have ye resist me again. I've been patient with ye, but the way ye argue with me in front of my men, well if ye were a man, I'd take ye to task for it."

She glared up at him with eyes as blue as the sky above and cheeks as flushed as fresh wild berries. Her skin was smooth and creamy, and rather than be furious with her for her insolence, he wanted to kiss her again. He wanted to lay her down on the grassy riverbank and stake his claim, make her shout with pleasure rather than ire, for he knew that the touch of his lips on hers quieted her. He had the pleasure of sweeping his tongue over hers and he wanted to do it again. To swallow her sighs of pleasure. Blood rushed to his groin. His cock grew hard and pressed hotly against her belly.

She could, without a doubt, feel his hardened arousal. Could see the lust burning in his gaze. Her eyes widened to the size of bannock cakes and her mouth formed a luscious, inviting pink O.

"Go and relieve yourself," he ordered, forcing himself to sound gruff, hoping to scare her into hiding behind a bush for privacy, because he wasn't sure if she didn't try to run that he wouldn't do exactly what his brain was telling him.

Her throat bobbed as she swallowed and he heard the sound of her roughly indrawn breath. Felt her tremble against him, and yet she did not move. Was she frozen in fear, or struggling with a desire of her own?

His hands slid from her waist to her rounded hips, and it took every ounce of effort he possessed not to grind his pelvis against her, to show her just want he wanted to do. Instead, he pushed her away and said through gritted teeth, "Go."

Brenna nodded, jerked away, whirling on her heel. She sought out her daughter, grasping her hand and tugging her behind the trees.

Theo had gathered his younger brothers and led them toward a copse of brambles.

Gabriel watched Brenna disappear with her daughter, comfortable in knowing that she'd not seek to escape unless all of her children were with her, and then he went to relieve himself as well, willing his erection to dissipate.

His potent desire for her frustrated him beyond belief. It was uncontrollable, fierce and caused a war within him. Not even his love for Ceana had ever brought about a yearning so intense.

'Twas madness.

And that madness only seemed to bolster the idea that he needed to get her to Dunakin and have Lamont take her away.

He returned to camp where his men were passing out bread and cold meat they'd taken from the castle. Brenna sat huddled with her children, smiling at a tale one of the young twins shared.

Gabriel sat on the opposite side of camp, as far from her as he could. He scarfed down his bread and meat, barely tasting the fare. Too distracted. Even the distance didn't keep his gaze away. He was drawn to her, watched her steadily, and when he realized he was smiling, he frowned and jerked his gaze toward the river in disgust.

He absently picked up a stick, pulled out his dagger and started to scrape off the bark. All the while he shaped wood, he watched Brenna. Kept his gaze on her as she led her tiny bairns to the river's edge where they dipped their hands in and washed their faces. Watched her do the same, rivulets of water dripping over her creamy cheeks to the length of her neck. The ride had been easy, but jarring enough that several loose tendrils fell free of her braid and floated whimsically around her shoulders and jawline.

Every move she made was fluid, easy, in stark contrast to the worry that pinched her face whenever she thought no one was looking, and even sometimes when she knew.

"My laird?"

Gabriel glanced up to see Theo standing before him. "Aye?"

"I beg a boon of ye, my laird."

Gabriel ceased his carving, giving the lad his full attention. "State your request and I'll consider it."

"I ask ye to be patient with my mother." The lad glanced worriedly over his shoulder to where she still crouched by the bank. "She has been through much and she..."

Theo turned his attention back to Gabriel, his lips pressed tightly together, and eyes squinted.

"What else?" Gabriel urged.

Theo cleared his throat. "For as long as I can remember my mother has..." He fidgeted, twisting his hands.

Gabriel waited patiently for what the boy had to say.

"My father was not a kind man. He did not love my mother. He did not value her for what and who she is."

"Ye think highly of your mother," Gabriel said.

"Aye. She is a saint."

Gabriel chuckled. "A saint, ye say?"

Theo straightened his shoulders. "Ye know nothing of her. But I gather ye will over the next few days and I simply implore ye to be patient with her. And..."

Gabriel stretched out his legs, hoping his position would set the boy himself at ease.

"Out with it, Theo."

"My mother needs someone who will care for her. Protect her."

"Aye. 'Tis the reason I came."

Relief flooded the lad's face, but Gabriel had a feeling Theo's train of thought did not remotely represent his own. What, exactly, was the boy suggesting? That Gabriel take her to wife? *Nay.* He kept himself from shaking his head and simply stared at Theo. Ignored the way his own chest swelled then tightened at the thought of a life tied to Brenna. He brushed off the idea of lying beside her each night, waking to her each morning.

Of their own accord, his eyes slid toward the river where she splashed her twins and smiled. *Mo chreach...* She was beautiful inside and out. From what he'd seen, everything he could want in a wife.

And it didn't hurt that her lands bordered the other side of Loch Portree. He'd control all of it if he did take her to wife.

But he'd also create an enemy of her if she thought that was the reason behind his doing so. Gabriel didn't want her as an enemy. Nay, he wanted her to admire him. Wanted her to desire him.

The idea took root, niggling irritatingly at the back of his mind.

"Thank ye, my laird. I know soon I'll have to return to Dunvegan, take my place as laird as I should, and I'd be ever so grateful to know that my mother is living out her days in happiness and safety. That my sister and my bairn brothers are safe until I can provide for them."

Gabriel nodded. "Will she not be overjoyed to reunite with her cousin?" he probed.

"'Haps." Theo shrugged. "They've not seen each other since they were children and I'm not certain they were close."

Would she be amenable to staying at Dunakin? With him? As his wife? He could force her. After all, he'd taken her castle, he could take her, too. But that had been done to her already and he didn't want a wife who was forced to be at his side. "There is a matter I'd like to discuss with ye, Theo, and I'd rather ye not tell your mother as yet."

The lad's eyes lit up. "Aye, my laird."

"I'd like to foster ye myself, with Clan MacKinnon."

Theo nodded emphatically. "I am grateful for the opportunity, my laird, and indebted to ye for it."

"Nonsense. Why were ye not fostered out before now?"

"Mother would not allow it."

"'Tis my understanding that your mother had not much power with your father."

Theo shook his head. "Nay, but my grandfather was kind to her, and he took up my training himself. When he passed on my father didn't seem inclined to send me away."

"I knew your grandfather. He was a good man." Gabriel purposefully didn't mention knowing Ronald as he had nothing good to say about the cur.

Theo shrugged. "As good as he could be. He did invade mother's lands and approve for his son to take her away and marry her." The lad straightened his shoulders. "I know not much about the way of things, but I do know some, and I know mother was just a bairn herself when she begot me. My sister is just eleven. Nearly the same age."

Inside Gabriel grimaced. He'd surmised that much about Brenna. He'd not be surprised if she insisted on being taken to a nunnery before she'd choose to marry him. With her fiery spirit, Brenna would be broken within a week by a domineering abbess.

"I'll not let such happen with your sister," Gabriel swore. And he'd not be the one to break their mother's spirit. 'Twas one of the things he admired most about her. And as much as he desired her, there was a part of him that held back at claiming her for himself. Perhaps fear that she would not accept him. And he couldn't take that kind of rejection again. Not when he'd already been through it twice before. "I'll invade your kin's land myself if Lamont tries otherwise."

Theo cocked his head in question. "Ye'll not keep her with ye, too? Is she to be fostered? Mother will be devastated."

"The only one I'll be keeping at Dunakin is ye."

Confusion marred his features. "But why? Are they going back to Scorrybreac, then? I dinna understand."

"Dinna concern yourself with it just now."

"But ye see, Laird MacKinnon, I do concern myself with it. I may be young, but I'm more a man than I am a boy. And I'm also a laird in my own right. As laird to laird, should ye not owe me the courtesy and respect I'm due?"

Theo sounded like his mother and Gabriel was impressed. "As your guardian, I'll give ye just what ye're due if ye question my rule again." Gabriel didn't raise his voice, but he made sure in his tone there was no room for argument. "Trust me, ye and your family are safe."

Without argument, Theo nodded. "I do trust ye. But know ye this, and I pray ye dinna take this any other way than how 'tis meant to be, I owe my mother my life, not because she bore me, but because of what she bore for me, and I'll see to it ye rest in your grave afore I see her unhappy."

Before Gabriel could respond, Theo turned on his heel and marched away. A good thing, too, because Gabriel might have been inclined to grip the lad by his ear and introduce him to a good lashing.

Then again, he had to respect what the boy said. He was fiercely loyal to his mother. So much so, that Gabriel smiled. The lad had ballocks of iron and one day, when he was well and truly a man, he'd be a formidable foe for anyone who stood in his way.

Gabriel tossed away his whittled wood and stood. Brenna had raised a good lad, *more a man*. She should be proud of such an accomplishment. Hands resting on his hips, smile still on his lips, he glanced back toward the river and caught her gaze. At first, she stared at him with measured trepidation, but then she smiled, giving him hope that perhaps there was a chance she wouldn't fight him.

By the saints, before they reached Dunakin, Gabriel was going to break through that tremulous barrier.

Chapter Thirteen

BY the end of the their second leg, Brenna's rear was screaming in pain. Her thighs were sore, her hands cramped, her back protesting the miles and miles of jarring terrain.

MacKinnon rode at the head of their procession, leading them along the river, over knolls and through valleys, and every once in a while, blessedly, through forest roads. Already she could feel where the sun had burned her on her cheeks and the top of her nose.

After spending so many years indoors, she was not quite used to the sun. She'd toiled in the gardens of the castle every once in awhile, but truth be told, she spent more of her time worrying over her children and their whereabouts than anything else. She'd personally overseen their studies, run the kitchen and kept as hidden away from her husband as she could. Especially lately, after the death of his father.

Though the old laird had not been able to come to her aid behind closed doors or if he was away, when he did take note of his son's cruel behavior, he attempted to put a stop to it. With him being gone, there had been no barrier between Brenna and Ronald's caustic temper.

She slowed her horse, thankful that the sun had started its descent and within an hour, earth would have a reprieve from its burning surface. For now, she was safe beneath a canopy of needles and leaves.

Their camp was not far from the river, in similar terrain to where they'd taken their noontime break. Firs and oaks reached high, letting the sun's light in, but its heated rays no longer blistered her skin.

She glanced to her children, who also had pink noses, but they didn't look as bad off as she felt.

"My lady," Gabriel approached her.

No doubt, he'd want to help her down. He'd tried to help her mount after the nooning, but mounting wasn't the issue she had. It was how far down the ground looked from atop her perch, and her fear that the horse would shift at just the right moment, causing her to fall. And with the fall, she'd scare the animal into trampling her and crushing her for good this time.

"MacKinnon," she drawled.

"May I assist ye?"

She pursed her lips and narrowed her eyes. Well, she didn't want him to know that she feared getting down. She at least had to make a pretense of not wanting his assistance. And it had nothing to do with the fact that she wanted him to touch her again. Nothing at all to do with the hardness of his body or the tingles that caressed her body when he touched her. "I'm perfectly capable of getting off this horse myself."

"Aye, most likely, but all the same, I'd not be a gentleman if I dinna offer."

"There's no need to pretend. We both know ye're not a gentleman," she retorted.

That only made him grin. "But I like to pretend." Without another word he reached for her and wrapped his strong, sturdy hands around her waist.

His touch was familiar and brought her comfort—as well as a rush of tingles. Ignoring the latter, she made an annoyed sound.

Bracing her hands on his shoulders, she fussed, "Put me down," though inside she wished he'd hold her closer.

MacKinnon's mind must have spoken to hers, for he did not put her down. In fact, her toes were not yet touching the ground, though she was off her horse and the length of her molded to his hard form.

Solid thighs. Thick, muscled chest. She could barely breathe. Her fingertips probed the corded bunch of sinew at his shoulders. Ronald had felt nothing like this.

Touching MacKinnon brought to mind the way he'd looked in the great hall with his shirt off as she'd mended the wound she'd created. He'd been so strong, smooth and fierce. Though she'd never had any feelings of desire before meeting him, it seemed he'd lit the wick of a candle just waiting to burst into flame within her.

What would it be like if he were to lie atop her? Kiss her as he had before? She couldn't imagine that he'd be as rough as her husband. Nay, indeed, it could be pleasurable. Or was that only her imagination? No women had ever shared with Brenna their dealings with a man. The only thing she knew was that there was pain. That joining led to being with child.

MacKinnon's kisses had to be a trick. They were what lured women into his bed, so he could inflict pain on them.

But even as that thought crossed her mind, something inside her argued against it. Aye, he'd been fearless and brutal with his sword against his enemies, but he'd been nothing but gentle with her children, and though he spoke roughly to her a time or two, he was also gentle with her. And his kisses... How could something that felt so good lead to pain?

"Please," she murmured.

He leaned in closer, his eyes taking on the same hooded look he'd had when he kissed her both times before.

"Put me down," she whispered.

Cobwebs seemed to clear from MacKinnon's eyes and he set her down, though she wavered on her feet. He kept his hands at her hips holding her steady. The pressure of his fingertips burned into the contours of her body.

"I fear the ride has taken its toll on me," she said with a nervous laugh.

"Apologies. We'll take it slower tomorrow," he offered.

Brenna smiled up at him. "That is kind of ye, but I'm sure I'll be fine by morning."

He nodded, and did let go of her then, leaving her feeling the loss of his embrace. Why did she always wish for him to touch her?

MacKinnon gestured toward her daughter. "She awaits ye, my lady. Best see to the wee ones."

She was grateful for their need of her and that it would put some distance between her and MacKinnon. "My thanks."

"Ye need offer me no thanks."

"But I will all the same." Brenna hobbled away, trying as hard as she could to walk with some dignity despite the scream of her muscles each step seemed to elicit.

"Are ye well, mother?" Gillian peered over Brenna's shoulder toward MacKinnon.

"Aye, love. Simply sore from the ride." Brenna glanced around to find Theo, who once more led Nevin and Kenneth to a place to relieve themselves.

"Oh."

"Are ye well?" Brenna asked her daughter.

"I'm quite well. I love to ride and I've never been so far from the castle."

Brenna couldn't help but smile at Gillian's enthusiasm. "An adventure ye're having. I'm so pleased ye've kept up your spirits."

"Have ye, mother?"

"Have I what?" They approached a thicket.

"Have ye kept up your spirits?"

Brenna grabbed her daughter's hand and kissed it. "As best I can, sweet child."

"All will be well. I can feel it."

"All will be well." Words she was coming to despise. Words she'd said to her sister. Words she'd whispered to her children. Words MacKinnon had vowed to her and now her own child, too. 'Twas as if they were all uttering words they couldn't believe in, didn't believe in, if only to convince the others there might be some truth behind them. "Come let us finish and get back to camp. Ye must be half starved."

MacKinnon's men were setting up a tent for her and her children when she returned. She insisted on helping set up camp, but though at first her offer was refused, they did send the boys off to gather wood and kindling for a fire.

"'Tis too warm for a fire," she pointed out.

"'Twill be cold once night falls," MacKinnon said.

"I want to help," she insisted.

"Nay." He crossed his arms over his chest and stared at her, willing her to challenge him.

The brute! Well, she'd not shied away from him yet and she'd not start now. "Let me set out the food at least," she protested.

He eyed her for a moment, then nodded for a guard to pass her their satchels of provisions. She and Gillian laid out the food on trenchers, consisting of the rest of the bread, some cheese, more meat and apples. The men all chatted, stretching out their bodies as they relaxed around the banked fire as she passed the food. In one of the satchels she even found a whole horde of honey cakes Cook had sent along. They were enticing enough she almost kept the bag for herself.

"Sit, eat," MacKinnon ordered her.

Brenna chose a spot near her children who ate with gusto. She swiped her skirts beneath her and sat upon the warmed ground. The sunshine had now mostly faded, leaving them in dusky light.

Several warriors stood guard while they ate.

When a skin of whisky accidently landed in her hands, Brenna didn't hesitate to take a nip. The liquid warmed its way through her body. Another sip and she'd be able to stretch out some of the tight kinks.

She passed the skin back to the warrior who'd given it to her, smiling with pride at being able to thwart his obvious intent at a joke. She supposed ladies didn't often indulge in harsh spirits.

The men sitting by her who'd watched her easily sip the whisky let out low whistles of appreciation.

She spied MacKinnon across the fire whose lips had quirked into a private grin. Sitting comfortably, leaning on one elbow, his legs stretched out on the ground before him, he appeared at ease in the wilderness. He nimbly cut slices from an apple, using the sharp tip of his knife to pop the pieces into his mouth. He gazed on her with an admiration she wasn't prepared for. No man had ever looked at her that way and she thanked heaven for the darkness, because the light of the fire didn't show off the blush she was certain colored her cheeks.

"Do you sing?" one of the guards asked her.

Startled by his question, she dropped her piece of bread on the ground, where Snow quickly gobbled it up. She broke her gaze away from MacKinnon to stare at the man who'd made the request. "Sing?"

"Aye, would ye sing us a song?"

Her gaze slid back to MacKinnon. Would he want her to sing a song? She'd sung lullabies to her bairns to lull them to sleep, but she'd not sung before grown men since she was a child, and the only song she remembered was a ballad her father had taught her and delighted in hearing.

She didn't know if it was the way he looked at her or the whisky that made her bold, but whatever it was, her courage was bolstered. "What of it, MacKinnon, would ye like me to sing?"

He stared at her through the camp, his eyes squinted. Then he popped in another apple slice and slowly nodded.

"*Am Bròn Binn* is the only ballad I know," she said. "And I warn ye, I've not sung it in many years." Clearing her throat, she worked up the nerve to sing. "*Chunnaic Rìgh Alba na shuain. 'N aona bhean bu ghile snuadh fòn ghrèin. 'S gum b'fheàrr leis tuiteam dha cion. Na còmhradh fir mar bha fhèin.*"

The King of Scotland saw in a dream... The fairest woman under the sun... And he preferred his heart's desire... Than to converse with men like himself...

The men were silent as she sang. And despite not having sung before a group in so long, her voice was not as rusty as she'd suspected. She closed her eyes and let the words flow, seeing the story behind her eyelids and recalling her family.

As she sang, a tear slowly trickled down her cheek. At the end of the ballad, she swiped it away and opened her eyes. The men all stared at her and then the whisky skin was thrust back into her hands.

"That was beautiful, my lady," MacKinnon said, followed by the appreciative murmurings of his men.

"Thank ye," she said softly, taking hold of the skin and sipping. Handing off the skin, she said, "The song was not the only thing my father taught me to like."

That got a laugh from the men.

"Will ye sing us another?" the warrior named Coll asked.

"I'm afraid today's journey has taken its toll on me. Perhaps tomorrow."

Brenna pushed to stand, indicating for her children to join her. Nevin and Kenneth gripped on to her hands and Gillian, too, stood, but Theo did not rise. She cocked her head staring at him and saw the determined set of his jaw. At fourteen summers he thought himself a man. Why should she take that away from him? A night of conversation and jesting with warriors would do the lad good. He'd not had that at Dunvegan.

She inclined her head in his direction and then in MacKinnon's. "I bid ye all good night."

MacKinnon stood, but before he could approach her, she whirled into the darkness with her children toward their tent. She had her boys make use of the brambles and Gillian, too. Snow kept a good watch, her eyes scanning their darkened surroundings. Thank goodness MacKinnon had allowed her to bring the animal. When they were finished, she led her children back toward their tent. There was enough illumination for her to see the darkened shape of it. They'd made her tent from their plaids and when she pulled back the flap, she could see that the floor had also been lined with blankets.

The men had done a good deed seeing to her and her children's comfort. She tucked them in, then whispered to Gillian to keep an eye out for her brothers as she went to wash her face by the river. When Snow tried to follow, she bade her stay to protect the children.

Judging by the laughter around the fire, the men had ceased with their proper talk and had let out the bawdiness that came out when men got together. She smiled as she sank down by the riverbank and dipped her fingers into the cooled water. With the sun down, the temperature had decreased significantly.

Brenna splashed the water on her face and rubbed it around to the back of her neck and over her chest. What she wouldn't give to strip off her clothes and sink into the cool water. To clean the grit of their long ride from her body, and to give her muscles a reprieve she was certain the chill waters would provide.

She still ached from their ride and all she could do was pray that on the morrow she was mended. If not, there was every possibility she'd not be able to walk herself to the privacy of the bushes should she need it.

"What are ye doing?"

The sound of MacKinnon's voice startled her so much from her thoughts that she jolted and lost her balance, pitching head first toward the water.

Strong hands on her shoulders balanced her, holding her steady. Instinctively, she reached up and put her hands over his.

"I was seeking a moment of solace," she said, hating the tremble in her voice.

"I'm sorry for startling ye."

She stood up, facing the river, his hands still on her shoulders. They stood that way for a moment, staring off at the moon above the water, the way it colored the darkened water to silver, and then he started to massage the kinks in her stiff muscles.

"Ye're tense," he said. "We'll take it slower tomorrow."

"That is not necessary," she said, the tremble gone from her voice. She bit her lip to keep from moaning at the magic he worked in her muscles.

"I'll not have ye bunching up like this all over."

It was on the tip of her tongue to suggest he simply continue working out those knots, but she held back. The whisky had been strong, else she'd not ever have muttered such improper things to a man.

"I'll be fine," she said instead, then stepped away, just out of reach. "Thank ye for your concern."

Even in the darkness his profile was handsome, strong. How was he not already attached? Then again, maybe he was, she'd never asked. But he'd only mentioned a mother at home. He would have mentioned a wife if there was one.

"Brenna," he whispered. His gaze was intense and she found herself motionless, paralyzed.

That thrill that ran through her veins picked up speed, making her heart skip a beat, her breath catch in her throat. She gazed up at him, watching the flicker of moonlight in his eyes. The muscle in his jaw clenched and unclenched and he licked his lips before blowing out a breath and looking away from her. He looked to be struggling with something. Could it be the same tricky emotions she found welling inside her? The war between desire and duty? Need and honor?

"MacKinnon," she responded.

Slowly, he turned his attention back to her. He looked so tense, almost angry, except that his lips were not thinned, not even pursed. They were partially open, and drew her attention to their softness, their firmness, the way he tasted.

"Ye can call me, Gabriel."

But before she could say his name, he'd closed the distance between them and gathered her in his arms. Warmth enclosed her and then she shivered. Tremors snaking over her entire body as the length of his hard form pressed and molded to hers. Zounds, but was this a dream? Was the way he felt, the way he made her feel, was it madness?

"I want to kiss ye, Brenna. And I need to do it properly this time."

Chapter Fourteen

SHE was frozen.

Feet rooted in place. Heart ceasing to beat. Lungs no longer able to pull in air. Even the blood in Brenna's veins stilled its rapid pace. For the span of several seconds, it was as though she were simply suspended in time. That she was floating above, looking down on a moment that would change everything for her.

MacKinnon—nay Gabriel—sought to kiss her. Was *going* to kiss her. Properly. As if their first two encounters had nothing on whatever it was he was about to present her with.

And she *wanted* whatever his proper kiss was.

Oh, Gabriel... The name itself was both powerful and heroic.

With only the moon to witness their embrace, she leaned closer, tipped her chin. This was wrong. 'Twas wicked. What respectable lady kissed a handsome warrior she barely knew under a blanket of stars, in the middle of the Highlands? What mother would drift away from her children to steal a moment of passion?

She would. She was. And she didn't regret it. At least not yet anyway.

His lips drew near.

All of a sudden, her heart rammed behind her chest, blood flowed, pounding in her ears. She sucked in a ragged breath, drinking in the scent of Gabriel—outdoors, leather, spice.

Every inch of her tingled, her knees wobbled slightly. She placed her hands on his chest, curling her fingers into his shirt, dragging the tips over his muscles. Marveled at the sound of his indrawn breath. Was it possible he felt as light-headed and heady as she?

"I *need* a proper kiss," she whispered, surprised at herself.

Something about this man brought out a woman inside she'd not known existed. A wanton who demanded to be put first, to be pleasured.

And what did she know of pleasure?

Only what he'd taught her so far and there was so much more she wanted to learn. If what he had to teach was even half of what he'd already imparted, then she'd be a happy woman.

"Saints, Brenna… What have ye done to me?"

His lips brushed softly over hers and she sighed, leaning into his mouth, pressing harder.

A surge of need was filling her, consuming her, propelling her forward. She wanted more. But he remained gentle, his hands at her hips a soft flutter, his mouth delicately sliding back and forth over hers.

They'd already been this close twice before, but now it was different. Not only because of the way his fingers massaged her or the way his lips warmly caressed hers, but because this time they both wanted it. Their first kiss had been one he'd stolen, a way to stun her, to show his power over her. The second had been startling, unexpected, a means to hush her. But this one... This was sensual, demanding. A fascinating exploration that left her breathless.

Brenna tugged against his shirt, demanding, needing, desiring.

The change in his kiss was quick, whirling her up in a gale wind. His head tilted to the side, his lower lip pressing to the crease of her own, the touch of his heated tongue sliding over her upper lip, and his hands... He kneaded her hips, tucked her body to his. And she didn't pull away from it. If anything, her body wanted to be *closer*.

She gasped with pleasure.

Aye, she'd dealt with her husband's invasive kisses, even practiced once as a girl with Cook's son at Scorrybreac. She was stunned, amazed, utterly floored that one man's skill with his tongue could be so different than another.

He did not thrust his velvet tongue into her mouth. He did not crash his teeth against hers. This kiss was not unpleasant or messy.

It was sensual. It was exotic. It was delicious. It was mind-bending.

And she never wanted it to end.

A soft moan escaped her and her boldness grew. She touched her tongue to his, drank in the low growl at the back of his throat. Their tongues colliding, sliding, swirling, tasting.

He nibbled her lips. Teased her. Delighted her.

Gabriel's hands trailed up over her spine and then back down with a slight pressure, sending a storm of shivers and tingles racing over her skin. Gooseflesh rose on her arms, her legs, and her nipples hardened into achy, needy buds.

Pressed to her belly was the long, thick length of his arousal. The sensation of its constrained power and desire sending a fresh wave of longing and pleasure coursing through her, settling between her thighs and causing her nether regions to quiver.

This time when she gasped it was with both enjoyment and surprise. These sensations whipping through her were new. This was all Gabriel. And once aroused, her body did not calm, nor stabilize, in fact it seemed to only grow more heated and insistent.

Caution was thrown to the wind as whispers of need and gratification filled her head. Just one night. Just one moment. No one would ever know…

How could a kiss take her sense, for it was, thrusting her into this titillating and fiery realm of seduction.

His mouth trailed to her neck, tracing a line in shivery, light kisses, and resting on the place where her pulse pounded. Brenna gripped his shirt tightly, leaning her head to the side to allow him better access, a soft moan escaping. A hand trailed from her hip over her ribs to cup her breast. At her roughly indrawn breath, he paused, but did not remove his hand. Sinking against him, she gave him silent permission to continue his wanton exploration.

The pressure of his hand on her breast, kneading the flesh, his palm grazing back and forth over her nipple was intense, and had her drinking in breaths that didn't quite make it to her lungs.

Gabriel's mouth pressed to her collarbone and he paused.

"Brenna…" he groaned. "Sweet, lass…"

She swallowed her stomach which had leapt into her throat and threaded her fingers through his short hair, tugging at the tendrils between her fingers. His lips roved lower, moving over her chest, fingers trailing beforehand and tugging at the fabric of her gown. What was he doing? Saints, but she liked the feel of his breath on her skin, his smooth, hot tongue on her flesh.

"Oh!" she cried out as his tongue flicked beneath her gown to touch the puckered flesh of her nipple.

She should not allow him to do this... Should pull away. Put distance between them. Return to her tent, but she couldn't. He was still doing it. His tongue delicate and hot fluttering lightly and deliciously over her sensitive flesh. The new sensations he elicited were heady, decadent and addictive. She was powerless to stop him. Her fingers wouldn't shove him away, but instead tugged him closer. Soft moans pushed past her lips.

And Gabriel... He was murmuring words that made her body sing and drove her up into the clouds to a place she wasn't aware existed.

"Lass, ye taste so good... Ye're skin is so soft... *Mo chreach,* but I love the sound of your moans... I want ye... I need ye..."

While he teased her breasts with one hand and his tongue, the other hand slipped from her waist to her thigh and he lifted, wrapping her leg up around his hip, tucking his arousal closer to her. She clung to him, both afraid to fall and afraid to let go.

He *wanted* her. *Needed* her. Desires she shared. Brenna longed to feel the length of him moving over her... inside her.

That was when she knew if she didn't stop him right that instant, she'd likely lay on the bank of the river and give herself over to him. Nay, not likely. She would. Was ready to do so right that moment.

An act she'd never enjoyed. An act she'd vowed never to do again once her husband was gone from this world. She was willing to give it all up because a kiss was so filled with pleasure.

But it wasn't just a kiss. It was Gabriel's kiss. Gabriel's intensity that drew her in, consumed her.

Threatened to tear down every stone carefully placed around her heart and soul. Already her walls were crumbling and if she didn't get away from him now, he'd breach her fortifications and conquer her as he had Dunvegan.

Gathering up her strength, she pushed against his chest. Lightly at first and then harder. She removed her leg from around his hip to put her weight back on unsteady legs. What was more difficult was tearing her mouth from his, but she managed it, instantly regretting the disconnect. Her body still thrummed, her heart still pounded and she could barely catch her breath, but she knew this was the right thing to do.

Gabriel grabbed hold of her hands at his chest. "My apologies, my lady, I know not what came over me." His voice was breathy, ragged. As gruff and heady as her own likely sounded.

Brenna smiled warily up at him, staring at the way the stars reflected in his eyes. "If 'twas anything like the way I felt, I know what came over us both. But..." She locked her gaze on his. "It shan't happen again."

He shook his head. "Brenna..."

"Shh... Dinna fear, warrior, I'll not hold ye t liberties taken. I'm not looking for another husband."

He frowned down at her, and fearing he'd demand she take him to the altar, she tugged her hands from his and stepped back.

"I promise, ye have nothing to fear from me in that regard." Even as she said the words, something tugged at her heart. Why? What was it?

I want him to want me for more than just a stolen kiss, proper or not.

The thought erupted unwelcome into her mind.

But he said nothing. Lips pressed together, his jaw hardened, he stared down at her with a vacant expression she could not read. Was it possible she'd read everything wrong? Had she been the one to kiss him, touch him, and he'd simply allowed it? Why did she suddenly feel so self-conscious?

She needed to get away from him. Get away from how he confused her, made her doubt herself, caused her to question all of the terms and values she'd set for herself. As a widow, the king could force her to remarry if he chose to. She was not completely out of the woods with that, but given that her son was old enough to soon become laird in full of Dunvegan, there was a good chance the king would allow her to live out her days in peace.

At twenty-seven, she was neither old nor young.

Her entire future was up in the air, and she'd be at the mercy of men, she knew, for the rest of her days, but if she could slink quietly, unattached, into the remainder of her life, she would.

Brenna whirled on her heels, unable to look at him anymore, unable to read his thoughts and coming up with a thousand different judgments he must be labeling her with.

"Wait." It was a softly given command.

But a command all the same.

And she wasn't going to allow him authority over her when he'd just so thoroughly ravished her and then broken her spirit.

Broken? Was that what he'd done? Was that what she truly believed?

Aye. She'd been crushed by his inability to respond. Even if she wanted to deny him a future with her, after a kiss like that, after his wanton caress, his wicked tongue, she wanted him to at least feel something, for it had rocked her world.

Brenna didn't stop. She marched with purpose back toward the camp, only to feel his fingers wrap around her arm and be tugged around.

"Get off me," she said through her teeth, trying to keep quiet and not draw the attention of the camp.

Was this where his entire demeanor would change? Would he turn into the monster some men did when given just the slightest chance with a willing woman? Would he now reveal himself to be no better than Ronald?

"Ye did not give me a chance to answer," he growled.

"To answer?"

His grip gentled and he let go. She could run now. She could escape him, but once more her feet were frozen in place.

"I dinna want your promise," he said.

"What?"

"Ye promised I had nothing to fear from ye. But, lass…" His lips curled into a grin that sent a tremor of heat through her and, once more, she was subdued, at his mercy. "If I've nothing to fear, ye'll not let me kiss ye again, and that would be a great loss for a man."

Her mouth fell open with a small noise of outrage. "Ye insult me. I'm not a woman who goes about kissing men for their pleasure. Ye might need to seek out a tavern for such. I'm a lady."

Gabriel chuckled. "I'd never suggest ye were a lightskirt, my lady."

"But ye did when ye suggested I might let ye kiss me again."

Fingers trailed from her upper arm down to her wrist and she fought against the sensations threatening to take hold of her again.

"Tell me ye dinna want me to kiss ye again, Brenna. Tell me ye didna feel what I felt."

She swallowed, her mouth suddenly dry. She tried to lick her lips, felt them tremble. "What did ye feel?" Her words came out whisper-soft and she instantly wanted to tug them back. To run to the safety of her tent and the innocence of her children.

Gabriel stepped closer, invading her space, her senses. He touched her throat with the tip of his finger. "My breath was quick, shallow. I thought it would cease, but it only increased in pace." His fingertip trailed up to just below her jaw where her pulse pounded. "My heart raced and I feared it would leap from my chest."

With every syllable uttered, her own heartbeat increased, her breath hitched.

Caressing his way over her jaw to her cheek, he tucked a loose tendril of hair behind her ear. "My body came alive with a need I could barely grasp. I'd be lying if I said I didna want ye, Brenna. I dinna understand it, but whenever I'm near ye, my thoughts are muddled, and the only thing I know for certain is that I want to touch ye."

Brenna wobbled on her feet.

Was this a dream?

She'd wake any moment.

Men, sensual, desirous men... They did not talk this way. Did they? Lord, what did she know of men or sensuality? All she knew was Gabriel and she would be content to know him and no other for the rest of her days.

When she'd asked how he'd felt, never in her wildest dreams did she expect such a thorough answer. Gabriel was completely upfront. And it was shocking. No one had ever been so openly honest with her.

"Is that how ye felt, lass?"

Zounds, but it was. Exactly.

Slowly, she nodded, unable to find her voice, certain that it would not come back, gone it was with her breath and her sense.

"What are we to do about it?" he asked. "Should we give in and kiss again? Should I give ye my dagger so ye can run me through for good this time?"

Brenna couldn't help but laugh at that. "I knew not who ye were when I did it and I fear ye'll never forgive me for it. At least not for a long time to come."

"Och, lass..." He cupped the side of her face. "I've already forgiven ye. In fact, I'd have expected nothing less of ye."

She raised a brow. "Should I be offended?"

"Only if ye wish, but that was not my intention."

"What is your intention?" Again the bold question was gone from her mouth before she could take it back. Had she not always practiced the art of thinking before speaking? Gabriel was not the only one with muddled thoughts.

"Which intention are ye referring to?"

She had to admit that her question was loaded. They were in a unique situation that he could answer in a hundred different ways. "Will ye let me go back to my tent" —*unkissed*— "or..." —*will ye ravish me?*

Gabriel chuckled, a jovial, teasing sound. He still cupped her cheek and he ran his thumb over her lower lip.

"Ye're an enchanting creature. Beautiful, tempting, and I'm drawn to ye like a moth to a candle flame. But, I think it best ye go back to your tent, my lady, else I do kiss ye again, and this time, I won't stop."

Brenna sucked in a ragged breath, nodding quickly. A kiss was one thing, to let him touch her breasts... scandalous. But more? She, herself, knew that anything beyond that was dangerous. Would only lead to torment.

She nodded, ducked her head and turned again. This time when she hurried away, he did not stop her. She all but dove into her tent. All four of her children slumbered, and when she looked at them, she felt both joy and trepidation. Snow snorted at her, as if to say, "*For shame, my lady,*" before she laid her head back down.

What had Brenna done?

Kissing the warrior who'd conquered them went against everything she'd promised. Threatened their safety. What if, in the morning, he decided he was angry for her wanton behavior? What if he cast her out? What if he left them all to their own defenses in the woods?

A few moments of stolen pleasure were not worth the lives of her children or their safety. On the morrow, she'd steer clear of him. She'd get up before the dawn to wash her face and relieve herself. She'd set out breakfast for the men and then she'd keep close to her children until it was time to leave. When he was near, she'd avoid all eye contact, and when he was far, she'd not seek him out with her gaze. When she woke, Brenna would pretend the man did not exist. 'Twas the only way to survive.

Brenna flopped onto her back, blew out a sigh and threw her arm across her eyes. Her body still sang with excitement. Traitorous. Despite how much she didn't want to remember, every second of their kiss replayed in her mind again and again. The slide of his lips, the caress of his tongue, the sound of his feral growl, the delicious press of his arousal, the decadent swirl of his hands on her spine, her hips, the way his fingers pressed to her pulse. His tongue on her breasts. His breath fanning over her sensitive skin. The words he'd said. The confession of how he felt when he kissed her, touched her.

'Twas enough to make her dizzy.

She sent up a prayer to heaven that MacKinnon woke up in the morning with*out* a clean conscious. That he, too, relived those moments with dizzying breathlessness. And she agreed to pay a penance for wishing such on him.

For, it was truly an evil thought, but if he were to wake up suddenly regretting it, not finding pleasure in it, seeking absolution for his wicked deeds, then she would pay the price for it.

Wicked deeds…

How could anything so beautiful, so amazing, be wicked?

She dug the heels of her hands against her eyes, rubbing furiously. Confusion warred inside her. She'd enjoyed it. She wanted him to kiss her again. And yet she feared it so much.

This must be why it was wicked, because one kiss from Gabriel MacKinnon and she was willing to surrender herself.

Chapter Fifteen

AN inferno had taken up residence inside his body.

Gabriel was certain of two things: first, the only way he was going to get blessed relief was to dive into the cool waters of the river, or to bury himself deep inside the welcoming warmth of Brenna's body. The second thing he was aware of was—he could not allow himself to succumb to desire.

Not when doing so would change the nature of his life, hers, her children's. Alter the landscape of the Isle of Skye, shift the powers between clans.

He stripped nude, leaving his plaid, shirt, boots, hose and weapons on the bank, and walked right into the darkened river. The blessed coolness of the water, suffused some of the heat from his skin, but there burned an internal flame he knew the river wouldn't touch.

Kissing her had been a wicked temptation granted.

Touching her breasts... exposing the pert pink nipples to his tongue... That had been a mistake.

A much needed misstep.

One he'd commit again if given the chance.

Which he wouldn't. He'd stay clear of her until he'd deposited her safely into Lamont's hands, and then as she rode away, he'd shout to her from a distance that he was keeping her eldest son to foster.

Then he'd hold up his shield, because she wouldn't stand for such without a fight. He'd have to let Lamont explain it to her reasonably, because Gabriel was certain if she rushed him, the only way he knew to calm her was to take her into his arms and kiss the breath from her. Kiss away her shouts. Her curses. Make her skin tingle with maddening need.

Ballocks!

He dove beneath the surface, submerging himself into blackness. Chill water covered his head and he felt free. He swam to the bottom, touched the mossy surface of rocks and mud, then pushed back to the top, dragging in a breath of air, before he pushed his muscles to the max.

Gabriel swam hard and long, until he could barely make out the tiny flickering orange light of their campfire. He was about to turn around when he heard something. Just the faintest jingle of horse tackle.

He stilled, cocking his head to listen better.

A man's cough. The stomping of a horse's hoof. There was someone on the other side of the lake who'd made camp. A coincidence? Or just a bystander passing through?

Gabriel was not yet on MacKinnon land. Aye, technically, MacLeod lands belonged to him, but that did not mean that a MacLeod would not try to fight him for it.

He swam closer to the bank. Whoever it was had not lit a fire. And a fire was not necessarily needed on a summer night. But it did beg the question of the person's intentions. Camped across the river, it was hard to say if the MacKinnon caravan was being followed or not by these intruders.

The closer he got the more he heard. There appeared to be at least four men. None of them slept, and, judging by the more than occasional belch, they were imbibing. Drunken men gave him nothing to fear when it came to skill, but their penchant for rash and hasty decisions was another matter altogether.

Though he had not a stitch on, Gabriel walked silently from the water, stepping precariously over the bank, wincing but making no sound when he stepped on the sharp edge of a rock with his bare foot.

With nothing but the light of the moon to guide him, he crept closer to where they sat. He finally spotted them leaning against a few trees, each nursing a skin of whisky or ale. Gabriel kept out of sight behind the trunk of a wide tree and listened to their obnoxious prattle; ready to depart, taking them for nothing more than slattern outlaws when their talk had him pausing mid-step.

"The bloody bastard will never know what's coming," one of them slurred.

"Aye, and when they come down on him, we'll be there to witness his blood sullying the earth as he stained the ground with our brothers'."

Gabriel listened intently. The men were set on revenge against someone, but they didn't mention a name, only what they were going to do when they reached the poor bastard. A snore issued from one, who promptly fell over. The other three grew silent for several minutes. Guessing they'd also passed out, Gabriel was about to sneak back to the water when he heard something that froze his blood.

"That bitch, Lady Brenna, is going to pay, too. When I get my hands on her I'm going to tear into her until she bleeds all over my cock."

"Pass her to me when ye're done."

Sick laughter sounded. "Gladly, and while ye fuck her, I'm going to fuck that saucy daughter of hers."

There was only one Lady Brenna that Gabriel knew in this area. Who else had a daughter whose castle had just been stormed? They weren't even off MacLeod land. The monsters were talking about raping the two of them. Gabriel's blood went from warm to raging hot.

These men must have escaped the battle, in hopes of gaining reinforcements. The closest place they'd head was Scorrybreac where the other half of the MacLeod army resided. The very destination of the MacKinnon warriors once Gabriel handed off Brenna and her brood.

Well, these arseholes weren't going to make it in time to warn their comrades. Nay, Gabriel was going to make certain of it.

Weaponless and naked, a lesser man might have thought it impossible to fight four drunken, likely armed, Highlanders. But to Gabriel, it was not only a challenge begging to be met, but a necessity. There was no way in hell he was going to let these scummy blackguards make it to Scorrybreac. And no way he was going to let anyone hurt Brenna or her daughter.

With only the light of the moon to guide him, Gabriel located the mounts of the fiends, whispering to the horses when they started to grow restless. Not expecting to find much, but eager for a weapon, he slipped his fingers beneath the blanket on one saddle and found the hilt of a sword.

Idiots.

Too keen on getting sotted, they'd not even bothered to see to the care of their horses. Or their weapons. Sorry bastards.

He tested the blade, it wasn't as sharp as he liked his own blades, but it would do. With the power he wielded in his body, he'd be able to do significant and deadly damage with any weapon. Beneath the next saddle, he found a second sword. He untethered the four horses and gently slapped their rears, sending them on their way.

Armed with two blades, he approached the mongrels.

Another had fallen unconscious from drink leaving only the two who had been talking about their desires for raping women.

"Good eve, bastards," Gabriel said with a grin he knew most likely would look like that of a madman, especially with only the light of the silver moon glinting off his nude form.

"What the..." The fiend on the right said, scrambling to stand. His face had a jagged scar from his forehead all the way down to his chin and Gabriel had to wonder if he had a hard time seeing out of his right eye.

The sod on his left struggled, falling twice before gaining his feet. "We dinna fancy cock," he finally managed.

"Well, a good thing that is, as I dinna plan to give it to ye. But I do plan to take yours. Not in the sense ye might be thinking, rather a more bloody affair really." He twirled the swords in his hands, his grin widening. "Who wants to go first?"

"Get out of here, ye bloody fool," the man with the scar said, pulling his sword from the scabbard at his side.

"Oh, I plan to, when I'm finished." Gabriel didn't give the fool a chance to answer, but rather arced his sword and brought it down toward him.

Drunk, and likely blind in one eye, the man had surprising reflexes. He raised his sword, crashing it against Gabriel's.

"A good block," Gabriel said. "But not good enough." He leapt back and swung this time with both swords in different directions—a skill he'd learned as a boy. He was able to wield different weapons in his hands, and neither his right nor his left was inferior. One of the reasons he'd been such a prized warrior was because he could fight two men at once, with two different weapons, and still win. His mind and body seemed to split so that he was able to do so. It also helped against lesser skilled men who wouldn't see his second blow coming.

Which Scarface's companion did not.

Gabriel sank his sword into the man's side at his waist, severing his body nearly in half, all while Scarface blocked the other blow.

With his bare foot he kicked the man over, dislodging his weapon, and he whirled on his heel to block the blow from the man at his back.

"Ye killed him. Wake ye fools!" Scarface shouted toward the two drunken men still out cold on the ground.

One of them stirred, muttered something.

Gabriel grinned at Scarface, who was backing away.

"Dinna run. Ye will not get far."

"I'll trample your naked arse with my horse!" The man turned to run.

Gabriel shook his head and followed.

"Where's my horse?"

The man was growing hysterical, once again proving that somehow over the years the MacLeod warriors had become soft.

"Gone. Now ye have to fight."

"I'm not going to fight ye. I'm going to kill ye."

He rushed at Gabriel just the way he'd expected—without thought. This one was even easier to dispatch of than his companion.

Returning to camp, the two other men still slept on the ground.

Gabriel hated to kill a man without at least giving him an opportunity to protect himself, but in this case he had no choice. If he didn't, then they would go about their merry way and warn the other MacLeods of what had happened at Dunvegan. They may even attempt to block their passage on the road with intent to cause Brenna and her children harm.

He couldn't allow that.

Gabriel nudged them both with his foot, trying to rouse them to make it a fair fight. He even considered dragging them through the water to take as his prisoners. But in the end, all was fair in battle, and these men were his enemies.

He said a prayer for them both and sent them to wherever it was they would end up, whether it be Heaven or Hell. Most likely with the devil.

There'd only been four horses, so he need not worry over any other men. He dragged all four heavy bodies to the river and pushed them in, then dove deep into the water to make the swim across and back toward his own camp.

By the time he reached the bank, several of his men waited for him.

"My laird, we were worried," Coll said.

Gabriel walked from the water, gripping onto his plaid that his second-in-command held out to him. He wrapped it around his hips, sluicing the water from his face with his palm.

Coll glanced out over the water, as if expecting something to rise. A nymph? A kelpie? "I feared ye'd drowned."

"Nay."

"There's blood on your back, my laird," another guard pointed out.

Gabriel glanced down to his side, seeing the blood dripping in rivulets from his previous injury. "Och, I think the stitches have come undone."

"Ye should not have gone for a swim." Coll said quietly, a slight shake of his head.

"Aye, I should have," Gabriel said harshly. "And I did a lot more than take a dip."

"What happened?"

"There were four MacLeods camped on the other side. They planned to warn those at Scorrybreac and send them back to Dunvegan." He kept to himself the vile things they'd threatened against Brenna and her daughter.

"Where are they now?" Coll squinted over the darkened river.

"Dead. Floating down river."

His men nodded. They knew his skill with a blade and his talent for fighting more than one man at a time.

"Think there are any more?" Coll asked.

"I pray not. But on the morrow, we'd best not tarry. I told the lady we'd take the day slower, but I fear we no longer can. We need to get them to safety quickly and then we need to secure Scorrybreac ourselves."

The men murmured their agreement.

"Shall I wake the lady to care for your injury?" Coll asked.

"Nay, I'll wrap it myself."

"But—"

"I said *nay*," Gabriel growled. Coll was the only man with enough ballocks and history to argue with him, but that did not mean Gabriel was going to let him get away with it.

Besides, that meant he'd have to face Brenna again, and though he'd had a swim and a fight, he wasn't certain enough time had passed between their sensual kiss and now for him not to feel the surge of heated blood barreling through him.

Gabriel gathered up his other garments and weapons. He sauntered back into camp and found a bag with the linens in it near a tree by the horses. Using the light of the fire, he examined his injury. 'Twas hard to see his wound in the dark, but there were darkened rivulets dripping down over his hip. It was bleeding and looked to be more open than before. He had definitely pulled out a stitch or two with the exertion of swimming and the skirmish. Gabriel rubbed on the salve Brenna had insisted they bring and re-wrapped his wound.

Luckily, battle rush still surged through his veins, and his skin was chilled enough from the water that he felt nothing.

After wrapping it up, he tugged on his shirt, pleated his plaid and redressed. Fully clothed, he sat at the base of the tree and leaned his head back on the bark, prepared to get some rest before the morning.

Dear God, he hoped the morrow brought a less eventful day than he'd had today. The past twenty-four hours had been a haze of violence and heated need.

His eyes dipped closed and he steadied his breaths. Gabriel had just drifted off to sleep when a blood-curdling scream startled him awake. He leapt to his feet, yanking his sword free of its scabbard, and eyes feeling bloodshot, ran toward Brenna's tent.

"Brenna!" he shouted.

Several guards were already there and a tousle-haired Theo climbed from the tent.

"'Tis all right," the lad said. "'Twas just my mother. She has… night terrors."

But that wasn't a good enough answer for Gabriel. "Let me see her."

Theo stared at him as though he were out of his mind. "She still sleeps," the lad whispered.

Gabriel shoved aside the flap and peered inside, seeing Brenna curled up on her side and shivering.

"She's cold," he noted. Without a thought, he unhooked his belt, his shirt coming down over his knees and tucked it around her.

When she sighed, snuggling into his plaid, something shifted inside him. Gabriel backed away slowly and then whirled on his heel, charging back toward his pack where he had a spare plaid and as far away from the woman who'd niggled her way inside his head.

Chapter Sixteen

GABRIEL'S scent was all around her.

Brenna stretched, breathing in deeply the spicy, woodsy scent of him. Then her eyes flew open, she gasped and sat straight up on the makeshift bed inside her tent, expecting to see him right there beside her.

She blew out a sigh of relief, when she came face to face with, not Gabriel, but Snow. Her dog, sitting tall, looked down at her and nuzzled her cheek.

Thank the saints, he wasn't inside the tent. Must have been her imagination, the recalling of his delicious and wicked kiss.

Except, she really *could* smell him.

'Twas on the blanket. Discreetly, she pulled it to her nose and sniffed. Aye, Gabriel. She'd not fallen asleep with his plaid, so how had she gotten it? Wrapped around her? Had he come into her tent? Did this mean that he didn't feel ashamed of what they'd shared and she didn't have to fear that he'd leave her in the woods to her own defenses? Or mark her a harlot for all of Scotland to condemn?

Brenna glanced around the tent. Her children still slept, and judging from the dim light streaming in through the tent flap, dawn had only just broken. Well, good. She'd wanted to wake before dawn.

Brenna crept out of her tent, with Snow whimpering to come with her. She snapped her fingers, allowing the creature to relieve herself as well.

Half the men had already risen and someone had set out bannocks to break their fast. Well, that was one less thing she'd have to do, she supposed. And she'd not have to face Gabriel to do it. That was good.

At the river, she washed her hands, sipped the water, then splashed her face. She could see the faint reflection of herself in the darkened water. She was a mess. Brenna took down her hair to fix it. Threading water through her long locks, she finger-brushed her hair, then re-plaited it.

Snow drank the water beside her, but went from peaceful to hackles raised in an instant. The dog started to growl at the water.

Brenna jumped back, afraid some beast would leap from the depths, but when none did, and she saw nothing, she snapped at her wolfhound.

"Snow, quiet."

But the dog did not listen. She growled menacingly at the water than leapt inside, splashing, seeming to wrestle with something.

"Snow! Get out of there!" Brenna called, fearful that her dog would be mauled by whatever creature lurked beneath the water's surface.

The dog splashed and tugged and then Brenna caught sight of a man's arm in Snow's mouth as she pulled his entire body from the river.

A man she knew. Vincent. Her late husband's second-in-command.

A man she feared.

He stared up at her lifeless, eyes bulging. His throat had been slit from ear to ear, gaping open at her just as wide as his slack mouth.

Dizziness consumed her and she backed away from the water's edge and the bloated, gray body of one of her many tormenters. She stumbled back and fell into strong arms, a silent scream on her lips.

"Brenna." A calm, cool voice whispered her name. 'Twas Gabriel. "He'll not hurt ye."

She trembled so hard she could not speak. Shook her head, tears filling her wide eyes.

"Come away from here," he said.

Gabriel called to Snow as he gathered Brenna in his arms and carried her back to camp. She wanted to snuggle close for comfort, but had vowed not to do so just last night, so she remained stiff against him.

Why was Vincent's body in the water? Who had killed him? Were they coming after her next? There was a murderer on the loose. And while Vincent deserved whatever rotten end he'd met, she and her children did not. Brenna glanced up at Gabriel, to tell him just that, to explain they were all in grave danger, but no words would come. Only a ragged, gasp for breath.

The men watched as he carried her toward the banked fire and gently sat her down on a log. He grabbed a skin of whisky and held it to her lips, but she pushed it away. She had to tell him. Had to make sure he knew.

"Drink. 'Twill take the edge off," he said.

She stared at the gray coals, shook her head. "Nay, thank ye. There is... We are in danger."

"No one will harm ye again," Gabriel said.

He sounded so sure of it, as though he himself would fight every man in Scotland to keep her safe. But why would he? He'd been the one to seize them. Why should he keep her safe? Aye, they'd shared several intimate moments, but... The touching of skin and lips did not mean anything. Men shared that with tavern wenches all the time. Just because she'd allowed him to touch her did not mean that he was now beholden to her. In the end, if it were his life or hers, she doubted he'd choose hers. Why then didn't she feel scared when he was around? Why was she filled with warmth? Because she was a fool and she wasn't going to let him know just how much of a fool she was.

She turned and glared at him. "This coming from the man who has captured my castle, my lands, and plans to do the same to my childhood home? This from the man who would take me away from what I know? Ye promise to keep me safe, but 'tis ye I'm in danger from."

Gabriel looked surprised at her reaction. He shook his head. "I take ye to safety. I've given my word. Ye've nothing to fear from me."

"So ye say."

"I swear it on my father's grave."

She wasn't going to back down, even if he swore over the burial grounds of every loved one he ever had. "Bold words, warrior. Leave me."

Jaw set and irritation flaring in his eyes, Gabriel stood. "Ye're a stubborn, spiteful wench," he said under his breath.

"I'm not your problem." She turned away from him, stood on shaky legs, grabbed several bannocks and marched toward where her children had gathered, their tent dismantled.

Vincent was dead. Ronald was dead. Thomas was locked in a dungeon.

The men she feared most could no longer harm her.

And yet, the man she feared not at all could do the most damage. Because while he claimed to protect her, even as he called her a spiteful wench, she knew, deep down, she wanted him to be by her side for the rest of her days. She knew she'd miss the way he could go from hot to cold then back to hot again. That she could move his mind as much as he could move hers was paramount enough that she had strong feelings for him. Not withstanding the heated kiss, the way she could still smell his scent on her clothes.

Well, she couldn't allow those feelings to grow beyond what they were now — tremulous imaginings and sparks of hope. She had to squash them. Toss cold water on the embers wishing to spark into flames.

She fed her children their bannocks, forcing herself to eat, and then guided them to their horses, taking the twins to the two warriors who'd held them the day before. When she'd seen them settled she approached her own mare, feeling that nervousness build in her belly. She ignored it. Stood right in front of the horse and stared it in the eye. It nickered at her, nuzzled her shoulder, and she stroked her palm from between its eyes down to the soft skin of its nose, then presented the rest of her own bannock cake.

"Do we have an understanding?" she whispered to the horse.

The mare bobbed her head, nibbling at the crumbs on Brenna's palm. Perhaps on this journey, she could forget her fear of riding. Could start anew. The mare she rode seemed pleased to help her with it.

Brenna mounted, situating herself in a comfortable position and waited for the call to move away from camp.

Gabriel avoided her all throughout the day. When they stopped for the nooning, she cared for her children and pretended not to notice him, though she couldn't help sneaking glances at him across the way. Everything about him was impressive, imposing and irresistible. It made her angry and renewed her desire to disregard him. A man with that much charisma could only be trouble.

For the first half of their journey that day, her body had not protested. She'd gotten enough rest that she felt she may make it through the day less sore than the day before, but as dusk approached and they still rode, she could feel the numbness of her rear turning to prickles of pain. At least she no longer feared riding — as much.

When Gabriel finally called a halt, she slipped from her horse and could have continued on to the ground in a puddle of screaming muscles. She sat silently as they ate their evening meal, then took her children and crawled into the tent, fast asleep, with Snow cuddled at her back, before her third breath.

The following morning she woke with the dawn and continued her regiment of making a pretense that Gabriel MacKinnon did not exist. And he seemed just fine with that, not so much as uttering a good morrow to her as he passed. Her children started to give her funny looks, but she avoided their questioning gazes and guided them to their mounts to begin this, hopefully, last day of their journey.

She bit her lip, wincing as she mounted, her muscles screaming out in pain at the rigorous activity. Lord, but whenever she got to where she was going, she needed to make riding a regular practice, else she'd have kinked and sore muscles to look forward to each and every time she took a journey.

They had a brief stop at noon as they'd done the other days, but then continued on.

Just when she thought she might fall off of her horse in exhaustion, the sound of bells ringing lulled her into a sort of haze. She was hallucinating now. Not good.

"Mother, is that Nèamh Abbey?" Gillian asked, her voice filled with awe.

Brenna widened her eyes, staring over the grassy knolls to a spot where they could see the very top of a bell tower. The sounds had not been a hallucination. The way the sun was sinking into the sky, it seemed to sit just on that tower, shining its light over the valley below.

She nodded.

"Have ye ever seen it before?" Gillian asked.

"Aye. When I was a child. My aunt was a nun at the abbey."

"Does she still live?"

Brenna had heard nothing from her family since being taken by Ronald. And married off. They'd not allowed her communication. And it didn't matter. Her mother and father had been murdered that day and her sister had run off into the wilderness. Likely all her family would despise her for surviving. The fact that her aunt had not reached out to her meant the woman was either dead or did indeed loathe her.

"I know not."

"I think he plans to take us there tonight," Gillian said.

Brenna swallowed her fear at perhaps coming face to face with her aunt. She prayed the woman was still alive, but also feared the disappointment she'd see in her eyes knowing Brenna had survived when no one else had. A quarter hour later, they approached the gates of the abbey, the bells still tolling.

Still on his horse, Gabriel lifted the iron knocker and not long after a tiny face appeared. He spoke softly to the nun behind the door, and then the great entrance was opened, but the men did not move.

"My lady," Gabriel called.

He waved her forward. The two warriors carrying Nevin and Kenneth also approached. With Gillian and Theo at her side, she advanced toward the gate.

"MacKinnon," she said, chin raised. "Will ye leave us here then?"

He narrowed his eyes. "Nay. I but thought ye and your bairns might like a chance to speak with the Lord, have a warm meal and rest in comfort this night."

Having not spoken in two days, he was still interested in her comfort?

She narrowed her eyes in confusion, but passed through the gates with him all the same.

A tall woman with poise approached, dressed in a black tunic, her hair completely covered by a white wimple and black veil.

The closer she came, the more familiar she looked. High cheekbones, black hair peeking through the sides of her wimple, blue eyes the same shade as Brenna's. Despite the creases in her face, this was, without a doubt, her Aunt Aileen.

"I am Mother Abbess." She stopped short, her mouth falling open as she stared at Brenna in obvious recognition.

Gabriel observed the interaction with intense curiosity, but she ignored him. As bold as he was, he'd no doubt ask when he felt the need to.

"My God," Mother Abbess said, then crossed herself. She broke out in a hopeful smile. "Brenna? Can it be?"

Brenna, half dismounted, half fell off her horse. She stumbled to right herself and then ran toward her kin, throwing herself into her arms, despite propriety stating she should bow first and kiss the superior woman's hand.

"How can this be?" her aunt whispered, stroking a loving hand over Brenna's hair. All of Brenna's fears of acceptance faded. Her aunt was overjoyed to see her. "By the grace of God, 'tis a miracle. Come. Come inside, my child. I shall have a warm bath drawn and a meal brought."

"My children," Brenna cried through the tears stinging her eyes.

"Children?" Aunt Aileen glanced behind Brenna where all four children now stood in a line. "Another miracle. Bring them. Come."

"My hound?"

Aileen shook her head and Brenna was ready to say, nay, that she, too, would remain outdoors, but Snow made her choice to move forward easier when she went and sat at Gabriel's feet.

Brenna allowed herself to be led inside, but just before she entered, she turned to see Gabriel. To mouth *thank you* to him. But the words lay stuck just beyond the workings of her lip.

He looked bereft.

And she couldn't begin to imagine what such an expression could mean. He looked almost as if she were abandoning him and yet they had no serious attachment. How was it then that her own heart tugged a little at being displaced from him?

She was reunited with her aunt, long lost to her, and she should be overjoyed. And, she was. But she also longed for Gabriel to be at her side. To experience the joy with her. Odd that she should feel that way.

Mother Abbess barked orders to the nuns they passed. She led them down a long, stone corridor and then unlocked a door with an iron key at her hip. As soon as it was opened, she stepped aside and allowed the nuns to enter, who worked with heads down to light a fire, dust off the furniture and snap white linen sheets onto the several cots.

A bed! Brenna did not think she'd be so pleased to see a bed again in her life. Even one as simple as these cots. She might collapse before the promised bath and meal arrived.

"Mother," Theo whispered, nudging her. "I…"

Brenna turned her attention to her son. His gaze was on the ground and he looked to be struggling with his words.

"Aye?" she urged, coming closer and stroking his arm.

Finally, he seemed to come to terms with what he wanted to say.

"I want to return to the men. I'm a man now, and this is…"

"This is what?" Brenna tried not to sound irritated. Tried not to sound betrayed that he would rather be with Gabriel than her. "This is God's house and your great aunt has provided ye with—"

Aunt Aileen touched Brenna's shoulder gently. "'Tis all right, my child. He wants to prove he's in no need of coddling. Let him go."

Brenna swallowed her protest, though it burned the back of her throat to do so. Her boy was growing up, and where he'd not found a figure he could admire in his own father, he had with Gabriel. She couldn't fault him that, MacKinnon was impressive and a good man.

A good man?

She frowned. Did she really want her lad to associate with a conqueror? With a man who'd stormed into their lives and... Och, but she could find little to argue the fact. He'd conquered them, but he'd gone out of his way to see they were safe, and had said many times he'd gladly hand over the reign of Dunvegan and Scorrybreac when her son was of age. What captor did such a thing? What abductor would allow her to walk into the arms of her kin at an abbey where she could permanently seek sanctuary, effectively freeing herself from him?

Aye, he was a good man.

"Mother," Theo continued. "I am safe with Laird MacKinnon. He holds my lands until I'm of age, will train me to be as good a laird as he is. Please, Mother."

She barely comprehended what he said. Could only see his tiny fists as he teethed his knuckles as a bairn. Saw him crawling on the wooden floor, playing and wrestling with other boys. The first time he'd ridden a horse, she'd witnessed it from her bedroom window and he'd looked up and waved goodbye. She'd feared for his life until the moment she'd seen him come back through the sea gate.

This moment was kind of like all of those. She'd watch him leave, fearing for his life and not knowing if she'd ever see him again.

Except, he'd be with Gabriel. And Gabriel had promised to keep him safe.

"All right," she managed, though her heart clenched painfully behind her ribs. "But do be careful."

Theo wrapped his arms around her, tugging her against his chest. When had her lad of fourteen summers gotten so big? He was nearly a foot taller than she now and it felt like, in just three days, he'd thickened with muscle.

Brenna nodded against his chest and pushed back, patting the spot over her heart. She swiped at her tears. "Go, then. Be well."

"Thank ye, Mother." His voice was filled with glee as he turned and jogged back toward where they'd come.

"Ye've raised a good lad," Aunt Aileen said, looking after Theo wistfully.

Brenna looked up at her aunt, feeling the weight of her transgressions heavily. "Before I seek comfort, I must make my confession."

Chapter Seventeen

BRENNA was related to the abbess?

This could put a significant hindrance on his plans to move forward. Would her kin insist she stay at the abbey until Ceana and Lamont reached them, rather than Gabriel taking her back to his holding at Dunakin?

Throughout the past two days his guilt at her comfort had grown considerably. Every time they dismounted, her gait grew stiffer, and though she tried to hide it, she winced with every step. Her spirit seemed to be depleting by the hour and try as he might to ignore her, he couldn't. When he'd spotted the abbey over the knoll, his first instinct had been to see if they'd offer her and her children a bed for the night.

Never in his wildest imaginings would he have guessed the abbess was her aunt. And it appeared she wouldn't have guessed it either. The two of them had been quite shocked to see one another. Stunned enough that he knew it was genuine.

Gabriel wiped down his horse while his men saw to their mounts and setting up camp outside the abbey walls.

"My laird." The sound of Theo's voice startled him.

"What are ye doing out here, lad?"

Theo puffed out his chest. "I'm a man and I want to camp with the men."

Gabriel looked behind the lad, hiding his disappointment when he didn't see Brenna standing there. "And your mother?"

"She has allowed it."

That was a step in the right direction. Perhaps if she could see that her son belonged with the men, she'd be that much more amenable to the idea of Theo staying behind with the MacKinnons for fostering.

"Good. Help Coll with setting up camp."

Theo nodded and walked with a bounce in his step toward Gabriel's second.

As the sun descended, the men sat in a circle around various campfires, drinking, eating and joking. Though they were near a holy place, they still took shifts for their watch. Those inside the walls of the abbey were generally thought to be safe from vagabonds and assailants, but anyone outside the wall and not wearing a religious habit was generally fair game.

Though he knew her to be in the safety of the abbey with her kin, her children, a warm bath and a bed not formed on the ground, Gabriel found himself staring at the doors, hoping she'd come out. That she'd say being outside with the lot of MacKinnons was preferable to inside the abbey. That being with him was a superior choice. He hoped to see her smile, hear her laugh, watch her discreetly watching him.

They'd not spoken much over the past couple days, and he missed their interaction, even when it seemed she'd bite his head off.

But he supposed this was good practice for when she went off with Lamont and Ceana. He'd likely not see her much, if ever, unless she managed a visit to her son. But Lamont lands were near the Lowlands and a rough journey that would take her weeks. With the way she'd fared in three days' time, he doubted she'd make the trek more than once a year.

If she stayed with him… If he could convince her…

Gabriel shook his head, leaned over to the guard beside him and grabbed the whisky skin. He took a mighty pull, hoping the liquor might knock some sense into him.

After all, Brenna was better off with her kin than she was with him and he'd damned well better start realizing it.

"WHEN I heard what happened to your mother—my poor, poor sister—and your father, I feared ye for dead," Aunt Aileen confessed.

After seeing that Brenna's children would be bathed and fed by the nuns, Aileen led her through the nave to the north transept indicating they should both kneel before the marble statue of Mary Magdalene.

"I feared much for myself," Brenna admitted, pressing her hands together and staring up at the effigy. "My sister... Kirstin... she..."

"She found safety in God's arms," Aileen said softly, a reassuring smile tugging at the corners of her lips.

It was enough to push Brenna over the edge. All this time, she'd had hope that her sister had somehow managed to be set free. But it appeared she had not. Her tiny body must have been found. But at least that meant she'd had a proper burial. All Brenna could do was pray she'd passed quickly, without pain. Her head fell into her hands as she sobbed.

Aileen rubbed her shoulders and said a prayer. "All will be well. Tell me what has happened that brought ye here today. Why do ye ride with the MacKinnon?"

Brenna dried her tears on a tiny linen square her aunt handed her. "The story is a dreadful one to retell, but I know I must."

She told her aunt about Ronald. Of her forced marriage to him. Of her bearing his children. Of the four who lived and the one who'd passed before it took its first, tiny breath. Then she told the truth of his death, the sin she'd committed in keeping that truth to herself. How Gabriel had conquered Dunvegan and, in doing so, captured her, though he said it was for her safety. That the MacLeods all believed her to be a murderess and her life was likely in danger because of it. How she'd sinned by kissing Gabriel, how she was wicked for her desires of the flesh, and how she betrayed her own self-vows by admitting she had feelings for him that went beyond simple esteem.

All the while she let her past and present spill from her lips in a torrent of sobs, laughs and ragged breaths, her aunt listened. And a miracle happened. She started to feel lighter, as though the weight of all that had transpired in the past fifteen years suddenly rose up off her shoulders.

"I am glad he brought ye here," Aileen said. "For now ye have more than one choice."

"Choice?" She glanced sharply at her aunt who knelt beside her. "I have no choices. They were taken from me. They are always taken from me."

Aileen smiled. "As a woman, aye, we oft think we have no choices. But look at me. I'm an abbess. And a powerful one, too. The Pope himself granted me Power of Jurisdiction. I have as much authority as a male in my position. Choices bless us when we least expect it."

Brenna swallowed, trying to understand the various paths Aileen may envision. "I see only one. That I should be delivered to my cousin, Ceana."

"Ye dinna see there are two other choices?"

Brenna searched her mind. "I could stay with ye. I could become a nun."

Aileen nodded. "There is that. Ye'd be welcomed here and, in time, ye might even take my place when I pass on. But there is a third choice. I see it plain as day and 'tis one I think would suit ye best."

Brenna shook her head, no other choice seeming possible or logical. "I dinna see it. Can ye tell me?"

Aileen cocked her head and studied Brenna. "Nay. I canna tell ye because ye're not ready to see it."

Brenna tried to ignore the flush of frustration that whirled through her. How could she see? She had no idea. All that she knew was that in the morning, unless she decided to become a nun, she'd likely leave this place. And what if she did stay and take her vows? What if later she realized that was the wrong choice?

An image of Gabriel flashed behind her mind's eye. She envisioned him sitting confidently outside the walls, laughing and jesting with his men. She imagined him looking toward her, that sensual smile curling his lips. A smile that was meant only for her. The one that he swung her way and made her think of his kiss, his lingering caresses.

Her cheeks flamed with heat and she ducked her head, whispering a prayer of forgiveness, for she not only sat before Mary Magdalene and her aunt, the abbess, but she was inside a holy place and thinking about the way Gabriel's kiss made her blood tingle.

She was truly wicked.

"Ye must follow your heart, child," Aunt Aileen said. "When ye trust in your heart, ye can follow the path that has been set out for ye."

Her heart… Her heart told her nothing right now. "I fear my heart has been broken for too long and shall never be mended."

"It may feel that way now, but ye're strong. Ye're like your mother. Resilient beyond measure."

"My mother? Truly? How can ye know?"

"Because, look at how much ye've endured. A lesser woman would have given up by now."

"Perhaps 'tis just that I'm stubborn." Gabriel's mutterings of that rang loud and clear in her ears.

Aileen chuckled softly. "Or 'haps, 'tis because ye're strong that ye're so stubborn. One must be stalwart in order to stick to one's convictions."

Her aunt had a point. From now on, perhaps Brenna should think of her stubbornness not so much as a curse, but a blessing.

"Then again, 'tis stubbornness that can sometimes lead us to a path we were not meant to follow. The inability to bend or see another way can lead us to pain, too," Aileen added.

Brenna let out a lengthy sigh. "Seems I have much thinking to do this night."

"Aye. I'll leave ye for a few moments to think and to pray. When ye've had sufficient time, ye know the way to your room. A bath and a warm meal will be waiting for ye." Aileen gently patted her on the back before leaving.

Only staying for a few moments longer, Brenna thought she might do her best thinking in the garden, though it was dark. She passed through the nave, the cloister and the garden at its center, preferring to walk its perimeter rather than sit on a bench as she'd been confined to a seated position for three days now.

Overhead, the black sky was star-studded and the moon was visible only as a half-circle. There were a few torches lit in sconces on the perimeter of the cloister. Even with the shadows that nightfall created, she felt safe behind these walls.

As safe as she'd felt in Gabriel's arms.

Brenna stopped dead in her tracks. Was that what her aunt had meant by her third choice? That Gabriel MacKinnon was her other option?

To what? Become his wife?

Cupping her hands to her heated face, she glanced up once more at the stars. Did she want to be another man's wife? Before now, she'd emphatically thought no. She'd been set on joining a nunnery. Living out her days in peace and praying the king never thought of her as a suitable match for any alliance.

She wanted to raise her children so they could grow up safe and with as many opportunities as they deserved.

Gabriel was a virtual stranger to her. She knew nothing about him other than what he'd presented to her thus far.

And, if she were honest with herself, that happened to be a lot. The man wasn't as much a stranger as she'd been trying to convince herself he was.

He was fierce. He was loyal. He was strong. He was good with children. Good with his men. Cared about his mother. His word was his honor and he had yet to break it that she could see. He was gentle. He was passionate. He was...

Everything a lass could ever dream of in a mate.

He did not bend over to her will, but challenged her. And yet, while he challenged her, she felt accepted. That even though he might disagree with her, he wouldn't push her or bend her to his will simply to prove he was more powerful.

Aye, she felt safe with him. But she also felt safe within the abbey walls.

Being safe was not a reason to be with someone, to pledge herself to someone. The fact that she felt she could be herself and not suffer backlash from it was, however, potent.

All of these things, tumbling through her mind, pushed her toward the third path her aunt had alluded to. But just before she stepped onto the newly lit symbolic trail, Brenna went rigid.

There was much more involved in a marriage than a simple journey through the Highlands could illuminate.

There was an intimacy involved in a marriage that she was certain she'd not be able to perform.

Gabriel MacKinnon knew how to kiss, that was certain. But…

She shook her head.

Staying here at Nèamh Abbey was likely the best thing she could do. Her children would be raised with a good education and Theo would be near both of his holdings. Soon he'd be old enough to take on his roles in earnest as Laird MacNeacail and Laird MacLeod. At the abbey, he'd be taught piety and fairness. Good qualities in a leader.

Decision made, Brenna headed back toward the room she'd been given. The three children who remained with her lay in bed, whispering to each other, and she couldn't help but smile at their innocent faces. She also couldn't help but feel the absence of Theo.

Behind a screen, she found the warmed bath. She stripped off her clothes and sank into the warmth. Every muscle thanked her. She scrubbed away the grime from their journey, washed her hair, and stayed in the water until it turned chilly.

When she climbed out and dressed in a night rail that had been left for her, she felt almost like new. This was the beginning of another new journey, the first choice of which she'd made on her own.

Brenna sat before the hearth and brushed her hair, letting the heat from the flames dry the wet tendrils.

On the morrow, she'd inform MacKinnon that his escort was no longer needed and that she and her children would be remaining at Nèamh. She'd send a letter to Ceana, telling her of her plan and thanking her for sending help when she did.

Gabriel would likely balk, but she'd explain that it was best for all parties, and that since his castle was not more than a day or two's ride away, he could even send her cousin here to speak with her. Ceana would be happy that she'd chosen this path, that she was no longer in danger. Because, that's what kin did. They supported each other.

Brenna fell asleep with a smile of relief on her face, but the only thing she dreamed about was the grin on Gabriel's face and his softly whispered confession of a racing pulse.

SLEEP was overrated.

Or at least that was what Gabriel tried to convince himself as he lay on the cool ground staring up at the stars and wondering what Brenna was doing.

If she'd not turned around to look at him before entering the abbey doors the day before, he might have been able to convince himself that she didn't care a fig for him. But she had.

She'd looked back and it had taken every ounce of willpower he possessed over the last several hours not to march over to the doors and demand entrance.

On the morrow he'd have to speak with her privately. He'd have to offer himself to her as a husband. There was no other way around it. She would never agree to be his mistress and he'd not ask it of her. The woman cared much about her reputation, for which he didn't fault her.

He admired her.

But he knew that he couldn't walk away from this abbey without her and he also knew that if Lamont tried to ride off with her—even though it wasn't because he was stealing her away—he'd lose his mind.

Gabriel craved her. Not just her body and her kiss, but her mind.

He craved seeing her smile. He craved arguing with her. He craved surprising her with a wink. He craved listening to her talk and seeing how she handled her children with such love and care.

Blasted, Lamont!

He'd been the one to put the idea of marriage into Gabriel's mind. 'Haps he'd known just how enchanting Brenna MacNeacail MacLeod was.

Well, it didn't truly matter.

All that did, was that on the morrow, he was going to ask her to be his wife.

Chapter Eighteen

BRENNA woke with the chiming of the bells for matins. She rolled onto her back, her body nearly free of the aches and pains she'd experienced from waking on the forest floor the previous few nights.

Her children slumbered peacefully, the two younger lads curled up together on a cot just as they'd been inside her womb. Gillian sprawled on her own as she always had, taking up more space than two grown men would need.

Slipping out from beneath her blankets Brenna tiptoed to the high window in her chamber to peek outside. The sun had just barely risen, but risen it had all the same. She couldn't help but wonder how Theo had slept. And Gabriel...

The Highlander was no longer her concern. She could not think of him anymore, other than the fact that he held her son's inheritance in his hands, and in a few years' time, he may or may not give it over to Theo as he'd promised.

Beyond that connection, she could not worry for his comfort, or hope that he'd slumbered as peacefully as she had.

Rolling her neck, she rubbed the muscles of her shoulders to work out the couple of kinks from sleeping in a new position and then stretched tall, her arms over her head. She yawned, feeling suddenly much more exhausted then she first had upon waking.

Perhaps even in a bed, her future decided on, she'd not found as much rest as she'd hoped for. In fact, the night came back to her in waves of tossing and turning. She felt unsettled. Disquieted.

Why should she be? Her choice had been to stay at the abbey. To have her children schooled by the nuns. To secure her future and follow the plan her aunt had laid out as a possibility — that she be groomed as abbess.

Brenna could do it. She'd always been up for a challenge and this would give her the opportunity to have her future in her own hands rather than that of another man. Why then did she feel so uncomfortable? Why could she not get Gabriel out of her mind?

She had to speak to him. She had to tell him what her plan was. Needed him to leave right away so that she no longer had to worry over this complicated stream of thoughts.

Resolute in her determination, she quickly refreshed herself behind the linen screen and dressed. She tied her hair up in a haphazard knot and shook Gillian's shoulder.

"I'll be right back. There is someone I need to speak with. Dinna let anyone in the room until I return."

"Even Aunt Aileen?" Gillian said in sleep-garbled tones.

"Ye may let the abbess in if she requests it."

Gillian sat up and stretched. "Aye, mother."

Secure in her children's safety, Brenna swung open the door to her chamber and came face to face with herself.

But, nay, 'twas impossible. How could she see herself?

Raven locks pulled tight, unlike hers in an unruly knot. Skin, soft and clear, minus the darkened circles beneath the eyes Brenna had become used to seeing in her own reflection. And this version of herself wore a nun's habit.

Was it a vision of her future? For if she went through with it, she'd look as prim and proper as this vision.

She closed her eyes. 'Twas only a vision. A trick of her nerves. Taking several breaths, she willed the vision to leave her. She'd not be honest with herself if she did not admit that the sight of her double dressed in such a fashion, and all that the habit required, did not send her into a tailspin of fear.

"It's really ye."

Brenna's eyes popped open. The apparition had spoken to her.

Her eyes blurred, mouth went dry, tongue tingly. The image reached toward her, touched her arm, and Brenna leapt backward, tripping over the hem of her gown. She stumbled several feet, while the identical woman lunged forward to help her keep her balance.

"We look just alike as she said." The nun laughed. "How did ye find me?"

"Find ye?" Brenna managed to say, though her throat felt swollen shut.

"Ye're in shock." The woman nodded knowingly. "I was, too, when Aunt Aileen told me ye were here."

"Here." Brenna couldn't seem to form any words other than repetitions.

"Aye. Come inside and sit."

The nun urged her back into the room with her children, ignoring Gillian's gasp. She pulled a chair from the stark table and pushed Brenna into it.

"Girl, get your mother a drink of water."

Gillian jumped to do the nun's bidding.

"How can this be? Kirstin?" Brenna whispered. "Aunt Aileen said ye'd died."

"Did she?" The nun cocked her head slightly in confusion. "I think not. She said she told ye I found shelter in God's arms."

"Aye, that is exactly what she told me."

The nun held out her hands. "And here I am. Safe and sound."

"Is it really ye?" Brenna pinched her forearm, expecting to bolt upright on the cot the nuns had provided her. But she didn't. Nay, she winced at the pinch and remained seated just where she was.

The nun laughed, grabbed the water from Gillian and held it to Brenna's lips.

"In the flesh, sister."

"I dinna understand."

Kirstin shrugged. "'Tis simple, really. I've been here all along."

"How?"

"Finn and I sought refuge here on our way to the MacKinnons."

Brenna gulped the water, hoping it would help relieve the violent turning of her stomach. "That is why Gabriel didna speak of ye. He didna know ye existed."

Kirstin shrugged. "Gabriel? 'Haps."

"Where is Finn?"

Kirstin's face fell. "That's a rather sad matter."

"Tell me."

"After leaving me here with Aunt Aileen, he went to find ye, but he never returned."

"Alone? He sought to come after the MacLeod army all by himself?"

Kirstin nodded. "Aye. We tried to convince him otherwise, but he said he'd not be able to live with himself if he didna try. He said honor required him to protect ye."

"Did no one ever find him?"

Kirstin shook her head. "'Twas as if he left me here and rode off into the heavens."

"I never saw him," Brenna admitted, grasping the cup tightly with two hands.

"I still pray for him to come back. I dream that when he left, he was swept up by a fairy and taken to a magical glen. Though I canna share that with any of the others here, they'd punish me for certain for such fanciful talk."

Brenna tried to smile, but she was certain it came out more like a grimace. "I've prayed nightly for ye both."

Kirstin dropped to her knees, resting her hands on the arm of the chair. "I thought ye dead, Brenna. That the MacLeod killed ye..." Tears filled her eyes, bringing on a storm in Brenna's own.

"We were so close, yet so far apart." Brenna shook her head, trying to see through the blur of tears. She grasped her sister's hands in her own.

"We heard rumors every once in awhile, that the MacLeod's son had taken a young wife, but then when we heard that she'd birthed a child, we discounted it. How could ye have birthed a child at such a tender age? A year went by before my menses started and since we are the same..."

Brenna chewed her lip holding back a sob as the memories of her hasty marriage and the ritual sacrifice of her new husband bedding her in front of the entire clan came back to her. Shame burned her cheeks. The old MacLeod had looked on, but when his gaze had met hers, she'd seen a change in him. He'd almost looked embarrassed to be the one who put it all in motion. He'd called the onlookers away, but he'd not stopped his son's forceful thrusts. She could still hear him grunting over her. Still feel that bereft, vacant sense of self that had come over her every time he used her thereafter.

"I had not yet started my courses either when I was wed," Brenna said. "But they began shortly after."

She remembered having her monthly just a few weeks after their union, how Ronald had raged about not being allowed into her bed for a whole sennight, and then as soon as she was clean, he'd taken her with a vengeance. A ruthless bedding that resulted in her son Theo's conception. As awful as it had been, she'd go through the pain and mortification of her husband's labors again and again to have all of her children with her.

Even now, she felt the humiliation of her past and his treatment of her. Felt it like a badge on her gown. Brenna lifted her chin.

"Mother?"

The sound of Gillian's voice startled Brenna from her living night terrors.

Kirstin jumped, too, the both of them seeming to have forgotten that the children were still in the room.

"Gillian, lass," Brenna said. "Come and meet my sister, Kirstin."

"Ye look the same," her daughter said, her voice full of whimsy, momentarily forgetting the horror of what she'd just learned about her mother.

"Aye. We are twins. As we grew up, none could tell us apart."

"Well," Kirstin said with a soft smile at Gillian. "That's not particularly true. Your mother was a fierce one. She always took care of me. So even though we looked alive, everyone knew the lass bossing the other about was Brenna."

Brenna laughed, the sound raw on her throat. It felt good to laugh. Her choice to remain at Nèamh was looking sounder by the minute. She'd get to live out her days with her aunt and her sister. She'd get the chance to spend the time she'd lost with Kirstin. Her children would get the chance to know their aunt and their great aunt. To see their mother as something other than Ronald's fearful wife. She could show them that she was strong, that her faith was true, and that happiness was attainable.

Nevin and Kenneth stirred, and when they sat up, looking back and forth between their mother and the stranger, their faces crumpled with fear and they burst into tears at the same time.

"Och, lads, there is nothing to fear." Brenna leapt from her chair and rushed to her children.

"There are two of ye," Nevin cried.

"How will we know which is the real ye?"

Brenna gathered them against her chest, still grateful to Gabriel for their transformation.

"This is my sister, Kirstin. Just as the two of ye are twins, sharing the same face, so am I."

"Ye are?" they said in unison, sounding completely awestruck.

"I am."

"How come we've never met ye before, Aunt Kirstin?" Gillian asked.

Brenna's jollity faded. How could she answer that question? How could Kirstin?

Brenna's immediate instinct was to protect her children from the answer. They knew that their mother and father didn't get along. Gillian knew that her father was cruel to their mother and the boys thought their mother a murderess. How could she explain the circumstances? Nevin and Kenneth were too young, but Gillian... she was likely old enough to know the truth, or least a variation of it.

Prepared to cut her sister off, Brenna opened her mouth, but Kirstin's reply left her silent.

"The Lord saw fit for me to come here and for your mother to marry your father. Without marrying your father, all of ye would not be here. Ye, see, He works in mysterious ways. Ways that are not always so plain for us to see at first."

The children nodded, seeming to accept her answer.

"Why did ye not speak of her?" Gillian asked Brenna accusingly. "Ye never mentioned her, or your aunt, or any of your family."

Brenna moved from the boys, hoping to pull her daughter in for a hug, but Gillian stepped out of reach, leaving Brenna's hands suspended in mid-air.

"'Twas painful for me to be separated from them all," Brenna said softly. "I knew not when I'd see them again. If ever."

Gillian shook her head, looking completely bereft. "Until this moment I would have said I knew so much about ye, Mother. But now I see there is a whole life ye kept from me. Ye didna trust me with it."

"That's not true," Brenna said, reaching for her daughter.

Still, Gillian backed away, and Brenna knew that she'd lied to her. She'd not trusted anyone with her past, even her children. But mostly, she'd not told them because she wanted to protect them. She wanted to protect Kirstin, to keep her memory as far from Ronald's mind as she possibly could. Who knew the depths he would go to in order to hurt Brenna?

"I'm sorry," Brenna said, locking her gaze on her daughter. "I did not tell ye, but it wasn't because I didna think ye could keep a secret. I didna tell ye because I wanted my sister to be safe."

"I'd not have hurt her," Gillian cried.

"I know, lass, believe me, I know ye would not. But someone else might have."

Kirstin stepped closer to Gillian, who allowed her to lightly wrap her arm around her shoulders. "Your mother is verra brave, child. She would do anything to protect those she loves. Has she ever protected ye before?"

Gillian nodded, her eyes meeting Brenna's. There was a sadness etched around her beautiful blue eyes. A melancholy that Brenna wanted to take away.

"She used to protect me, too," Kirstin said. "She still does. Because that is the type of person she is, your mother. A defender."

"But..." Gillian's lower lip quivered. "Who protects ye, Mother?"

"Ye protected me yourself, child, on the road when MacKinnon asked about the horse."

Tears spilled in giant drops down her daughter's cheeks. "But who will protect ye when I marry? Or when I join the church?"

"God. I..." Should she tell them her decision? Perhaps that was the right thing to do to show Gillian that she did trust her, to let her into her confidence now. "I've been doing some thinking. I will ask MacKinnon to leave us here. I will join the church like my sister and my aunt."

The reaction on her daughter and sister's faces could have been mirror images. They both looked shocked. And not particularly in a good way.

"But what of MacKinnon?" Gillian said, sounding outraged.

"What does MacKinnon have to do with your mother?" Kirstin asked.

"MacKinnon can go to the devil," Brenna cursed, more to herself than either of them. "MacKinnon will continue to hold Dunvegan and Scorrybreac, I imagine, until Theo is ready to take his place."

"But what of us?" Gillian asked.

"The four of ye will stay here with me." Brenna's gaze flicked to her sister. "I was going to ask Aunt— Mother Abbess—if we could stay. If the children could be educated here. I would take my vows. Give coin to the abbey." Coin she'd need to retrieve from Dunvegan.

Brenna did not mention becoming abbess herself one day. Why had Aileen said she'd groom Brenna instead of Kirstin?

"Vows?" Kirstin mouthed, the word barely coming off her tongue.

"Mother! Nay! I will not stay." Gillian stomped her foot, the first show of true defiance Brenna had seen in her daughter in a very long time.

"What?" Brenna was shocked.

"I wanted another adventure, not to be locked up behind these stuffy walls just like a prisoner as we've been in our home for so long."

"Gillian!" Brenna rushed under her breath, a warning in her tone. "Dinna speak that way of the abbey."

Kirstin laughed. "She sounds a lot like me."

Gillian crossed her arms over her chest and pouted. "I had different plans."

Nevin and Kenneth had crept closer, listening intently to the conversation.

Plans? What sort of plans could a girl of nearly twelve have? Then she was suddenly reminded of how, at that same age, all choice had been ripped away from her.

"I know ye might want something different, but this will be best for all of us."

Gillian bit her lip and didn't speak.

"Mother," Nevin said, tugging at her skirt. "I dinna think it's best for all of us. Gabriel will be awfully sad to never see us again."

Gabriel? Since when did her children call him Gabriel?

A tapping sounded at the door, cutting off any replies she could have spoken. Brenna stared at the wooden expanse, as if she might somehow develop a magical power to see beyond closed doors. Nobody moved. The knock sounded once more.

"My lady? Laird MacKinnon wishes to speak with ye."

Brenna jerked her gaze toward Kirstin. "Help me."

Chapter Nineteen

GABRIEL marched, hands held behind his back, from one end of the vestibule to the other. The sun shined down onto the abbey courtyard. A practical garden of herbs, fruits and vegetables grew along the perimeter. Not an inch of space wasted on anything that could not be used as a resource.

What was taking the lass so long?

He'd sent the nun in search of Brenna a quarter of an hour ago and still she'd not reappeared. Her son, Theo, had insisted on staying outside the gates, certain in the way of youth that they all get on their way quite soon. Perhaps secretly afraid that once he'd stepped foot back inside the abbey his mother would force him to remain there forever.

Gabriel chuckled. As a lad, he'd often thought along the same lines — that once a freedom was given, it would soon be taken back when his elders realized the extent to which they'd granted him liberty.

Och, at this rate it would be the morrow before she exited her chamber. Soon — a distant hope.

For Gabriel, soon would be right after he and Brenna had exchanged vows in the chapel. Then they'd be on their way, arriving at Dunakin as husband and wife.

The thought made him shudder with both excitement and trepidation.

He'd not set out on this journey to bring home a wife. Indeed, he'd not left Dunvegan, conquered and tossed their leader in the dungeon, expecting to have a spouse upon his return.

Being married put quite a damper on his plans. He'd originally planned that as soon as they arrived at Dunakin and restocked their supplies, he and his men would be heading toward Scorrybreac to take the castle. But a wife would cause a delay. Not only because he now had to take his time to exchange vows, but it would be best if he consummated the marriage, too, else she changed her mind while he was gone, or worse still death could befall him and she'd inherit nothing.

But the added time was necessary, for he'd not leave Nèamh without her as his wedded wife. Then on to Dunakin.

Brenna and her children would have to remain behind when he traveled to Scorrybreac. But before he left he'd introduce Brenna and her brood to those at the castle. Though his mother would help her to become accustomed, he'd stay on a day or two to be certain they all adjusted well. That would mean more time added before he could depart, but necessary all the same.

A woman's place was at home, tending to the hearth and servants. Keeping house. And Dunakin was not a small castle. Nor was it the size of Dunvegan. She'd have an easy time acclimating to her duties.

As her place was there, she'd understand, and he'd not have much to worry over. She'd wish him well on his journey to take back her childhood home.

If that were the case, then why, when he pictured Brenna standing on the steps of Dunakin as he rode away, did she look so formidable? Why did it seem that his wife would not be as compliant as he wished? As she should be? As was dictated by man for a hundred thousand years?

Because she was Brenna MacNeacail MacLeod, and the woman did not stand down for anyone, let alone a man she despised—which at the moment seemed to be him, mostly.

Well, perhaps she did not despise him all that much. He'd seen the look in her eyes on more than one occasion that spoke of an interest far beyond simple curiosity. Had felt her melt in his arms, drank in her soft sighs of pleasure. He could tame her, aye.

"My laird." Her voice startled him, as did her willingness to finally acknowledge his position.

Was it possible he worried for naught?

Gabriel slowly turned to face Brenna, finding it hard not to step back when he finally caught sight of her.

She stood before him, raven hair in a severe knot. Not a lock out of place. Incredibly unusual for her. He'd come to be used to the unruly look about her. It seemed to add fuel to her fiery persona. But this...

Brenna was dressed in a nun's habit.

Neat as a black and white holy package.

And the only way she'd have dressed as such, was if she...

"What are ye doing in those clothes?" he demanded, refusing to believe she could have taken her vows so quickly.

She glanced down, examining the dark wool as if expecting to find a stain. Seeing nothing out of place, she glanced back up at him curiously.

"They are my clothes," she answered.

"Nay, they are not. Go and change." He crossed his arms over his chest, challenging her to deny him.

The brash woman simply raised a brow and stared him down. "I'll not."

"No wife of mine shall take her vows."

"I am not your wife." Her words were spoken evenly, with an air of challenge.

Gabriel took a few steps forward, leaving enough space between them that he couldn't easily reach for her as he wanted to. He didn't want to frighten her. "But ye *will* be."

She stared at him a moment and then laughed, a tinkling sound as beautiful as the ringing of bells. "Is that your idea of a jest?"

Gabriel narrowed his eyes, surprised she would find him funny. Though he suspected the jest was most likely on him. He'd have to work a lot harder to convince her to marry him, he could see.

"'Tis a good match. And it makes sense. I promise in time, ye'll understand."

She cocked her head to the side. "How so?"

"Ye're in need of a husband. I'm in need of a wife. I also hold your son's birthright under my protection. And soon Scorrybreac will also be mine. Why should ye not? 'Tis for the good of everyone."

"Hmm…" she mused, a twinkle in her eye that set his nerves on edge.

The woman was toying with him. So like her and yet he found it grating on his nerves. How dare she toy with him? He was proposing a future for her—a way to save her and her children. Why could she not see that?

"Ye may be in need of a wife, but I am not in need of a husband, I can promise ye that, warrior."

Gabriel arched his brow. "Every woman needs a husband."

"Ye are wrong there. For ye see I've given my life to God. He and no other will hold my heart."

Gabriel felt the burn of anger in his chest. "Ye canna be serious."

"I swear it." She made the sign of the cross over her chest and forehead.

Gabriel straightened, hands fisted at his sides. "Ye would deny me?"

She pursed her lips, staring at him in that unnerving way that made him want to turn around so she couldn't see his face. "*I* would," she drawled.

Gabriel bared his teeth, feeling his anger build to a menacing and dangerous level.

"What will ye do with your children? Scatter them to the wind? What kind of mother abandons her children?"

"I assure ye they'll not be abandoned."

"Ye have no idea what ye're doing," he warned.

"Enlighten me then." She spread her arms out so gracefully, as though she'd dance, then folded her fingers neatly back in front of her waist.

"Ye will lock yourself behind these walls like a coward, forgoing everything ye've ever had and everything ye deserve," Gabriel admonished.

Again that curious turn of her head as she studied him. "And what is it that ye think Brenna MacLeod deserves, my laird?"

Gabriel scoffed at her use of third person. "I dinna have to answer that. Ye should know by now."

"I might. Then again, ye've said I have no idea what I'm doing. 'Haps I'm not aware of what is deserving either."

"If that's your choice, then I canna do anything to make ye change your mind. But know this, your lad is coming with me. Theo will foster with me until he is old enough to rule Dunvegan and Scorrybreac himself."

Brenna's face fell and she glanced toward the ground as though this were grave news she'd have to impart on a grieving mother. "That is not a choice ye can make, sir."

"I have every right to make it. I besieged Dunvegan. It could be mine. By all rights the land, castle and inhabitants *are* mine. I was gracious enough to take ye and your children from there, to bring ye to your cousin, to offer ye and your children a better life, and ye have spat on me and my generosity."

"I have done no such thing, sir. I have done nothing but assert the choices a woman, a mother, in such a position would wish to make. And ye have tried to take away the right to choose."

"Ye have no right! Do ye not see? I have been nothing but kind to ye. Tried to allow ye to make some choices on your own, but ye dinna see the right of it. Ye will not choose the right path."

Brenna's mouth fell open and she shook her head, backing away. "The right path has been chosen. Of that I'm certain, for a man such as ye would never be able to hold the heart of a woman."

Gabriel felt as though he'd been punched in the gut. He spoke rashly, harshly, and he'd lied. For he believed she had a choice. He'd not gone into her home with the intention of becoming the monster he was acting like now. But the ache of her denying him was more painful, made him angrier, than he'd ever been before.

"Brenna, wait." He held out his hand, hanging his head in shame.

"Ye dinna have permission to call me that." She whirled and ran, leaving him alone in the vestibule.

Gabriel stared long in the direction she'd gone, willing her to come back. Willing his feet to move. He'd thoroughly embarrassed himself. He'd lost his temper. He'd allowed his anger and jealousy to take hold and now she'd denied him what he truly wanted.

If he left now, she'd never forgive him. He had to find her. To apologize. To try once more to get her to see his way.

Glancing around the courtyard, there was no one in sight. No one to tell him that he couldn't follow in her footsteps.

He took off at a jog, his weapons clinking at his hips. He slowed his gait to keep the clanging noise down. The corridor she'd taken off in was dimly lit. He glanced at each door he passed, as if he would somehow know just which one she'd entered. For fear of breaking into the privacy of a holy woman, he didn't test any of the closed doors. Several nuns stared at him silently from one open room to the next. None with eyes as blue and enchanting as Brenna's. They shook their heads at him with shame.

Ballocks!

By the time he got to the end of the hallway he'd not seen her at all, nor been able to discern which door she might have gone in. This time, when he retreated the way he'd come, he slowed to listen at each closed door. There was one with voices and he could have sworn one of them was hers.

Should he knock? Should he simply barge inside and demand she marry him straight away?

Nay, nay, nay.

Being demanding had sent her running down this corridor to begin with. He needed to use a bit more finesse. She'd just come from a horrible situation and likely didn't want to repeat it. She'd only be reminded of her husband if he treated her in the same manner.

Gabriel had to control himself if he were going to make her see reason, give her cause to accept his apology.

Stealing himself for another round of battling wills, he tapped lightly at the wooden door.

The voices within went silent.

Then the handle turned and Brenna opened the door. She gasped.

"What are ye doing here? Ye must leave. Ye're not allowed here."

"Gabriel!" Nevin shouted shoving his way past Brenna and wrapping his tiny arms around Gabriel's thigh. Kenneth quickly followed suit.

The two of them jostling, bounced the door wide open.

Once more, Gabriel was surprised at what he found.

There were two Brenna's. One nun and one unruly lady — the nun tried to block his path, but the unruly one, she stood stoically in the back of the room.

He glanced between them, understanding dawning, then he glowered at the one in the habit. "Ye're not Brenna. Ye tricked me. Ye allowed me to believe ye were Brenna."

She bit her lip, but said nothing.

Thinking back on their conversation, she'd cleverly answered each of his questions without actually telling him she was or wasn't Brenna.

"What are ye doing here?" Brenna asked from across the chamber, her voice sounding tired.

"I came to apologize. To ask if I could try again." Gabriel didn't even flinch at the sound of pleading in his tone.

She shook her head. "Ye need not waste more of your breath on thoughts of... that. I've made my decision. And ye'll not be taking my son."

"Brenna, please." Gabriel stepped further into the room, traveling the center with the two boys still holding tight to his legs. Their giggles were a sound he'd miss if he never heard it again.

"When we were by the water bank," she started. "Ye said some things that were beautiful. Words that made me think there was a chance... That all of my hopes of happiness could be realized."

"I meant what I said."

"But ye didna," she said with a subtle shake of her head. "Not truly. Ye were swept up in the moment. Disillusioned by a physical reaction versus one that came from the heart."

"That is not true." Gabriel shook his head, reached out his hand to her, wanted to feel her slim fingers thread through his.

Brenna did not reach for him. "Ye hardly know me."

"I know ye. I know ye well enough to have thought something was off when ye came to me in a habit. And I was right. It wasn't ye."

"It does not matter. I cannot accept your proposal."

"Proposal? Mother, what is he saying?" Gillian piped in. Having been quiet and reserved by the hearth, he'd not noticed her there.

"Come, children. Let us give them a moment alone." The nun gathered the three young ones, but then glared at Gabriel. "I'll not be closing the door, and I'll not be far. Just outside in the corridor. Behave as a gentleman, else the wrath of God come down on ye."

"On my honor," Gabriel promised with a slight bow.

She ushered the children out of the room, leaving them somewhat alone.

"My sister told me what ye said." Brenna spoke softly, chewed her bottom lip when she was finished.

"I wish she hadn't."

"Why?"

"Because I would have liked to have told ye myself." Gabriel ran his hands through his hair. "And I'd have liked to omit the parts that were unsavory and bastardly of me."

Brenna smiled. "Aye, ye were not the most kind of men."

"I do apologize." He walked briskly to the door, leaned out, and said to the nun, "I'm verra sorry for my harsh words. They were not meant for ye, and quite honestly, they were not meant for Lady Brenna, either."

"I'm sorry for tricking ye, my laird. I'll certainly pay a penance for having done so."

Gabriel smiled. "I'll not tell if ye won't."

"I cannot lie."

He nodded. "I understand."

Gabriel turned back to Brenna. "Ye didna tell me ye had kin at the abbey."

"I didna know they were here."

"How many are there?"

"Just my aunt and my sister."

"Your twin?"

"Aye."

Gabriel wanted to be close to her. To hold her. To force her gaze from her boots back up to his face. To ask her to share her troubles with him, because he could see there were many. He stepped closer, but she held up her hands.

"Ye must go. And ye must leave Theo with me. We'll be safe here. Happy. The children will gain a good education and my future is secured."

"I offer those things to ye as well."

She shook her head. "Ye offer those things, but with a price."

"What price?"

"The price of my obedience, my soul. When I was forced to wed Ronald, it was both a blessing and a curse. A blessing because it gave me four amazing children, but a curse because it stole so many years from my life. So many years spent in misery and fear."

"And ye think I would do that to ye? I am not, nor will I ever be, Ronald MacLeod."

Brenna shrugged. "'Haps not now. But the words ye thrust upon my sister were..."

"Rash. Foolish. The words of a jealous man. The words of a man desperate to gain the acceptance of a woman."

"I cannot." Her voice was so low, he barely heard her.

"I will keep ye safe."

She lifted her eyes to his. "I do believe ye would keep me safe. And I believe ye would treat my children well. I do. They have all taken to ye like I've never seen them take to another, besides me, afore. But..."

"But what?" Gabriel stepped closer to her and she didn't back away, giving him just the slightest bit of hope.

"Safety is not enough, Gabriel," she whispered.

"What more do ye want? I will provide ye with it."

"I'm sorry. I wish I believed ye."

Chapter Twenty

THERE had been many difficult choices Brenna had made in her life, but allowing Gabriel to walk out of her chamber door might be the one she'd regret the most.

The moment his back disappeared from view, her chest tightened and she crumpled to the floor, no longer able to stand.

"Brenna!" Kirstin said, rushing into the chamber. "Did he hurt ye?"

Swiping at her tears, Brenna shoved to her feet, dragged in a deep breath and composed herself.

"I apologize for scaring ye. I had a moment of... A relapse in judgment. I am fine now. He's not hurt me any more than I've hurt myself." Brenna's heart broke at the sorrow she'd seen come over his face when he'd left her chamber. Felt the stab of loss greatly. Had to force her feet not to run after him, to assure herself she'd made the right decision.

"Ye love him," Kirstin said.

Brenna's legs trembled, threatening to dump her onto the floor once more. Love? Nay. She did not even know what love was, other than the love she had for her children. For her sister. For her family. Love Gabriel?

The thought made her chest warm, heated her cheeks. But it wasn't because she really did love him. Nay, perhaps it was embarrassment that her sister would think so. That she'd collapsed upon his leaving and the thought that she'd never see him again had struck her so deeply in her core.

Was it true?

"I dinna love him." She shook her head, frowning. "I've not loved a man before and I'll not love one now. There is but one path for me in this life, and it is here, with ye, serving God and His people."

Kirstin frowned, studying Brenna hard. Unable to keep her sister's scrutinizing stare, Brenna turned away.

"He is sending Theo inside. Will ye bring him to me?" she asked meekly. "Please?"

Kirstin clucked her tongue before answering. "Do ye think it prudent?"

"What?" Brenna snapped her gaze up. "He's my son."

"That I approach Theo, when we've not yet met? I'd not shock him as I did the other three."

"Oh." Brenna had not thought of that. "I will go and greet him then." And perhaps she'd see Gabriel once more. She stilled at the doorway. "I fear…"

"I will go with ye, Aunt Kirstin," Gillian said. "Mother, ye stay and rest. I'll ask for a soothing tea to be sent."

Brenna turned grateful eyes on her daughter. "Thank ye."

Gillian frowned. "I may not agree with ye, Mother, but I'll not naysay ye either. I know ye've only got our best interests at heart."

When had her daughter grown up so much?

They left her chamber, the twins begging to go with them, and whooping with glee when Kirstin acquiesced. When Brenna was all alone, the silence echoed off the plaster walls.

What would she do without Gabriel in her life? Seems that the only happiness and relief she'd felt had been with him.

Now he would be gone.

Would her happiness remain or would it disappear on the horizon with him?

Brenna walked to the hearth lifting the poker to jab at the unlit logs and ash, trying to convince herself that she'd made the right decision.

There was no going back. She'd not take the path he'd offered her, even if…

Even if what? She loved him?

She could not! She didn't even know what love was.

Hadn't she already established that?

Then what was the ache she felt in her heart at knowing he'd not offer for her again, that he'd go off and find another lass to marry? What was the flutter in her belly every time she thought of him kissing her or his whispered words of adoration? Why did her knees go weak when he walked into view? Or the thought of him make her heart beat fast?

Brenna shook her head and stabbed mercilessly at the ash. Rubbish. Utter nonsense.

"I dinna think ye'll make it flame by doing that." Theo's voice sounded behind her.

Brenna jumped, dropping the poker painfully on her foot. She winced and bent to return it to its place beside the hearth.

"Theo, my son." She rushed toward him, tugging him down for a hug. He wrapped his strong, gangly arms around her. "Ye look like ye've grown another foot."

"It's been only a day since ye last saw me. Less than that, in fact."

"Aye. I suppose it has." Brenna let her son go, but then grabbed on to his hand. "I have something I need to discuss with ye. Come sit down."

Theo's face darkened, as if he expected bad news. And she supposed in a way, he was going to get just that. He'd grown very fond of Gabriel and how the warrior had incorporated Theo into his ranks, allowing him to train and be the man he wanted to be.

They sat opposite each other, and she kept her gaze on his, took his hands in hers.

Taking a deep breath, Brenna let it out slowly, and spoke in even and gentle tones. "I have decided that we will stay here at the abbey."

"Here? All of us?" Theo's brows drew so close together they could have been one.

"Do not frown so," she soothed.

"I dinna want to stay here. There are only women here. No warriors." Theo yanked his hands away and jumped up.

"Aye, that is true." Brenna leaned forward, urgent in her need to convey her message. "But ye will gain a good education, and when its time to take your lands back, ye'll be well prepared for it. A just ruler."

"But I'll not be able to protect my people without the proper training."

"But ye will. Ye will be educated here."

Theo shook his head. "Nay, Mother. There are no warriors here to teach me. None that I can emulate while becoming a warrior myself. I cannot be laird of the MacLeods, or the MacNeacails, if I am not a warrior."

"But ye'll be a man of God. Your people will respect that."

"I dinna doubt they will respect me having an education in a place such as this, but they will doubt me as a ruler when I canna protect them even from the weakest enemy. Do ye not want me to gain my inheritance, mother? Do ye wish me to be a priest? To make a life in the church?"

Brenna shook her head, not having expected such resistance, nor for his arguments to make such sense. Her heart clenched and she could feel herself losing.

"Mother, I ask ye to let me go with Gabriel. He will train me. He will show me how to protect my people. He can even take me to my holdings so I become familiar."

Why did her son have to speak reasonably? Why did his path have to be so different from her own?

"I dinna want to let ye go," she whispered. "What if ye stayed here for a time, and worked with the tutors, learning other ways to be a ruler, and we could hire a warrior to come and teach ye to fight if that is what ye want."

Theo shook his head slowly, his gaze never leaving hers. "It is not what I want, mother. I want to go with Gabriel."

Tears stung her eyes. His desire to leave her and forge his own path was a crushing blow. Would Gabriel take everything from her? Her head dropped into her hands and she dragged in a cleansing breath, trying to keep herself from bursting into tears.

"I am not ready to let go of ye," Brenna said. "And I am still your mother."

"Ye'll always be my mother and I'm not asking ye to let go. I'm asking for ye to let me foster with Gabriel. I've not had the chance to do so yet and it's past overdue. Ye know this. I'll not be far from ye and I will visit with ye often. I promise. Please, mother. Please let me do this. I *need* to. I *have* to."

Deep in heart, she knew he was right. In order to be a good leader, he needed to be trained by one. And Gabriel MacKinnon was a good leader.

"Ye promise ye'll come to visit me often? Every week?"

Theo raised a questioning brow. "Mother, truly? The other warriors will laugh at me."

Brenna sucked in a ragged sob, trying to keep the tears from shedding. "All right, every month, then?" She wasn't willing to back down on that.

"I will come the last Sunday of every month, and I will stay until Monday if his lairdship allows it."

"He must allow it." Her voice wobbled and Theo returned to her, taking her hands in his. She gripped them tight, rubbing her thumbs over his knuckles as she'd done when he was a bairn.

"I'm certain he will. If not because I request it, but because it is what ye desire."

"Me?" 'Twas hard to hide her surprise.

"Laird MacKinnon cares deeply for ye, Mother. Everyone knows it."

"Everyone?"

Theo shrugged as if it were old news. "Aye."

"How?"

"Because he's been beating them up one by one since he left your chambers." The lad laughed as if she were silly for not having known that.

Gabriel was beating everyone up? He was hurting that much? "I dinna understand."

Theo waved his hand. "'Tis the way of men." He stood, gave her his hand and pulled her to stand. "We must be off then. Scorrybreac will not wait."

"Ye will go to the siege!" She shook her head vehemently. "Nay, ye canna!"

"I canna allow other men to fight my battles for me. I must go. I must show my people that I come for what is mine." Theo stood, his chest puffed out just a little more than it had been before.

At fourteen, and borne of herself and a selfish monster, Theo had turned into a young man she was proud of. What she feared most of all was that she'd not get to see him be a man in truth. Going to a siege was preposterous. She understood his thirst for adventure. He'd never been allowed such before and in just a few days, he'd had a mighty taste of it. But that didn't matter. She'd not allow him to go to battle!

"Please, go with Gabriel to foster once he's taken Scorrybreac. Stay with me that long, I beg ye."

Theo laughed. "Mother, ye dinna beg. And I will not. Scorrybreac is mine and I want to be there. Gabriel has promised to keep me safe. Ye need not worry."

But she would, until she heard he was safely behind fortified walls with a hundred guards to keep him safe. But Theo glowered down at her and she saw as much stubbornness in him as she saw in herself. She could hold him back all she wanted, but in the end, if she didn't let him go, he'd only sneak out when she wasn't looking.

If she were going to gain his trust, there was nothing she could do but relent. "Last Sunday of the month," she whispered.

"Aye, mother. I promise."

This time, when she crumpled to the floor upon seeing a man she cared for leave, she did not stop the tears from falling, nor push away the comfort that her sister provided. She sobbed on Kirstin's shoulder until she was too exhausted to take another breath.

A week went by with no word.

Brenna spent her days in the chapel praying, refusing meals most days, only to eat cold porridge upon the sun setting.

The children had been saddened by Theo leaving, but seemed to understand, more than Brenna did, his reasoning. Or else they just accepted it a lot more readily than she did.

Kirstin had taken to gathering Gillian in the morning and giving her chores between lessons, while the twins were taken off by two saintly nuns for their lessons. Saintly, because the lads were so full of energy, by the time the nuns returned them in the late afternoon, they looked as if they'd been to battle themselves.

Brenna had been spending so much time in the chapel praying for Theo, she'd lost touch with her other children. Guilt riddled her soul, for she couldn't seem to balance her grief with the need to mother her remaining children.

Brenna pushed off her bruised knees and walked sedately through the nave on her way back to the chamber she shared with her children.

"Brenna."

Aunt Aileen stood in the center of her path, blocking the way.

"Mother Abbess," she said, dipping into a curtsy.

"'Tis time for ye to return to us." Aileen stood, hands folded in front of her, chin thrust forward, her stance holding no room for argument.

Brenna looked on curiously. "But, I have not left."

Aileen smiled indulgently, as though Brenna were a child in the midst of denial.

"Ye have. There is no need to deny it. Ye've been present in the flesh, but your mind has been far from here."

"I pray for my son who has gone to war."

"Ye dinna pray for another, as well?"

Brenna frowned. What was Aileen trying to say? Trying to make her admit? Had she thought of Gabriel? Aye. He had her son. Had she prayed for his safety? Aye. Because if she didn't, who would keep her son safe?

"I pray for all the MacKinnons," Brenna answered.

"Come sit with me." Aileen turned on her heel and headed for a bench in the garden.

Brenna sat beside her, back stiff, stomach rumbling. The scent of herbs wafted on the summer breeze and she sucked in an aromatic breath of it.

"Have ye eaten today?" Aileen asked.

"Nay. Not as yet. But I will."

"Sister Kirstin told me what happened between ye and the MacKinnon." Aileen's voice trailed off in a way that spoke volumes. She wanted to know the story.

"Nothing happened." Brenna shrugged casually as if there had indeed been nothing between the two of them.

"He wants to marry ye." Aileen said it as if it were a fact. Which it was, at least it had been.

"Wanted. But he'll find another easily, I'm certain."

"Why did ye choose to stay here?"

"Because I want my children safe. I want them educated. I want to serve God, to thank Him for keeping me alive and blessing me with my children."

Aileen plucked a sprig of chamomile rubbing the flower between her fingers and then bringing it to her nose. "Are ye certain?"

"Aye."

"Then why have ye not yet come to see me about taking your vows?" The question was spoken so calmly, so softly, yet her words seemed to shout and echo around the garden.

"I..." Why hadn't she?

The truth was, Brenna had not even thought of it. Not once. She'd been so focused on her prayers for Theo and Gabriel that she'd done nothing else. Thoughts of her future had not crossed her mind.

"I will come to ye tomorrow, Mother Abbess."

Aileen smiled at her, tucked an errant tendril behind Brenna's ear. "I think ye'd best wait."

"Wait? Nay. I've made my choice," Brenna insisted

"Patience is a virtue. Not only because we must learn to wait for what we want, but also because learning restraint and piousness are the keys to becoming a good servant of God."

"I am patient." Though her voice did not express such a virtue at the moment.

Aileen smiled indulgently. "As am I. So we will wait."

"Until when?"

"Until God tells us it is time." Aunt Aileen stood and pressed a kiss to Brenna's forehead. "Come to the kitchen and get a warm bowl of porridge and some figs."

"I will be fine with the cold porridge in my chambers."

"I know ye will. But I offer ye better fare and I wish for ye to accept it."

Brenna's stomach rumbled even louder. "All right."

She followed her aunt to the kitchen where the cook quickly scooped a warm bowl of porridge from an iron kettle on the hearth. She slathered a hunk of brown bread with butter and pushed them across the preparation table toward Brenna.

"Thank ye." Brenna prepared to leave the kitchen.

"Ye can eat here," Aileen said, pulling out a wooden stool.

"Will ye eat with me?" Brenna asked.

Her aunt shook her head. "Though I will pour each of us a glass of wine."

She grabbed two cups and a jug before taking the stool beside her.

Brenna swallowed the wine slowly, wincing slightly at the bitter taste.

Aileen laughed, sipping the red liquid easily. "I've gotten used to the wine. Enough so that it tastes quite refined."

"Why is it bitter?"

"It is cheap. We are not extravagant here."

"I will get used to it." Brenna nodded into the cup.

"'Haps."

Brenna was silent for a moment, eating the warmed porridge and grateful for it. Warmed up, the bland oats tasted remarkably better than they did cold — which is how she'd been eating the past week.

"Your daughter, Gillian, is worried about ye," Aunt Aileen said. "She is a verra caring and empathetic child. She cares much for ye."

Brenna smiled. "She is a joy. A marvelous joy."

"Ye're a good mother."

"I wish I was better."

"We all wish we were better than we are." Aileen sipped the last of her wine.

"Is that a sin? To wish myself better?"

"Nay, lass."

Brenna stared down into her half-eaten bowl. "I miss my son."

"He will return."

"I pray he does." Glancing up at her aunt, a woman who looked so much like her mother, she was grateful to have found her, to feel the love of her kin.

"And when he does, he'll come with the MacKinnon. What do ye wish of him?"

"I wish him well."

"That is all?"

Nay, that was not all. There was so much confusion jumbled up inside her. Had she made the right choice? Had she doomed herself to have had love and then lost it?

Was it truly love?

Her belly did a little flip and her chest tightened. Her mouth went dry and her fingers started to tremble. Heat filled her face, sliding down over her chest, to her thighs.

"I dinna know," Brenna admitted.

Aileen smiled. "'Tis a sin to lie. Even to one's self."

Chapter Twenty-One

DUNAKIN looked exactly as Gabriel had left it. Well-fortified and peaceful. The exact opposite of his current mood. He grumbled to his men, growled to himself and was generally unpleasant.

Why did the sun have to shine so bright today? Why not another storm as they'd had on their way to Dunvegan? Och, preparing for a siege with the mud sluicing in his boots would have been much more preferable.

They rode over the bridge toward the gate of Dunakin, the men as sullen as their leader.

Once the portcullis was raised, they rode into the center of the bailey and dismounted. They'd need to change out their horses and gather supplies.

"My laird," his mother, Lady Cora, said. "Ye look to be in a hurry, when ye've only just returned."

A sweet smile covered her face and he couldn't bear to wipe it clean. Praying for patience, Gabriel approached her. He took a moment to embrace his mother before issuing another order to his men.

"We are," he said to her. "We're on our way to Scorrybreac."

"And who is this?" Cora asked, her gaze on Theo.

"Brenna MacNeacail MacLeod's eldest son."

His mother pinned him with a questioning gaze. "Why is he with ye and she is not?"

Ignoring the latter question, he said, "Theo MacLeod will foster with the MacKinnons until he reaches an age to rule his holdings."

"More than one?"

"Ye know there is, Mother. Dunvegan and Scorrybreac."

She smiled. "I thought maybe ye'd take Scorrybreac for yourself."

Theo's mouth fell open. "Laird MacKinnon has more honor than to steal land under the guise of protection."

Cora inclined her head, as though she'd expected the lad to say as much. "And where is Lady Brenna and the rest of her children?" He'd hoped with her current trail of thoughts she'd forgotten that he hadn't answered her yet…

"They are at Nèamh Abbey." Gabriel frowned. "Where they'll remain."

"Why is that?"

His mother's line of questions was starting to irritate him. The muscle above his eye twitched, sending a painful piercing across his skull.

"She wishes to take her vows and have her children educated by nuns."

"But not this one?" Cora pointed at Theo as though the boy weren't there to see it.

Gabriel drew in strength from somewhere to deal with his mother's plucky attitude this morning. She seemed primed for a fight.

"He remains with me." Dismissing her, he asked, "Where is Lamont?"

"He returned to his lands."

"Why?" Gabriel roared.

Cora did not even flinch. She seemed to expect such a reaction. "He thought there would be no need for him to stay."

"How could he think such a thing? He's the one who asked me to rescue them for Ceana. Brenna will be devastated to learn that he's abandoned her."

Cora shrugged daintily. "I suppose he didna think that once ye rescued them, they'd be going back to the Lowlands with him."

Gabriel's mood darkened all the more. "I see."

Lamont had suggested that he marry Brenna from the very beginning. The man had been so set on the thought he must have left shortly after Gabriel did. Bastard.

"Are ye certain she'll be devastated that Lamont has left... or ye?"

Gabriel wasn't going to take her bait. He knew where she was going and he wasn't willing to follow. "Theo, go and pick out a new horse. We leave within the hour."

"Ye will not take a bit of time to rest?" Cora asked.

"Nay. The sooner we leave, the easier a time we'll have with the siege at Scorrybreac."

Cora didn't say anything, just watched as Theo sauntered toward the stables. "The lad is your rival and ye take him under your wing."

"He is no rival of mine. I've offered him and his siblings my protection."

"And their mother?"

Lord, but his mother wasn't going to let it go. Gabriel groaned inside. "She has it as well."

"Ye have feelings for her."

"Hardly. She's a stubborn, argumentative wench. She stabbed me. I'll have the scar on my back forever."

Cora snickered. "A lass as tiny as she stabbed ye in the back?"

"'Tis not nearly as funny as ye make it out to be."

"Quite a tale to tell your heirs."

He ground his teeth, the scraping noise making him wince. "I'll not bother."

"Hmm... Well, 'tis a shame it didna work out for ye to marry her."

"Mother, dinna meddle in this."

"I would never. But ye do need to take a bride. Ye need an heir. Especially now that ye've taken on such a responsibility to the MacLeod and MacNeacail clans. Ye're essentially the laird of the isle, son."

Gabriel had not thought about it that way until she mentioned it. He would rule the Isle of Skye from coast to coast for the next four years. The most powerful man on the isle. Such knowledge should make his head swell. Should make him cocky. Would make a lesser man wield his power in a way that harmed others. But not Gabriel. He would keep the isle safe. Keep the lands safe from enemies.

"Only for the interim. I'll not abuse the trust they've given me."

"I didna doubt ye would."

Gabriel grunted. "I need to prepare for our departure."

"I wish ye and your men well, and hope your siege is fruitful. I'll pray for ye all."

"Thank ye, Mother."

When she walked away he waited for several moments, expecting her to turn back around to continue questioning him, but surprisingly she did not.

Gabriel continued advising his men. Once they had enough provisions, fresh weapons and horses boarded onto one of the MacKinnon galleons, they set sail. Across the firth was MacKinnon lands, and though they could reach Scorrybreac by horse, it would take twice as long. If the castle was as protected as Dunvegan, they'd be able to moor the ship at the MacKinnon port, and essentially walk right into the castle.

The wind was just right, pushing them quickly across the water at a pleasing clip. Scorrybreac rose from the peninsula it sat upon over the firth, growing in size with every passing moment. But unlike Dunvegan, the castle seemed to be better fortified.

Even from this distance, he could hear the warning bells sounding at their approach. The toll made him smile. At last a battle that would be worth fighting. Had the usurpers been warned? Was there more than one party of MacLeods who'd escaped his siege at Dunvegan?

There was no time to think on it. From the battlements, flamed arrows were shot toward the pier, lighting it on fire. They'd not be able to moor there.

"Lay the anchor!" Gabriel shouted when they were close enough to swim toward land.

The way the men on the wall were prepared to fight, he doubted this siege would take long. There'd be no rest for the weary and his men were ready to defeat the enemy. In fact, he predicted he'd be walking inside Scorrybreac's great hall by nightfall.

"Prepare to jump overboard," Gabriel ordered.

"My laird," Theo said, worry marring his features. "I canna swim."

"What?" Gabriel jerked his gaze in the lad's direction. "How is that possible? Ye live on an isle."

"There are a great many lessons that can be missed even when the opportunity to learn seems within reach."

The lad had a way of speaking and a maturity that struck Gabriel as being much older than he was. He would make a good leader some day.

"Today your opportunity presents itself. Ye'll learn to swim in order to take your lands back, lad."

"Or I'll die trying."

Gabriel nodded, though he had no intention of letting the boy suffer any injury, let alone die. "Your mother would be proud."

"Aye."

"We'll jump in and ye'll have to kick as hard as ye can toward the surface. Drag in a breath of air, not water. Move your arms like this." Gabriel showed him how to move his arms in arch-like motions and Theo mimicked him. "'Tis harder than it sounds, but I think ye've got enough determination in ye to get to the bank."

"Aye, my laird. I'll not disappoint ye."

The anchor was lowered and the men prepared to jump, removing their plaids and boots as the weight of the wool when soaked would only make it harder to fight. Ease of movement overshadowed any thought for modesty.

"We fight in our shirts, weapons at our hips." Gabriel showed Theo the sword and daggers at his hip and the baldric strapped to his back with his claymore.

Theo eagerly disrobed, and made sure his belt was tight, his weapons ready, and he did it with a grin. Gabriel found his spirit invigorating.

They climbed onto the railing, and a breath later, were plunging into the cool depths of the firth. Gabriel was quick to gather himself, and proud to see that Theo had managed to kick his way to the surface, though he sputtered.

The men were already swimming with vigor toward the shore. Arrows rained down on them through the water, but luck was on their side and none hit their mark. Prepared to grab hold of the boy's nape if needed, Gabriel swam beside Theo at a painfully slow pace until Coll came up beside them.

"Go, my laird, I'll stay with the lad."

Gabriel nodded, needing to direct his men and the siege. He pushed ahead, a rush of excitement fueling his movements and pushing his limbs through the water with increasing speed. The shouts of the men on the wall were met by the threats and growls from his own men. Music to his ears.

Feet on the bank, Gabriel grabbed a flaming arrow from the ground and rushed the gate, jamming the fiery tip between two planks and ignoring the singeing pain to his palms. Several of his men followed suit, until the gate of Scorrybreac was littered with arrows and fire licked with a vengeance up and down the wooden boards.

From the other side, he could hear men shouting. They'd try to put out the flames with water from their well, and they'd not risk pouring burning oil from the murder hole above them, because doing so would only set the blaze alight all the more.

Theo reached Gabriel's side, a grin on his face as rivulets of water cut paths over his young cheeks.

"We did it," Theo said.

"Not yet," Gabriel warned. They'd only just begun.

Splashing sounds cut through the hiss of the fire as the men indeed tried to put out the flames from the other side.

"Rams!" Gabriel shouted.

Three warriors rushed forward, each holding on to a battering ram as long as they were tall and a shield to ward off arrows and stones from above. They didn't stop running, but slammed their timber into the weakening door.

From above a fresh rain of arrows split the air. Gabriel grabbed Theo, thrusting him out of the way and narrowly missed the deadly pelting of arrows that sank into the earth near his feet.

Unlike when they'd swam in the water, this time the arrows hit a few marks. His men shouted in pain, but none fell. They broke off the shafts and left the pointed tips in their skin. The three warriors battering down the door, thrust their rams with renewed vigor against the flames, the gate shuddering under their power.

"Again!" Gabriel roared.

Amidst the arrows, stones were thrown from above. One hit him painfully on the shoulder, but he pushed through the pain, as did all of his men. They would fight to the death with not an inch of their flesh unscathed.

This time when the three warriors slammed their rams against the gate, the wood cracked with a resounding boom. They wasted no time rushing back and slamming forward, splintering it all the more.

Gabriel kicked out, crushing the blazing wood with his bare heel. His men followed suit until they'd finished breaking down the gate and rushed inside, weapons drawn. There was not a second to lose as the MacLeod warriors met them with a wall of steely blades.

Gabriel attacked the first man he saw, his arched sword clanging hard against his foe's blade. The man blocked each of Gabriel's attacks, but was not quick enough. With a fake attack to the right, he drew his dagger and stabbed left, sinking it between the fiend's ribs. One man down, he moved to the next. Another down, he spotted Theo. The boy had skill with a sword, but the man he fought against was too powerful.

Judging the distance, Gabriel surged forward, but he wasn't going to make it. The warrior knocked Theo to the ground, and poised to strike a deathblow. The only recourse Gabriel had was to throw his weapon. He didn't hesitate, arching back and flinging his dagger forward. It hit the mark, slicing through the man's neck and knocking him off balance just as his sword fell, giving Theo enough time to roll to the side and away from the blade.

Gabriel retrieved his weapon and held out his hand, pulling Theo to his feet.

"Stay with me. We'll fight, back to back."

Theo nodded, all color drained from his face, and blood having spattered across his cheeks from the strike in his enemy's neck.

With the lad's back pressed against his, they sought out their next opponents. The bailey was full of chaos as MacLeods fought MacKinnons. These warriors were better prepared than those at Dunvegan, however incredibly odd that was, considering they were ruled by the same man.

Theo parried with one man while Gabriel battled another, and when Gabriel downed his, he whirled to fell Theo's adversary.

The entire battle may have lasted fifteen or twenty minutes at most, but at long last, the MacKinnons succeeded. Gabriel stood, blood soaking his skin, shirt and weapons. His breathing was labored, but he didn't care because, unlike their enemies, he *was* breathing, which was a different story from his enemies.

Relentless, there had been only one option: win.

"My laird," Theo said, kneeling before Gabriel. "Ye will always have my loyalty and can rely on me to be your ally in all things from this day forward."

Gabriel pressed his hand to the lad's head. "Ye've done well, Theo. Ye fought for your lands and ye won. We are allies, and I will protect ye, but I dinna expect ye to agree with me in all things. Ye must have your own mind, but I will demand your respect should ye feel the need to voice your difference of opinion."

"Aye, my laird."

Gabriel turned in a circle taking in the carnage. Servants peeked from windows and from whatever barrel, wagon or structure they'd hidden behind.

"Come and greet your laird!" Gabriel shouted, his voice harsh from the bellowing he'd done in battle. A deafening silence echoed in the bailey. Gabriel grabbed Theo's hand and yanked it high. "Laird Theo MacLeod. Son of Brenna MacNeacail!"

Gasps rose from the silence that had initially greeted him.

"Pledge your allegiance to him and to me, for I am your laird's guardian."

Slowly, as if expecting to have their lives extinguished, men, women and children came out from their hiding places.

"How do we know he is who ye say he is?" an older man asked, his limbs shaking from fear.

"My mother is Brenna MacNeacail," Theo said, his voice booming. "Ye only need look at me to know."

The man tentatively edged closer until he was only a couple feet from the lad. His old rheumy gaze regarded the boy up and down, staring hard at Theo's eyes. Then he nodded.

"I recall your mother. Ye have the look of her." He shook his head slowly, regret softening his features. "I wish we could have done more for her."

Gabriel gritted his teeth, wishing the same, but Brenna had told him herself that she'd do it all over again because of her children.

"She is safe at Nèamh Abbey," Theo said. "With my sister and my brothers. And my Aunt Kirstin, too. She wished me to tell ye all how verra much she misses ye."

They bowed one by one in front of both Gabriel and Theo, speaking their vows of loyalty.

"Spread the word to your kin that your true laird, a laird of your blood, has returned," Gabriel advised.

"Tell them that MacKinnon has my trust. That he will protect us all!" Theo added.

While the people went to spread the word about the siege to the rest of the MacNeacails, Gabriel and his men cleaned up the bailey, burying the dead and tending the injured. They were brought food and ale. Thankfully the galleon had not caught fire from the rain of flaming arrows and was brought back to the pier. The horses were housed in the stables, and the men's plaids and boots were returned to them.

As night began to fall, exhaustion kicked in, and Gabriel sank into a tall, wooden chair by the hearth, prepared to catch a few hours of sleep.

"My laird?" Two MacNeacail clansmen burst into the great hall, startling Gabriel.

He grabbed his sword and was on his feet, the tip at one of their throats. "What?"

"We've just had word from the village." They hesitated.

"Out with it."

"They say some two dozen MacLeods passed by there hours ago. They must have escaped during the battle."

Gabriel gritted his teeth, feeling that familiar pounding in his head that he had come to associate with rage. And fear.

Theo had rashly told his people where his mother was. *Ballocks!* If the MacLeods wanted vengeance on the boy, on Gabriel, they would go straight to Nèamh.

Chapter Twenty-Two

"YE have a visitor." A young nun, sulking, interrupted Brenna from one of the new duties she'd taken on to pass the time, and to try and prove to her aunt that she did, indeed, intend to take her vows, despite the realization that she loved Gabriel.

Brenna stood up from her spot on the floor in the nave and tossed the sudsy linen into the bucket of water she'd been using to scrub the floors. Honorable work, and a chore that had to be completed.

"May I ask who, sister?" Brenna asked politely.

If she were going to live among the sisters of Nèamh, she needed to learn to speak the way they did. With respect and without names. They were all *sister*, save for Mother Abbess.

"A lady. She awaits ye in the courtyard." The sister turned, walking away in a huff.

Brenna dried her hands on her apron and tried to clear the frown from her face. It would seem that while she tried to respect the sisters, some had yet to warm to her. She'd heard the rumors. They believed she would rise quicker in the ranks than a lot of them due to her familial status. They thought her spoiled. Little did they know.

Kirstin had gone through the same thing and it was only when she formally renounced her intention to be groomed as a future Mother Abbess that she gained respect from the other nuns.

Who could be visiting Brenna? And a lady at that?

She knew of no ladies that would come to see her. None that knew her whereabouts. 'Twas very odd. And yet, the visit did not seem to send alarm bells to anyone but herself.

Brenna cautiously approached the courtyard, a million and one variations of who would await her passing through her mind. One being that the nuns were playing a trick on her, the other that it was a MacLeod warrior dressed as a lady that would then run her through.

Neither of those was the case.

Standing in the center of the courtyard was, indeed, a lady. Slim and incredibly tall, she stared at one of the fig trees as if contemplating its life cycle. Her guard stood in the corner, pretending that neither of them existed.

"My lady," Brenna said, dipping into a curtsy.

The woman turned and Brenna could see there was something familiar about her, but she did not recall ever meeting this woman before.

"My, ye are bonny," the lady said. She sauntered forward, her eyes raking Brenna from top to bottom and back again. "Ye've not yet taken your vows."

'Twas a statement rather than a question. And the second time someone had pointed it out. Almost as though they were accusing her of putting it off. Of avoiding her own fate.

And, maybe she was.

Brenna squared her shoulders and met the grand lady's challenge with a hard stare. "Not as of yet, but I do intend to verra soon. May I ask ye to introduce yourself to me? I'm afraid I dinna recall your name."

The woman waved her hand in the air. "And why should ye? We've not seen each other since ye were a girl. I am Lady MacKinnon, but ye may call me Cora."

Lady MacKinnon? Could this be Gabriel's mother? Cora was not a common name... It had to be her. "I would not feel right about addressing ye in so familiar a fashion."

"Why?" A slow smile spread on her face. "We're practically family."

Brenna cocked her head, staring at the woman. "How so?"

"Your son will be living with me at the castle while he fosters."

Disappointment soured Brenna's belly. What had she expected? That the woman would say her son had fallen madly in love with Brenna and that they'd be family once they wed? She'd have to, of course, set the woman straight...

But even the idea of telling her the truth only saddened her.

She missed Gabriel. More than she wanted to admit.

"Aye, he will."

"Ye're not happy with the situation." Once more the lady made her words a statement of fact rather than a question.

Brenna refused to answer, partly because she had no idea what exactly she would say, and partly because she was afraid she'd blurt out the truth of it.

"Well, I can see why my son respects ye."

That was a shock. Brenna tried to hide her reaction to Cora's words. Gabriel, respected her? It was almost worth a laugh and a holler of excitement.

"He admires ye. I've not seen him speak of a woman as he has of ye. I've not seen him so distracted by one either."

"I'm flattered," Brenna managed.

Cora inched forward, stopping a foot away, and squinting her eyes as she searched Brenna's face. "I'll be honest with ye, Brenna, from one lady to another. Will ye listen?"

Did she have any other choice? If she turned away, Brenna had the idea this woman would only follow her, so she nodded instead.

"Come back to Dunakin with me. Dinna choose this as your life. Make your life with my son."

The woman's words shook her to her very core. Brenna's knees started to weaken. How many times would she be tested? How many times would she have to choose differently than where her heart pushed her?

"If he doesna make ye happy, I will personally escort ye back here. But I beg ye to give him a chance."

Brenna closed her eyes, breathing deep and trying for a moment to compose herself, to escape the intense scrutiny of Lady Cora MacKinnon.

"I canna," she said weakly.

From the moment she'd met Gabriel, the stone fortification she'd built for protection around her heart and soul had slowly started to crumble. Piece by piece it was coming apart, and Cora had just ripped another large chunk away, leaving her nearly exposed.

"Aye, ye can. I saw it in your eyes. Ye admire my son. Why should the both of ye suffer needlessly? I would not have come all the way out here if I did not believe there was a chance at a happy future for the both of ye."

Cora's words were convincing. Achingly so.

Brenna shook her head, trying to force herself to erase every image that came to mind when she considered the woman's suggestion.

Her heart beat so loudly behind her ribcage that it literally pounded in her ears. She shook her head, the pounding growing louder, quicker.

Cora grasped her arm and jerked her back to the present.

"Something is wrong," Cora said.

Her guard was immediately alert, yanking his sword from his scabbard.

Brenna's eyes snapped open. "What?"

The pounding grew louder and Brenna realized it was not the pound of her heart, but someone banging on the front gate of the abbey.

Nuns rushed past her, going in the opposite direction. Cora snagged one by the hand and whipped her about.

"What is happening?" the lady asked.

"We are under attack! Two dozen armed guards are battering down the gates!" The nun yanked free and ran with the others.

"What if its Gabriel?" Brenna said, thinking perhaps the nuns had mistaken his enthusiasm for entry as menace. She started for the front entryway.

"Dinna go, child," Cora begged. "My son would request entry, not force his way in."

"My lady... I must protect ye," the guard warned Cora.

Brenna worried her lower lip, but the choice to run was made for her when Cora said, "What about the children? They are your priority."

"Aye." Brenna ran toward the chamber where the wee ones would be going through their studies and Cora followed with her guard, but when she opened the door, the children were not inside. "Where are they?"

Frantic with fear, she dropped to her knees and looked under each cot, but came up empty-handed.

"One of the nuns must have them," Cora said.

"Aye. We must find them."

Brenna raced back down the corridor and out into the cloister, but her way was blocked by a dozen fierce and angry warriors.

Warriors she recognized immediately as MacLeods and men who'd disrespected her numerous times in her own home.

"There ye are, my lady. No need to run, now. We'll just be taking ye along with us."

Cora's guard stepped in front of them both.

"Ye'll do no such thing," Cora said, putting her tall, lengthy body in front of Brenna's.

"We dinna want to hurt ye, my lady, but be assured, we will if ye stand between us and Lady Brenna."

"Ye'll not be touching either of the ladies," the guard said, "else ye garner the anger of my laird."

"Have ye no respect for position?" Cora added. "For God's own walls? Lady Brenna has sought sanctuary here and ye have no right to come within these walls for purposes of violence." Cora stood her ground.

Where were the children? Lord, Brenna prayed they were somewhere safe.

The men laughed. "A rousing speech to be sure, my lady. And ye're right. We dinna come with the intent to inflict violence on anyone, only to collect a fugitive and bring her to justice. Now, if ye will step aside so we may keep our word. I have no qualms about killing your guard. Tell him to stand down."

"What is the meaning of this?" Aileen rushed from the nave in a wave of black robes. "How dare ye enter our sanctified walls with weapons drawn?"

"Och, another nun. Shall we teach ye a lesson for interrupting the duties of a clan's guard?"

"Ye vile filth, get thee gone!" Aileen bellowed, pointing toward the battered gate.

Without warning, one of the guards lashed out, catching Aunt Aileen hard on the cheek with his gauntlet. Crimson showed where he cut her creamy skin. Her mouth fell open in shock and then her eyes rolled as she slowly tipped forward.

Brenna rushed to catch her aunt before she fell, but one of the guards grabbed her around the waist, not allowing her to go any further. Aileen fell with a crash to the ground, eyes closed.

"Nay! Get off me!" Brenna screamed, struggling against her captor.

The MacKinnon guard jumped into action, fighting off several MacLeods.

"Let her go!" Cora shouted, beating her fists on the man's arms.

"Take her!" shouted the guard and several others stepped forward to secure Gabriel's mother in their grasps.

Brenna bucked against her captor, the back of her head butting against the man's face. That only made him tighten his grip painfully and then he tossed her over his shoulder with a painful smack on her rear.

"I think I'd rather see her punishment handed out here, where everyone can watch," the beastly bastard said.

Brenna continued to beat at the man's back, kicking his front, too.

Just inside the cloister, the man slammed her against a column, holding her head against the marble. She searched for Aileen. For Cora. For her children, but saw none of them.

"Dinna struggle and it will be quick. Struggle and ye'll wish ye'd died when the MacLeods first invaded your lands all those years ago."

No matter what he did to her, she'd never wish for that, because wishing such meant her children would not exist. Keeping that in mind, she bucked hard, and stomped even harder on the bastard's foot.

He howled in pain and punched her in the side of the head. Tiny stars filled her vision.

"Get the rope!"

Even though her vision was blurred and pain filled her head, Brenna fought. She refused to remain still. She screamed, she writhed, she kicked. It took the guard several minutes to subdue her with the rope, cut so tightly around her middle that she could barely breathe as they pinned her to the column.

The cold tip of a dagger pressed to the back of her neck, just where the bones of her spine met.

"Move and ye die," said the man behind her. "Quicker," he added, confirming her fears that they'd come seeking retribution for their laird's death.

Tears stung her eyes, and she whimpered, keeping still. No matter what, she had to hold out as long as she could.

Beyond the men's jeers, the strange echo of her own breathing and the beating of her heart, she could hear Cora's sobs and curses.

Brenna closed her eyes and sent up a prayer to the heavens to save her or to at least make it quick. To keep her children from harm. Would they kill her and then massacre her children?

The knife slid down the top of her gown and sliced, cutting the fabric and chemise all the way to her waist. Chills snaked over her exposed back.

"The whip!" the man called.

He would whip her. Tear into her flesh one strike at a time. It would be a slow and painful death.

"Gabriel," she whispered. "Keep them safe."

"Confess," the guard said. "Say it loud enough that we can all hear it before we gain our reward."

Brenna remained silent. They were already getting enough from her as it was. She'd confess to nothing.

"Confess!" The guard's bellow echoed ferociously in the cloister and the sound of his whip cracking against the ground sent a shiver of fear violently up her spine.

When she remained silent, he cracked the whip against the ground once more and bellowed his demand. Brenna shook violently, but the only words to come out her mouth were prayers for mercy from God.

"We take your silence as an admission of guilt. Ye are hereby charged with the murder of your husband and your punishment is one hundred lashes."

A death sentence. But she'd expected nothing less. Not from the MacLeods. Not when they'd all watched her torment over the years. Not when they'd all remained silent as she, only a child at the time, was raped on a wedding night that should not have occurred.

Brenna wrapped her arms around the column and braced herself for the sting of the first lash. If she were lucky, she'd lose consciousness after the first ten or twenty, and then she'd feel no more.

She closed her eyes and imagined happier moments in her life. The extreme rush of love she'd felt upon meeting her children for the first time. The feel of their tiny fists wrapped around her finger. The sound of their sweet voices when they told her they loved her. The look in Gabriel's eyes when he gazed on her, the feel of his lips touching hers. The way her children had glommed onto him, how he'd taken them under his wing. When she was gone, he would protect them. They would be happy. Safe.

The whip sang through the air, the first strike ripping painfully against the side of her back. All the air left her lungs in a single, loud sob.

Chapter Twenty-Three

BLOOD tunneled through Gabriel's veins at a rate that rivaled the speed of his horse. Rather than going back to Dunakin, he and his men had taken their horses and ridden straight for Nèamh. Exhaustion was forgotten and fury and fear ruled him.

He sent a messenger to Dunakin to warn his men of the possibility of attack by the MacLeods and orders to keep his mother safe.

They'd been riding like the devil was on their tails for the better part of a day and a half, with barely a break to water their horses. The poor animals would surely need a rest after such abuse. But there was no other way to go about it. They had to get there and they had to get there quick. The MacLeods had a good few hours' advantage on them, thank heavens it wasn't more.

If they were lucky, the men would not be allowed entrance into the abbey, and then he'd be able to engage them in battle outside the walls. Gabriel prayed, whispering a litany like a mantra, that the nuns had not opened their gates, that the MacLeods were not cunning enough to weasel their way inside.

Oh, Brenna…

He'd missed her face, the sound of her voice, even the petulant thrust of her chin. But until the moment he'd known she was in danger, he'd not been aware of the extent of his feelings.

Emotions ran deep and strong within him, clutching their way around his heart.

Gabriel loved her. Loved her with all his being. Loved her far greater than he'd ever loved another. If he lost her… his life would be over. There was no living.

Beside him, Theo was silent as they rode, his brow scrunched up in a ferocious frown, and his teeth bared. The lad regretted leaving his mother behind. Regretted having chosen his future over her. Gabriel had tried to tell him that it wasn't his fault. Tried to explain that the fault lay entirely with Gabriel not insisting she continue on with them for her protection as he'd originally planned, but the boy didn't want to hear it. Refused, turning his obstinate eyes toward the horizon and the way to Nèamh.

"Riders approaching!" Coll shouted.

Gabriel turned toward the sound of thundering horses coming from behind. MacLeods? Was it possible they'd beaten them to the abbey? They were less than an hour's ride away now.

Gabriel faced two choices, stop and engage whoever approached and risk Brenna's safety further, or outride them.

He chose the latter.

"Onward!" he bellowed, leaning over his horse and kicking its flanks.

The men roared their agreement. Dust from their horses' hooves surrounded them in a choking cloud, but it didn't matter. Gabriel was barely breathing as it was.

The bell tower to the abbey rose up from the valley beyond and on the wind the sound of those bells tolled a warning.

They were too late. The MacLeods were there.

The bastards had better pray that God struck Gabriel where he rode now, for if he reached them, they'd wish the devil had taken them instead.

Behind them, the riders still approached, shouting, but Gabriel ignored them. He wasn't going to stop until he was through the gates of the abbey and Brenna was in his arms. Not until she was safe and he declared to her just what she meant to him. How much he loved her and how much he desperately wanted her to be his wife.

If she denied him, he'd spend the rest of his days trying to prove to her he was worthy.

The closer they came to the abbey, the more his rage burned inside his chest. He could see the gates were flung open and the cries and shouts of outrage sounded on the wind between tolls of the bell.

Bloody hell, but he prayed the bastards weren't massacring everyone inside.

Gabriel bellowed a war cry, raising his sword onward, and his men followed suit. They rode straight through the gates and into the courtyard, immediately set upon by the MacLeods who'd taken up their arms and stood in a line, trying to block their way. They were no match for Gabriel and his men. They sliced through the six men standing guard and leapt from their horses to advance into the cloister.

"My laird!" Gabriel turned in time to see some of the men he'd left at Dunakin riding through the gate. They'd been the ones following. The man, bent over his horse and out of breath, managed to say, "Your mother is here."

His mother? Holy Mary... He had two women to protect and the children.

"Theo, go and find your sister and brothers. I will find your mother."

The lad made a face, intent to protest, but Gabriel cut him off with a hard glare and a shake of his head. "Go. Do as your laird commands."

Theo pressed his lips tightly together and nodded. As they approached the cloister, Theo slunk off down a corridor with Coll and several MacKinnon guards beside him in search of his siblings and Gabriel's mother, Lady Cora.

A wall of men stood before Gabriel, blocking his view of the cloister, their teeth bared. Not a nun was in sight and he guessed they'd all holed up as soon as the bastards had attacked.

"Get out of here. This is not your fight," a warrior close to his own height growled.

"Aye, the bitch is ours," said another.

They parted just enough that Gabriel saw Brenna's abused body slumped against a column.

Fury, swift and fast, blazed inside him and all Gabriel saw was red. He wasn't sure what happened next, only that he was barreling toward Brenna and the man wielding the whip behind her. Two bloody, angry stripes were slashed across her back. She was tied at the wrists to the column, and clung desperately to it, trying to stay upright, shoulders shaking.

"Gabriel," she sobbed.

"Brenna!" Gabriel bellowed, then arched his sword, attacking every man in his way.

His men followed suit, attacking without mercy.

Gabriel cut through the men quickly, slicing, cutting and hacking his way toward Brenna until he was face to face with the man holding the whip.

The warrior puffed out his chest, grinning with malice. "Get back, ye heathen," the man said, snapping the whip against the ground. "We're exacting a right and just punishment. I ought to tie ye to the column with this bitch for killing my men."

Gabriel could have laughed. The MacLeod warrior's bravado was infuriating. "Ye watched me kill these men. And still ye challenge me? Before ye can blink, I'll have that whip coiled around your neck."

The man opened his mouth to respond, fingers curling tighter around his whip, but before he could move an inch or utter a syllable, Gabriel disarmed him and flattened the man to the ground, his heel grinding against the bastard's neck, along with the length of corded leather.

A gurgling noise came from deep inside the blackguard's throat. Gabriel didn't care. This man had laid those marks on Brenna's back. This man had tied her there, cut her gown and exposed her to the lot of them. This man had tormented her unjustly. No one touched *his* woman without paying the ultimate price.

With his men putting down the rest of the MacLeods around him, Gabriel cut off the man's breath for the last time.

Less than a second later, he was cutting through the ties at Brenna's wrists and gathering her into his arms. His fingers trembled as did hers. As soon as she was loose, she thrust herself into his embrace and collapsed. He caught her up, one arm beneath her legs and the other around her back. She whimpered against his neck, clinging to him, her tears wetting his shirt. Gabriel turned away from everyone, hiding her exposed skin and wishing he could take her wounds away, give them to himself to ease her pain.

"Gabriel!" his mother rushed forward, holding out her hands. "Let me care for her."

But he didn't want to let her go, even into the care of his mother, a renowned healer. If he could trust anyone with Brenna's care it was Lady Cora. But he just couldn't let her go. He tightened his grip, her small body curled against him, their heartbeats pounding against one another and he shook his head.

Mother Abbess approached, eyes imploring, a cut on her cheek. "Lady Cora is right, we need to tend to her back afore infection has a chance to set in. If we get a salve on them quick, her scars will be minimal."

Scars. The lass would forever bear the mark of that evil bastard's whip.

Warm blood trickled from the stripes on her skin, sliding over his arm, making his anger rise once more. If he could, he would kill the bastard all over again.

The rest of the MacLeods had been dispatched of, and his men, under the direction of Coll, were taking the bodies from the cloister outside where they could no longer desecrate the grounds. Gabriel's own bloody sword lay at his feet.

He raised his regard to Mother Abbess. "I apologize for raising my weapon in your holy sanctuary."

She straightened her shoulders, eyes just as fierce as Brenna's meeting his. "If I'd had a sword, I would have raised it myself."

Behind Cora and the abbess stood Theo with the twins tucked behind him and Gillian staring defiantly onward.

"Mother," Theo choked out. "This is all my fault."

"Nay, lad, there's naught ye could have done against all the men who tried to seize the abbey," Gabriel said.

"Aye. Ye'd only have gotten hurt or worse," the abbess said.

Still, Theo shook his head. "Nay. 'Tis still my fault. They sought to punish her for something I did."

Silence filled the cloister, save for Brenna's voice which weakly brushed against Gabriel's chest. "Dinna say another word, Theo."

"What?" Gabriel asked, glancing down at Brenna.

She'd stopped trembling, clutched his shirt tighter. "Tell him to remain silent."

"Nay, Mother," Theo said. "I'll not. I've hidden behind your skirts long enough. The truth needs to be told and ye need no longer protect me from my actions."

Brenna shuddered against Gabriel, tried once more to feebly resist her son's argument, but Theo stood taller, puffing out his chest. He cut off his mother's attempt to silence him.

"I killed my father. It was not my mother."

The quiet that followed was so palpable, so tangible that even the wind seemed to understand the need for it and ceased to whistle.

"The man was a fool, a tyrant and I grew tired of his treatment of my mother. Of me, and what he planned to do with my sister was the last straw."

Brenna stiffened.

"What did he plan to do with your sister?" Gabriel asked.

"He was already negotiating her marriage to our cousin, the heir to the MacLeods of Lewis. It would have secured his line in the north, but Gillian is not yet twelve. And our cousin is a foul-tempered arse, pardon my language. He'd have treated her worse than my father treated my mother."

Gabriel nodded.

"I couldn't let him do it. We argued. He threatened to have me whipped at the stake in the bailey, and the last time he'd done that, I made a vow I'd never let him do it again. In a fit of rage, I grabbed the first available weapon—a fire poker."

"That's enough," Brenna said. "Ye need say no more."

"But, mother, they must know."

"Ye've said enough. They know now."

Theo's lips trembled, but the anger and righteousness in his eyes spoke volumes. He did not regret his actions. The only thing he regretted was letting his mother take the blame for it.

"Whip me, my laird. Tie me to the post. I'll gladly take the punishment meant for me. Add as many lashes to it as ye want for having caused my mother harm."

Gabriel shook his head. "I'll not punish ye, lad. Your bravery saved your sister, your mother, and likely your little brothers from pain. Aye, 'tis a sin to murder, and an even greater sin to murder one's own father, but in this instance, I believe God will forgive ye. For ye acted in self-defense and in defense of your family. Ronald MacLeod acted not as a loving sire, but an enemy and a threat to the safety of innocents. Ye dinna have to answer to me, but to your people. But, for what it's worth, I thank ye for saving this precious woman." Gabriel gazed down into Brenna's eyes. "For I love her with every breath I take, every beat of my heart and every ounce of my being."

Brenna's eyes widened, tears filling their depths and for a moment, he feared she'd push away from him, demand to be let down and run screaming from the abbey.

Instead, she clutched him tighter and smiled. "I love ye, too."

Gabriel's heart swelled near to bursting and a tingling sensation prickled its way over his entire body. How good it felt to hear those words, to know they were meant for him, that the feelings inflaming his heart and rocking his soul were returned.

"Ye have no idea how good it feels to hear ye say that," he whispered.

"Oh, aye, but I do, for I've never heard it before and the sound of those words uttered from your lips fills me with such joy. I think I could float away now and be happy forever."

Those around them seemed to melt into the background. Gabriel only had eyes for Brenna and he wanted to tell her a hundred more times just how he felt.

He pressed his forehead to hers. "I love ye. I want ye to be my wife. I want to wake up each morning to your smile. I even want to calm ye when ye rave at me. I want to share in the happy moments of your life and comfort ye in the sad. I want to take away your pain and give ye all the joy ye deserve. Say, aye, Brenna. Say ye'll do me the honor of being my wife."

Her lips curved into a trembling smile. "Aye! Gabriel MacKinnon, conqueror of my heart. Aye!"

Conqueror of her heart? "Och, lass, 'tis ye who have conquered my heart and soul. I thought I could never love again, but what I found was I never loved before. Ye have me caught up in a maelstrom I never want to be free from."

Then, right there in the center of the abbey with everyone there to see, he pressed his lips gently to hers.

Chapter Twenty-Four

One week later...

BRENNA snuggled close to Gabriel on his horse. He'd not left her side since arriving at the abbey, nor let her ride her own horse all the way from Nèamh to Dunakin.

Her back had healed nicely and, though there were still scabs, it no longer ached.

"I canna wait for ye to see my home," Gabriel said.

Brenna leaned her head back against his shoulder. "Our home."

"Och, ye're right, lass. *Our* home. I really like the sound of that."

Before leaving the abbey at dawn, in the presence of both of their families, they'd exchanged their vows. A small, quiet affair that left them both eager to travel to Dunakin where they could begin their lives together.

All seemed right with the world. Brenna had finally found happiness, love, and hope for the future. Scorrybreac and Dunvegan were safe from MacLeods, and though her brother-by-marriage was still a prisoner, she knew she had nothing to fear from him. As long as MacKinnon was in control, there was little fear that the MacLeods of the Isle of Lewis would retaliate.

Though in four years time when Theo took his place as laird, she did worry the MacLeods would finally make their move, having bided their time. But that was several years from now, and she was confident that Gabriel would help him, when and if he needed it.

Gabriel's arm slipped around her middle and he nuzzled her neck. Her skin prickled, tingling. They'd not had a chance to be alone, to be intimate, at the abbey, and she looked forward to having him all to herself when they arrived. At least for a little while.

The children were all completely ecstatic to have Gabriel as a stepfather. They smiled up into the warmth of the sun, the soft wind rustling their hair.

Before leaving the abbey, she'd been sure to thank her aunt and sister. With both of them hinting to different choices she could make, but not pushing her either way, only pointing out the facts, she'd been able to realize on her own the depth of her feelings.

Saints, but every time she thought about how she'd let him walk away, her breath caught and her heart did a flip in panic. Brenna squeezed Gabriel's arms around her.

"What are ye thinking about?" he asked softly.

"Us."

"Aye? What of us?"

"Just how happy I am ye came back to me." She snuggled closer, feeling the warmth of his body sink into hers.

"Och, lass, 'twas my plan all along." He traced the shell of her ear with his lips sending frissons of need racing along her skin. Over the last week, they'd shared a few quick kisses, and she was now officially tangled up in a ball of need. "When I walked out of that abbey, there was no way in hell I wasn't coming back to claim ye."

They approached the castle, an impressive stronghold somewhere between the size of Dunvegan and Scorrybreac. Attentive guards lined the walls. Brenna smiled, not having expected anything less.

They clopped across the short bridge and beneath the portcullis, through the gates and into the bailey.

Men, women and children rushed forward to greet their laird and his new wife. They shouted their greetings and color filled Brenna's cheeks. When she'd been brought back to Dunvegan with Ronald, there had been no fuss. This was a wholly new experience. Everything with Gabriel was.

He was a better man. A better laird. Just plain better.

A true hero.

Gabriel dismounted behind her, then held out his hands to her. Rather than balk at his help as she had so many times before, she smiled and placed her hands into his large, sturdy ones.

"I didna think ye'd ever let me help ye," he chuckled, sliding his hands up her arms and then around her waist. He lifted her, swinging her effortlessly down.

"Welcome home," Cora said to them dismounting from her horse. "Ye'll be mistress now."

Brenna, grabbed hold of her new mother-by-marriage's hand. "But I hope ye'll help me."

Cora nodded, smiled, a flash of relief in her eyes. Gabriel had told Brenna that his mother had mentioned being tossed aside once he'd married, and though Brenna was excited about her new role as Mistress of Dunakin, she didn't want to diminish in any way what Cora had achieved.

"I'd be happy to show ye around. But I'll tell ye the same thing my mother-by-marriage told me." She leaned forward, speaking in low tones. "This is your house now. Ye're the mistress and ye'll want things done your way. I'll be here to help ye, but I'll not be in the way."

Brenna grinned. "That sounds nice to me, but I do hope we can become close friends. For too long I've suffered without the companionship of a lady."

"It would be a pleasure. Now come inside, I should show ye—"

"Mother," Gabriel interrupted. "If I could beg a boon of ye... Would ye mind terribly keeping the duties of mistress for one more night?"

"Oh..." Cora's eyes widened as understanding dawned. "Right, aye. I'll have a tray sent up. And some wine."

The lady ran into the castle, pointing and ordering the servants about. Brenna wasn't certain her face could get any hotter. Part of her wanted to tunnel back in time to her first marriage, how she'd been bedded in front of the clan, but the other part of her, forced her forward, to face her new husband knowing he'd not put her through such humiliation.

"May I?" he asked.

"What?"

Gabriel swooped down and lifted her up into the air. "I want to carry ye to our chamber."

Brenna laughed with pure joy. "They way ye've spoiled me the last week I may get used to never walking again. Will ye feed me, too?"

"If that is what ye wish. I'd do anything for ye, Brenna. I hope ye know that."

She touched his cheek with her palm. "I do. I really do. I love ye so much."

"And I ye." Gabriel marched across the bailey, up the keep stairs and didn't stop there. Up the circular stairs he took her and down a corridor lit with torches.

When they entered his chamber, several maids who'd been tidying up scurried out.

"Smells of herbs in here," he mused. "Cinnamon, like ye."

Brenna laughed. "They made it smell sweet."

Gabriel twirled her in a circle, his nose pressed to hers. "Is that what ye think, that ye're sweet?"

"Dinna ye?"

"I do. And I aim to taste just how sweet every inch of ye is." He brushed his lips over hers, tasting the seam of her lips and drawing out her breath.

Brenna tightened her hold around his neck, feeling her body grow all tingly. Her nipples hardened, between her thighs throbbed. Though her body was inclined to simply acquiesce, to bare all to him, her mind wanted her to hold back. To go slow.

"Oh, pardon me..." drawled a servant from the door.

Gabriel lifted his lips from hers, barely glancing toward the door with a subtle nod. The servant carried in a tray full of delicious smelling food, and behind her was an army of more help carrying in wine, goblets, linens, a tub and steaming buckets of water.

Her husband carried her toward the hearth where he sat with her on his lap as they watched the workers prepare the overlarge tub and set out the food and wine on the table. When they'd completed their tasks, the servants ducked out with bows, their eyes not quite meeting Brenna's or Gabriel's.

"A glass of wine, my love, while the bath cools from boiling?" Gabriel asked.

"Aye. A wee bit."

He lifted her, settling her on the chair.

"I can get it," she protested.

"Nay. Tonight I will serve ye."

She couldn't help but think again about how different this was than when she was married before. And she needed to stop comparing them, because there was no comparison. Ronald was so far off from Gabriel it was as if they were born in different worlds.

The wine gurgled from the jug into two cups. Gabriel carried them both over and sat opposite her. He clinked his glass to hers. "To us."

"To us," she mirrored. The wine went down smooth, quite a bit tastier than what she'd grown used to at the abbey.

Gabriel leaned forward, set his cup down, then lifted her boots to his knees. He unlaced them, removing each one and setting her toes to wriggle free in their hose.

"Such tiny feet," he chuckled.

"Compared to yours, aye, but rather long for a lady of my size."

"Let me see."

Brenna gasped, her breathing suddenly erratic. "See?" she asked. Gabriel had not yet even seen her bare toes and here they were married.

"I plan to see all of ye before the night is through, love."

Brenna drank another gulp of wine and nodded. "Aye."

Gabriel slid his hands up her calves to just behind her knees where he tickled the flesh there. She giggled, squirmed, felt relief in how natural this seemed.

He unlaced the ties of her hose and rolled each one down slowly until both of her bare feet rested on his bare knees. The hair from his legs tickled the bottoms of her feet and she giggled. She wasn't sure her feet had ever actually touched a knee before.

"Perfect pink toes," he mused, stroking their length.

"If ye say so."

"I do." Gabriel lifted one foot and began to massage the arch, the heel, the ball just below her toes.

Brenna found herself moaning in pleasure and leaning back into her chair. "Ye're quite talented at that, husband."

"I aim to please my wife."

If he was this good at massaging her feet, how good would he be at massaging the rest of her?

His fingers trailed upward, rubbing her calves and once more tickling the backs of her knees. He palmed the back of her thigh, just above her knee and paused.

"Will ye let me…"

She nodded before he finished. As nervous as she was, he seemed to have the magic touch at putting her at ease.

"Come here."

Brenna stood, crossing the short distance to stand between his knees. His hands were still on the backs of her thighs and they roved upward slowly, spanning the space just beneath her buttocks. She gasped, bit her lip, closed her eyes.

Gabriel's forehead came forward, resting on her belly. She heard his own ragged draw of breath and she swore his fingers trembled ever so slightly on her skin. Rather than forge upward to cup her rear, he caressed lower all the way to her ankles.

Brenna ran her fingers through his short hair, over his shoulders, massaging the thick muscles and holding herself up as her legs had gone quite wobbly.

Heart pounding, body trembling, she'd never felt so exquisite, except when in his arms. Light filtered through the two arrow-slit windows, slicing across the floor and lighting up the bath.

"Shall I bathe ye?" she asked, wanting to both touch him, but also please him.

Gabriel looked up at her, his eyelids lowered, a heady smolder in his gaze. "I think we should bathe each other."

Brenna's mouth fell open, not having suspected he'd answer that way, but eager for it to be the case. She nodded.

Gabriel stood. "Do ye want to undress me?" he asked.

Her heart clenched. What a kindness he afforded her, offering to be first. Already they'd shared their souls, but not yet their naked forms. And he knew her fear, knew her past and how joining made her nervous.

Brenna nodded. She reached with trembling fingers up to the brooch pinned at his shoulder holding his plaid in place and tugged. The pin came free and the strip of plaid slid from his shoulder, over his chest and down to the floor. For some reason, she couldn't bring herself to look into his eyes as she undressed him, but rather found herself staring at his throat, at the small indent at the base of his neck where his collarbones met.

Her fingers shook all the more as she tried to untie the laces of his shirt. After several attempts, she finally finished, and the shirt fell open to reveal tanned, muscled skin with the barest hint of blond chest hair.

Without hesitation, she splayed her fingers over his heart, feeling the beat against her palm.

"Your heart beats just as fast as mine," she whispered.

"Aye, love."

"I thought ye'd be... Less nervous."

Gabriel chuckled, a throaty, heady sound. "I'm not nervous, lass."

She flicked her gaze up to his. "Then why?"

"I'm exhilarated. I'm alive. I'm in love. I'm filled with desire for ye. All these things make my heart pound."

"Oh..." she breathed out, leaning forward to press her lips to that small indent that kept redrawing her gaze.

Gabriel inhaled sharply and she took that as an invitation to explore a little further. Brenna slid her tongue out to taste his smooth flesh, which only seemed to make him breathe harder.

"Och, lass, if ye keep that up, we'll not make it to the bath."

"Ye like this?"

He nodded. 'Twas no wonder. She'd liked it when he put his tongue on her skin, too.

"I like it a lot."

Brenna smiled, pleased. She tugged his shirt from where it was tucked in his belt and he wrenched it over his head revealing his torso. Corded muscle rippled beneath smooth skin. Brenna held her breath as she stared at him, ran her fingers lightly, tentatively over his chest, his stomach. Up close, nearly nude, he appeared bigger than before. Stronger. And yet his hands gently touching her elbows and stroking up the backs of her arms trembled, too.

When she looked up at him, Gabriel's eyes locked on hers and his lips descended to capture her mouth in a searing kiss. She was swept up in all the new sensations, new feelings. And she wasn't scared. The fear she'd felt at first had disappeared as swiftly as it had come. With her husband, she felt comfortable, safe. Loved. Pleasured.

His strong arms wrapped around her, circling her back and tugging her close against him. Her breasts crushed to his, her bare toes touched his boots, and she wrapped her arms around his neck, fingers threading in his hair, head slanting to accept more of his kiss.

"I dinna think I'll ever get enough of your kiss," he murmured against her mouth.

His fingers deftly untied her gown as he kissed the side of her neck, her collarbone, then came back to drink in more of her mouth.

Rapture filled Brenna and she was once more struck with the happiness she felt with Gabriel. One stone at a time he'd torn away her defense, knocked away her fears and showed her that together they were strong.

And it wasn't only that he made her happy, he allowed her to be her true self, the person she was always meant to be. He reveled in her many moods, her various desires, her hopes and dreams. He didn't make her feel inferior, or that her place in this world was not as good as his. Nay, he treated her with respect, reverence and love.

Gabriel wrapped his hand around hers and dragged her palm over his chest, over his flexing abdominals and to his belt.

"Please, love, undress me. I want to see ye, to feel your skin on mine."

Brenna tucked her fingers into the straps of his belt and pulled, feeling the leather slide. As she did so, Gabriel threaded his fingers through her unruly hair, capturing the sides of her face, his thumbs rubbing her cheeks as he kissed her.

She let go of his belt, her fingers still pressed just below his navel. His plaid unraveled, pooling at their feet in a whoosh of warm air. She gasped at the sudden loss of fabric and the unexpected feel of his arousal brushing her fingertips. His skin was soft and she shivered. Gabriel let out a low growl.

"Zounds, lass…"

Brenna gently untangled herself from his embrace. "If we dinna get into the water soon… 'Twill be too cold to enjoy."

"Och, ye naughty, lass…" Gabriel winked.

"Naughty?" She raised a questioning brow, trying as hard as she could not to look down, though her eyes were drawn to the golden trail of hair leading from his belly button southward.

"Aye… Ye want to get in the tub with me."

Oh, aye, the thought had crossed her mind to enjoy a warm bath with him. The idea was decadent, wicked. And Gabriel certainly knew how to bring out the wicked side of her.

"Together…" she drawled out. "Aye."

"We need to get ye undressed."

She was ready to reveal herself to him and ready to look.

"Oh…" she gasped. Ronald had not been as beautifully built. Not as enticing. Not as well-endowed as her new husband. And while the sheer size of him should have scared her, she found herself only growing more and more interested.

Gabriel closed the distance between them, continuing to unravel her from her gown until she, too, stood before him unclothed. The air in the room felt oddly chilled and yet she was hot as an inferno.

He grinned at her and swept her up in his arms, stepping into the bath and settling her on his lap in front of him. His chest to her back. Her buttocks to his hard arousal. She shivered and leaned back against him, the warm scented water sloshing around them in delicate waves.

Arms encircled her, his fingers splaying over her abdomen, thumbs brushing the undersides of her breasts.

She gripped his hands and pressed them to her breasts, wanting the same sensations to coarse through her that he'd elicited before. Gabriel was eager to please her, cupping her breasts and plucking at her nipples.

Brenna moaned, arching her back. When she did so, her buttocks ground against his thick shaft, prompting a low groan from Gabriel.

"Och, lass, that feels wickedly wonderful."

Brenna arched against him again, finding that delicious tendrils of sensation were snaking their way along her limbs and between her thighs throbbed with the need for... Him.

Gabriel seemed to sense her need. With one hand still at her breasts, he trailed his fingers down her belly to the tuft of dark curls at the apex of her thighs.

"Mmm... This is even better than I imagined," he moaned.

But she couldn't answer him, couldn't breathe. His hand caressed over her mound, cupping her sex. Brenna cried out at the contact, never having felt such pleasure before. And then there was more. His fingers slipped through her folds, stroking over a tender spot, then downward, entering her in soft, even thrusts.

All thoughts left her as pleasure and need took hold. Gabriel kissed the side of her neck as he stroked her into oblivion. She reached up behind her, gripping the back of his neck and tilting her head even further to allow him access to her skin. This was unlike any other bath she'd ever experienced.

And she didn't want it to end.

Of their own accord her hips began to tilt up then back in time with the motions of his hand. Heat pooled in her core, thrumming outward. Between gasps, she moaned, unable to catch her breath. Her heart pounded in her ears. Decadent pressure mounted in her womb, curling around her core and threatening to cause her to ignite. And then she did. Bursts of pleasure sprang from somewhere inside her, mounting in waves.

Brenna cried out, her body stiffening and then trembling violently and uncontrollably.

"That's it, love," Gabriel crooned. "Ride the waves…"

"Gabriel," she gulped when she was finally able to find her voice. "That was…"

"A beautiful climax. I want to see ye do it again."

"I want to do it again," she breathed, rolling over so she faced him, her taut nipples brushing over his chest in a way that made her entire body shiver.

Gabriel gripped her hips, lifting her slightly. "Put your legs around my hips," he crooned.

Brenna did as he suggested, and when she sat down, his hard arousal brushed over her sensitized flesh and she moaned.

"Ye're so responsive. I love it." He tugged her forward, kissing her hard on the lips, driving his tongue inside, then backed away. "I'm sorry… I was overzealous. It's just, ye make me so — "

"Excited?" she cut in. "Me, too." And then she gripped his face between her hands, pressed her lips to his, claiming him as he'd done to her so many times. She licked his lower lip, nipped it with her teeth, then drove her tongue into his mouth to meld with his.

"Saints, love," he groaned. "Ye'll be the death of me."

"No, death, only pleasure."

Growing bolder, she reached between their bodies and gripped his shaft, sliding the smooth, wet skin against her palm.

"Och, lass, so much pleasure. The way ye touch me..." He groaned. "I'm likely to find release in your hand."

"Do it," she urged, wanting him to feel as good as she did.

"Not so soon... I want to be inside ye."

She slid the tip of his arousal through her folds. "Like this?"

"Aye, but deeper."

She stilled, worried for a moment that it would hurt.

"Go slow," she said.

"As slow as ye wish," he said.

Gabriel wrapped his hand around hers and together they guided his erection toward her opening. Their gazes locked as he entered her, slowly, exquisitely... lusciously.

When he'd buried himself fully inside her, she collapsed against him, searching out his mouth in a kiss to rival all kisses and finding just want she wanted.

With his hands at her hips, he gently coaxed her to move back and forth. With each roll of her hips, he thrust in, pulled out, drove back in. Leisurely plunges that left her breathless and had that delicious pressure building once more in her core.

Gabriel tore his mouth from hers, scraping his teeth over her chin, suckling her neck. He cupped her breast and lifted, bending his head lower to take her nipple into his mouth. As if the sensations whipping through her couldn't get any better, now there was this...

Water sloshed over the sides of the tub with their movements, but she cared not. The only things she cared about were the two of them and the pleasure coursing through her.

"Brenna, my love," Gabriel said, his voice low and strained. "God I love ye…"

"I love ye, too, more than ye know."

"My life would not be complete without ye."

"Not at all…" she moaned, riding him harder.

Gabriel groaned, claiming her mouth once more, and with the touch of his lips on hers, her entire body sparked again. She jerked against him, quivering around his arousal, and drinking in his own groan of release.

When they both settled, and the water had truly grown tepid, Gabriel pulled her from the tub, dried her with a soft linen and carried her to bed.

"Now, I shall feed ye, lass, just as I promised when we arrived."

Brenna laughed. "A wife could get used to such pampering."

"Then I shall endeavor to surprise ye often."

And then he kissed her soundly.

THE END

If you enjoyed **CONQUERED BY THE HIGHLANDER***, please spread the word by leaving a review on the site where you purchased your copy, or a reader site such as Goodreads or Shelfari! I love to hear from readers too, so drop me a line at*

authorelizaknight@gmail.com *OR visit me on Facebook:*
https://www.facebook.com/elizaknightauthor. I'm also on
Twitter: @ElizaKnight. If you'd like to receive my occasional
newsletter, please sign up at www.elizaknight.com. *Many
thanks!*

Stay Tuned for more books in the The Conquered Bride Series — A spin-off of the Stolen Brides!

Coming this fall – *Claimed by the Warrior*

Have you read the Stolen Bride series?

The Highlander's Temptation
The Highlander's Reward
The Highlander's Conquest
The Highlander's Lady
The Highlander's Warrior Bride
The Highlander's Triumph
The Highlander's Sin
Wild Highland Mistletoe — a Stolen Bride winter novella
The Highlander's Charm

Want something a little extra steamy? Have you read the Highland Bound Trilogy?

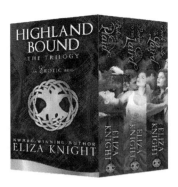

Behind the Plaid
Bared to the Laird
Dark Side of the Laird

Read the sequel to the trilogy!

Highlander's Touch

ABOUT THE AUTHOR

Eliza Knight is a *USA Today* bestselling indie author of sizzling historical romance and erotic romance. While not reading, writing or researching for her latest book, she chases after her three children. In her spare time (if there is such a thing…) she likes daydreaming, wine-tasting, traveling, hiking, staring at the stars, watching movies, shopping and visiting with family and friends. She lives atop a small mountain with her own knight in shining armor, three princesses and one very naughty puppy. Visit Eliza at http://www.elizaknight.com or her historical blog History Undressed:
www.historyundressed.com

Made in the USA
San Bernardino, CA
14 July 2016